ROYAL EXPOSÉ

Praise for Jenny Frame

Longing for You

"Jenny Frame knocks it out of the park once again with this fantastic sequel to *Hunger For You*. She can keep the pages turning with a delicious mix of intrigue and romance."—*Rainbow Literary Society*

Hunger for You

"I loved this book. Paranormal stuff like vampires and werewolves are my go-to sins. This book had literally everything I needed: chemistry between the leads, hot love scenes (phew), drama, angst, romance (oh my, the romance) and strong supporting characters."—*The Reading Doc*

The Duchess and the Dreamer

"We thoroughly enjoyed the whole romance-the-disbelieving-duchess with gallantry, unwavering care, and grand gestures. Since this is very firmly in the butch-femme zone, it appealed to that part of our traditionally-conditioned-typecasting mindset that all the wooing and work is done by Evan without throwing even a small fit at any point. We liked the fact that Clementine has layers and depth. She has her own personal and personality hurdles that make her behaviour understandable and create the right opportunities for Evan to play the romantic knight convincingly…We definitely recommend this one to anyone looking for a feel-good mushy romance."—*Best Lesfic Reviews*

"There are a whole range of things I like about Jenny Frame's aristocratic heroines: they have plausible histories to account for them holding titles in their own right; they're in touch with reality and not necessarily super-rich, certainly not through inheritance; and they find themselves paired with perfectly contrasting co-heroines…Clementine and Evan are excellently depicted, and I love the butch:femme dynamic they have going on, as well as their individual abilities to stick to their principles but also to compromise with each other when necessary." —*The Good, The Bad and The Unread*

Still Not Over You

"*Still Not Over You* is a wonderful second-chance romance anthology that makes you believe in love again. And you would certainly be missing out if you have not read *My Forever Girl*, because it truly is everything."—*SymRoute*

Someone to Love

"One of the author's best works to date—both Trent and Wendy were so well developed they came alive. I could really picture them and they jumped off the pages. They had fantastic chemistry, and their sexual dynamic was deliciously well written. The supporting characters and the storyline about Alice's trauma was also sensitively written and well handled."—*Melina Bickard, Librarian, Waterloo Library (UK)*

Wooing the Farmer

"The chemistry between the two MCs had us hooked right away. We also absolutely loved the seemingly ditzy femme with an ambition of steel but really a vulnerable girl. The sex scenes are great. Definitely recommended."—*Reviewer@large*

"This is the book we Axedale fanatics have been waiting for...Jenny Frame writes the most amazing characters and this whole series is a masterpiece. But where she excels is in writing butch lesbians. Every time I read a Jenny Frame book I think it's the best ever, but time and again she surprises me. She has surpassed herself with *Wooing the Farmer*."—*Kitty Kat's Book Review Blog*

Royal Court

"The author creates two very relatable characters...Quincy's quietude and mental torture are offset by Holly's openness and lust for life. Holly's determination and tenacity in trying to reach Quincy are total wish-fulfilment of a person like that. The chemistry and attraction is excellently built."—*Best Lesbian Erotica*

"[A] butch/femme romance that packs a punch."—*Les Rêveur*

"There were unbelievably hot sex scenes as I have come to expect and look forward to in Jenny Frame's books. Passions slowly rise until you feel the characters may burst!...Royal Court is wonderful and I highly recommend it."—*Kitty Kat's Book Review Blog*

Royal Court "was a fun, light-hearted book with a very endearing romance."—*Leanne Chew, Librarian, Parnell Library (Auckland, NZ)*

Charming the Vicar

"Chances are, you've never read or become captivated by a romance like *Charming the Vicar*. While books featuring people of the cloth aren't unusual, Bridget is no ordinary vicar—a lesbian with a history of kink...Surrounded by mostly supportive villagers, Bridget and Finn balance love and faith in a story that affirms both can exist for anyone, regardless of sexual identity."—*RT Book Reviews*

"The sex scenes were some of the sexiest, most intimate and quite frankly, sensual I have read in a while. Jenny Frame had me hooked and I reread a few scenes because I felt like I needed to experience the intense intimacy between Finn and Bridget again. The devotion they showed to one another during these sex scenes but also in the intimate moments was gripping and for lack of a better word, carnal."—*Les Rêveur*

"The sexual chemistry between [Finn and Bridge] is unbelievably hot. It is sexy, lustful and with more than a hint of kink. The scenes between them are highly erotic—and not just the sex scenes. The tension is ramped up so well that I felt the characters would explode if they did not get relief!...An excellent book set in the most wonderful village—a place I hope to return to very soon!"—*Kitty Kat's Book Reviews*

"This is Frame's best character work to date. They are layered and flawed and yet relatable...Frame really pushed herself with *Charming the Vicar* and it totally paid off...I also appreciate that even though she regularly writes butch/femme characters, no two pairings are the same."—*The Lesbian Review*

Unexpected

"If you enjoy contemporary romances, *Unexpected* is a great choice. The character work is excellent, the plotting and pacing are well done, and it's just a sweet, warm read...Definitely pick this book up when you're looking for your next comfort read, because it's sure to put a smile on your face by the time you get to that happy ending."—*Curve*

"*Unexpected* by Jenny Frame is a charming butch/femme romance that is perfect for anyone who wants to feel the magic of overcoming adversity and finding true love. I love the way Jenny Frame writes.

I have yet to discover an author who writes like her. Her voice is strong and unique and gives a freshness to the lesbian fiction sector."
—*The Lesbian Review*

Royal Rebel

"Frame's stories are easy to follow and really engaging. She stands head and shoulders above a number of the romance authors and it's easy to see why she is quickly making a name for herself in lesfic romance."—*The Lesbian Review*

Courting the Countess

"I love Frame's romances. They are well paced, filled with beautiful character moments and a wonderful set of side characters who ultimately end up winning your heart...I love Jenny Frame's butch/femme dynamic; she gets it so right for a romance."—*The Lesbian Review*

"I loved, loved, loved this book. I didn't expect to get so involved in the story but I couldn't help but fall in love with Annie and Harry...The love scenes were beautifully written and very sexy. I found the whole book romantic and ultimately joyful and I had a lump in my throat on more than one occasion. A wonderful book that certainly stirred my emotions."—*Kitty Kat's Book Reviews*

"*Courting The Countess* has an historical feel in a present day world, a thought provoking tale filled with raw emotions throughout. [Frame] has a magical way of pulling you in, making you feel every emotion her characters experience."—*Lunar Rainbow Reviewz*

"I didn't want to put the book down and I didn't. Harry and Annie are two amazingly written characters that bring life to the pages as they find love and adventures in Harry's home. This is a great read, and you will enjoy it immensely if you give it a try!"—*Fantastic Book Reviews*

A Royal Romance

"*A Royal Romance* was a guilty pleasure read for me. It was just fun to see the relationship develop between George and Bea, to see George's life as queen and Bea's as a commoner. It was also refreshing to see that both of their families were encouraging, even when Bea doubted that things could work between them because of their class differences...*A Royal Romance* left me wanting a sequel, and romances don't usually do that to me."—*Leeanna.ME Mostly a Book Blog*

By the Author

A Royal Romance

Courting the Countess

Dapper

Royal Rebel

Unexpected

Charming the Vicar

Royal Court

Wooing the Farmer

Someone to Love

The Duchess and the Dreamer

Royal Family

Home Is Where the Heart Is

Sweet Surprise

Royal Exposé

Wild for You

Hunger for You

Longing for You

Dying for You

Wolfgang County Series

Heart of the Pack

Soul of the Pack

Blood of the Pack

Visit us at www.boldstrokesbooks.com

ROYAL EXPOSÉ

by

Jenny Frame

2022

ROYAL EXPOSÉ

ISBN 13: 978-1-63679-165-4

This Trade Paperback Original Is Published By
Bold Strokes Books, Inc.
P.O. Box 249
Valley Falls, NY 12185

First Edition: August 2022

CREDITS
Editor: Ruth Sternglantz
Production Design: Stacia Seaman
Cover Design by Tammy Seidick

Acknowledgments

Thanks to my editor Ruth and to all the staff at Bold Strokes Books. Your hard work is greatly appreciated.

To Mum and Dad
Thank you for all your encouragement
and for showing off my books proudly!

PROLOGUE

An orange prison uniform lay discarded on the floor of a cheap motel bathroom. Dressed only in jockey shorts, she leaned on the sink as her dark shoulder-length hair and face dripped with water. On the side of the sink lay a hair colour kit, and a powered razor waited ready to change her appearance.

She looked into the mirror and asked herself, *Who am I?* At that moment she shuddered as her mind played the sounds that tortured her from prison. Screams, shouts, and pleading. She squeezed her eyes shut for an instant and then opened them, hoping the noise would be gone.

It was for the moment, but past experience had taught her that the nightmares she had seen and heard were never too far away. One thing was for certain—she didn't want this appearance a single minute longer.

She was sick of her life. Going from one character to another was affecting her badly. So badly that she didn't know who she was any more and worried that she had lost who she truly was.

"Who are you?" She slammed her fists down on the rim of the sink.

She stood up and prepared for the painful part of the image change. She turned on the hot tap to create steam. It would help with the process of removing the Intelliflesh.

Intelliflesh was an artificial skin compound, which, when stuck to your flesh, bound to your nerves, giving the artificial skin sensation. It was used in the movie industry and more infamously in the sex toy business.

But this Intelliflesh had been used to change her face. This was the longest sustained period of time she'd had to use a mask to change her appearance. Ripping the fake skin from your nerves always hurt, but it would be so much more painful now that it had been attached so long.

She grabbed a tub of removal cream and took the top off. She hesitated. This was going to hurt, but she was just as worried about seeing her true image underneath. She couldn't hide any more.

Before she could change her mind, she applied the cream around the circumference of her face and just below her hairline. She had done this process many times, and experience told her to do it as quickly as possible.

She sliced into the flesh at her hairline, just to give her something to grip, then pulled it off as quickly as she could. Her skin burned as the flesh ripped from her own. Inch by inch she pulled it, until it was finally free.

She discarded the mask and touched her own skin, watching herself in the mirror. It felt raw and foreign. It was her face, but she was disconnected from it, especially as her eye colour was still brown, not her natural colour of blue.

It was time to decide. She had lived as so many people before. Could she be herself again?

"Who do I want to be?"

She wasn't sure, but she wanted to try to find herself. "I want to be Casey James."

On the edge of the sink was a roll of tools. She picked up a handheld laser device, put it to the correct setting, and held it close to her right eye. The laser would reset her eye colour to the one she was born with—blue.

It was strange to see the deep brown turn slowly to blue, and it would take time to get used to it again. Would she be able to feel like Casey James again? She quickly lasered the other eye and turned her attention to her hair. She took a bottle of solution and rubbed it through the strands before stripping away the dark brown colour with another laser.

She watched her natural blonde locks slowly return to the crown of her head. It wasn't long till she had her own colouring back. She looked at her watch. This had taken too long—she'd have to cut her hair later.

Apart from her looks, there was one more thing that could make her feel her own identity again. She picked up a pair of old-fashioned dog tags and held them to her heart.

"Help me find my way back."

She put them round her neck and quickly put on a T-shirt and jeans, then packed up the discarded Intelliflesh and the prison uniform. Now she had to get far away from this place. She was in no doubt there would be people looking for her soon.

After all her tools and hair and make-up equipment were safely in her rucksack, she grabbed a baseball cap and placed it on her head. She stopped briefly to look at her new appearance.

"I'm Casey James." Even to her own ears, Casey sounded like she was trying to convince herself of that fact. She opened the bathroom window and dropped her bags outside. There was no way she was going out the front in case she was seen.

Casey jumped out the window into the alley at the back. She looked around and saw nobody about, so she got the bag with the Intelliflesh and prison gear and stashed it in the motel trash bins.

Then she headed off into the night, not knowing if Casey James was still part of her soul.

CHAPTER ONE

The noise and chaos of the streets of New Delhi were making Poppy King's anxiety much worse than usual. She kept looking at her watch, and time seemed to be going too fast. Poppy was late for her flight home. It was her own fault for forgetting to set an alarm.

"Do you think we'll be much longer?" Poppy asked the taxi driver.

"No. Not long."

Poppy grabbed on to the door handle as the driver suddenly cut across two lanes of traffic. She had spent her last night in India with her team from UNICEF, having a going away party at a local restaurant and bar. The noise wasn't helping her headache, and as soon as she got checked in for her flight, she would need to take some painkillers. *If* she got checked in, that was.

Finally, the taxi arrived at the airport and pulled up with a screech. Poppy got out quickly, and a member of the airport staff approached with a luggage trolley, while the driver got her luggage out of the boot.

She paid the driver with a healthy tip and hurried inside with her trolley. The airport was packed, which was going to make getting to check-in even harder. She tried to navigate her way through the crowds of people as best she could and got onto a moving walkway, which would take her to the next floor.

Her big sister Lex would give her a good-natured lecture about being late. Poppy didn't think Lex had been late in her life.

This was the end of a big adventure, but hopefully the start of a new one. After studying fashion in Denbourg, and a brief internship at a Denbourg fashion magazine, Poppy had decided to follow her big sister's example and give her time to working for a charity.

Since her passion was the clothing industry, Poppy had taken a placement offered by UNICEF. She joined a group of workers travelling the globe, helping the enslaved and poorly paid child workers in the garment industry.

It was rewarding work, and UNICEF were extremely happy to have someone with Poppy's public profile, not that she liked that fact. But now the time felt right to come home and start working on her next big adventure, if she could get to the plane on time.

As Poppy neared the top of the moving walkway, she had the feeling she was being watched. She turned around, but the crowds of people made it impossible to pick out anyone. She put it to the back of her mind and rushed as much as she could to check in. Because she was so late, there wasn't a big line at the desk.

"I'm not too late to check in, am I?"

The woman on the desk looked up, and recognition spread over her face. "Not at all, madam."

She took her phone out, ready to scan her e-ticket, but the lady said, "It's already been taken care of, ma'am. You can make your way up to the Platinum Lounge."

Poppy screwed up her eyes and gave her a sceptical look. "Lounge? But I have an economy ticket."

"You were upgraded, ma'am."

"Why and how?" Poppy asked.

"Perhaps these people may help?"

Poppy hadn't noticed the two people in black suits standing near the check-in desk, and now they started to walk towards Poppy.

She sighed, knowing instantly from their clothes and their stiff postures that they were palace secret service, protection officers.

The woman was striking, and tall for a woman. Her choppy collar-length brown hair with blonde highlights hung loose. She looked formidable and strong, but utterly feminine.

"Ms. King? I'm Chief Bohr." Bohr showed her identification. "Could you follow us to the VIP lounge, and we can talk about why we're here?"

"Who sent you?" Poppy asked.

"Crown Consort Lennox, ma'am, but I can tell you more once you are secure."

Lex. How many times had she told her? Poppy sighed but said, "I'll check in my suitcases first."

"Don't worry about that." Bohr pointed to the big man beside her. "This is Mattius. He'll get your bags checked in for you."

She had no choice but to follow. Since she was sixteen years old she had wrestled with the constraints of her big sister's position.

Lennox King was the spouse of the Queen of Denbourg and was herself Crown Consort. Poppy loved the Queen. Rozala had become the kind of sister she'd never had. Whereas Lex was very much in tune with her masculine side, Roza was as feminine as you could get, sharing Poppy's attitude and her love of clothes and make-up.

This was the part she didn't like. As Chief Bohr led her through the airport, doors seemed to miraculously open, and crowds parted as directed by other suited and stiff security people.

Poppy got looks from the other passengers, wondering no doubt why she was being escorted through the terminal like a queen herself. Bohr led her to an elevator.

"This will take us to the VIP lounge, Ms. King."

"It's Poppy. Please call me Poppy."

"Of course," Bohr replied.

Another couple of people tried to get on the lift, but Chief Bohr said firmly, "I'll send it back down to you," then closed the doors quickly. Poppy saw the commuters' angry faces as the doors shut.

"Did you have to do that, Chief Bohr?"

"There are threats everywhere, Ms. King." Then she smiled. "I'll explain everything when we get to the lounge."

The doors opened into a plush airport lounge full of smiley airline staff, all too much for her mood. There was a reception desk, but the man behind just nodded to Chief Bohr and said, "Welcome, Ms. King. Anything you need, just let me know."

"Thank you."

Bohr led her to one of the comfortable couches. Poppy had been in one or two of these lounges before, when she travelled with Roza and Lex, but she liked to be treated normally. She travelled and lived simply. She wasn't royal, but people liked to brand her as royal by association.

A waiter came over and said, "Could I get you both anything to drink?"

"Latte with an extra shot please," Poppy said.

The waiter looked to Bohr, and she said, "Double espresso please."

"So, Chief Bohr, what is this about?"

"Please, call me Jess. I'm only *Chief* to my team." Jess gave her a big smile. She seemed more relaxed since she'd gotten Poppy up to the lounge.

"Jess, then. What's going on?"

"I'm sorry for the surprise at the check-in desk, but we didn't want to intrude on your night with your friends."

Poppy scowled. "You were watching me last night?"

"Yes, Mattius and I arrived yesterday morning," Jess said.

Poppy was more than annoyed. "Look, I don't like to be watched—" Just as she was about to launch into a tirade, the waiter arrived with the coffee. "Thank you," Poppy said as the waiter placed the cups on the table.

Once he was away, Jess looked around at Mattius, who gave her the thumbs-up sign.

"What was that all about?"

"Just checking that Mattius had screened your coffee."

"For what?"

Jess lifted her espresso and took a sip. "Anything…that shouldn't be there."

Poppy shook her head. All this fuss was so over the top. "I live a private life, I'm not royal, and I don't know how many times I've told my sister and sister-in-law that I don't need protection."

"I'm sorry, Poppy, but you do for at least your trip home. I can tell you more on the plane, but there have been threats against the Queen's family, and you are part of that family. We're just doing our job, and that is to get you home safely—then you can talk to your sister about it."

"Okay, fine, I'll go along with this until we get home," Poppy said.

Jess smiled. "Thank you."

The other secret service agent arrived at the table and said to Jess, "It's time for boarding, Chief."

"Thank you, Mattius."

Poppy looked at the clock. "Wait, it's too early. They aren't boarding for another hour."

Jess stood up and buttoned her jacket. "You are boarding first, Ms. King."

"I haven't even had my coffee." There was no point fighting it. "My sister better have a good excuse for this."

Poppy took one sip of coffee and then followed Jess, internally cursing her sister Lennox all the way.

❖

Casey James swirled the remaining alcohol-free lager around the bottle and thought, *I need something stronger.* She could still hear the distant shouts of pain and fear in the far reaches of her mind. Non-alcoholic lager just didn't cut it.

Jon, one of the barmen at Gold's, walked over and said, "You look as if you need something stronger."

"I do, but I've got the bike with me."

"Oh, you got it? Honestly, I don't see you in nearly a year, then you're here every day, now you might be leaving again? Why do you come here, Casey?"

"The company," Casey said with a smile.

Jon was a friend. Well, as close to a friend as she could have. She only really counted two friends in her life, and the other was more like family. Jon only knew who she was on the surface and also was very aware that there were parts of her life that she didn't talk about. He never pushed it.

Jon brought her a second bottle of lager and joked, "God, your social life is bad. On the house."

"Thanks. It's just a bad mood. We all get them."

Casey might have joked about the company, but in a way it was true. Coming to Gold's bar in Denbourg's capital of Battendorf was as close to a social life as she had.

Jon wiped the bar. "I won't say cheer up, because that always puts people in a worse mood."

"I appreciate that."

"Can I help with anything? Is it woman troubles, family, work?"

"You know I never have woman troubles, Jon. Relationships are too complicated for me," Casey said.

This was very true. The nature of her work meant she couldn't ever form any attachments, or she would risk blowing her cover, and her career.

"I'm just going to head back to the office and see Goldie before I go," Casey said.

"Okay."

Casey took her beer and walked back past the stairwell, which led to a second floor with pool tables, then past the T-shaped stage where

Gold's put on some special evening entertainment. Casey had missed them since she'd been away. It was something that both she and her brother had loved.

Casey got to the bar manager's office, knocked, and walked in. Goldie was on the phone but smiled and waved her in. Casey put down her lager on the desk and waited until he finished the call. Then Goldie stood and walked over to the edge of the desk, sat down, and crossed his arms. He was tall, around six foot four, and was dressed a lot less flamboyantly than he usually was in the evenings, but even still, he wore a finely knit, short sleeved gold sweater, which popped against his dark black skin, and tight blue jeans.

Goldie had the benefit of being effortlessly thin and could wear almost any feminine clothes he liked, if they accommodated his height. Anyone could tell how much Goldie loved to show his gender nonconformity, by his dressed-down outfit. To complement his clothes, he wore light make-up with purplish-blueish shadow and deep wine coloured lipstick.

"Have you decided yet?" Goldie asked.

"I think so. I'm hoping to go in the morning."

"I've only just got you back, Case."

Casey felt guilty. It had been a long time since she was separated from the only person she considered family any more.

"I know, but"—Casey rubbed her face with her hands—"I need to do this. I've lost something of myself, and I have to find it again if I can. I don't know any other way."

Goldie let out a breath and stood up. He put a hand on her shoulder and squeezed. "I know this assignment was the most difficult you've had to do, and there are things that you've done that you're not proud of. But good came out of it. You did a service to all those who have lost someone."

Casey touched the dog tags that hung around her neck. "I know, but every job I do costs me."

Goldie pulled Casey into a tight hug. He was the only one, apart from her regular employer, who knew what Casey did.

"I love you, Case, and Albie would be so proud of you."

Casey gulped hard at the mention of her brother. Albie and Goldie had been partners when she'd came to live with Albie, and they'd been like parental figures to her.

"Thanks, Goldie, but I need to make peace with myself."

Goldie cupped her cheeks. "Do whatever you have to do, as long as you stay safe and come back to me, my little treasure."

Casey smiled and shook her head. "I'm thirty-two years old. You're not meant to call me that any more."

Goldie just patted her cheek and grinned. "You'll always be that little angry sixteen-year-old we brought to live with us."

Casey nodded and said, "I'll drop by in the morning before I leave, okay?"

"Make sure to do, treasure." Goldie gave her a wink.

Casey, smiled, shook her head, lifted her bottle of lager, and walked out into the main bar. She'd just finish it and head home.

Jon walked over to her. "Hey—" He was interrupted by the boos and shouts of the other patrons.

They both looked up to the large holograph TV screen up on the bar wall. It was footage of Thea Brandt on-screen. That was bound to bring out consternation in any Denbourg national. Just over nine years ago, Thea orchestrated the assassination of King Christian and his heir, Crown Prince Augustus, bringing Princess Rozala to the throne. That act had scarred the nation and the lives of the military personnel caught up in the aftermath of the assassination.

"Did you see this story, Casey? That famous undercover investigator—Lucian—got a big story about Thea Brandt."

Casey knew only too well what the story was about but pretended she did not. "No what's it about?" Casey asked.

"TV up five," Jon said.

"This morning a news story broke about criminal mastermind Thea Brandt, by award winning investigative journalist Lucian. Lucian, who we now know is a woman, spent six months infiltrating Thea's gang of criminals on the inside. Lucian describes that far from being dismantled, Thea Brandt's world criminal network has been rebuilt in the nine years she has spent incarcerated. Thea is controlling it all from jail with the help of fellow inmates and prison guards she's bought off. Lucian also discovered that a so-called kill list has been drawn up by Thea and her associates, and plans made to implement it. On that list is Queen Rozala, her family, and several government officials. The governor of the prison has been suspended until a full inquiry can be implemented."

"If Lucian came into this bar," Jon said, "I'd shake her by the hand and give her as many free drinks as she wanted. Anyone who stops Brandt deserves a medal. I'd always thought of Lucian as a man, though."

Casey shut her eyes, and images of what Lucian had to do to gain access and to earn Thea's trust flashed across her eyes. Because she was Lucian and that was her story.

As she had on many other investigations, Casey had let her inner darkness come and take over, but the more she visited the dark side, the more difficult it seemed to get back to her normal self, and the more she questioned which was her normal self.

That's why she had to get out. Lucian had retired, and Casey was going to spend some time finding the answers she needed.

"You assumed Lucian was a man?"

Casey tensed. She knew that woman's voice instantly.

Jon said, "Well yeah, it's usually a man's name, but I suppose I shouldn't stereotype like that."

"Probably best," the woman said.

Jon turned to the patron who had just sat down and asked, "What can I get you?"

"Gin and Dubonnet, please."

"Of course. Give me a minute," Jon said.

He was obviously flummoxed by the unusual drinks order. If Casey hadn't known her by voice, the unusual choice of drink gave her away. Annika Ivanov.

Once Jon moved off, Casey said without out turning around, "I didn't think I'd find you in a bar on such a busy news day."

"There's always the next story, Casey. You know that."

Casey turned around to look at her just as Jon delivered her drink.

"Thank you, barman."

Annika was looking as elegant as ever. At fifty-five years old, Annika did not look her age. She took care of herself and was an extremely beautiful woman. She had medium-length ash-blonde hair and wore the very best of designer business suits. Annika was the CEO of the Ivanov multimedia company. The family business was over a hundred years old, and in that time the family had acquired digital newspapers, TV news stations, and other multimedia interests from all over the world.

It was Annika who'd given Casey her first job, the woman who first saw a spark in her, to whom she owed her whole career.

"How did you track me down?" Casey asked.

"I know you like to drink here when you are in Battendorf. I know Goldie is here. I have my contacts." Annika smiled.

"Oh, I know you do. What is it you want?" Casey said that in a much harsher voice than she meant to.

"Charming."

Casey shook her head. "I'm sorry. It's just the way I'm feeling at the moment."

"It's okay. I know you go through an adjustment period when you finish a job," Annika said.

Adjustment period was an understatement, especially with this last job. The things she heard and saw haunted her.

"What did you want to see me about?"

"I've had a tip-off—"

"No," Casey said. "I told you this was my last job. I'm retired."

"I never thought you meant it. You can't retire at thirty-two," Annika said.

"I can when I don't know who I am any more."

"You are the best investigative journalist I have ever worked with. You have so much more to give, new people to expose, and people to help."

In her mind Casey saw herself holding down a fellow inmate while they received punishment for apparent crimes against Thea's prison regime. It made her feel sick.

"I can't do it any more, Annika. When you start to become what you're investigating, it's time to retire," Casey said as she swirled her lager around the bottle.

Annika put her hand on hers and whispered, "You could never be like Thea. You have saved lives by exposing her prison setup. The Denbourg royal family, for example."

Casey ran a hand through her floppy blonde fringe. "Maybe, but it's just too much. To get this story I had give it every ounce of my energy, and it's left me feeling empty. Besides, my cover is getting exposed. People know Lucian is a woman now."

Annika took a sip of her drink. "What are you going to do instead? This has been your life."

"I know, but it's time to reassess. I've bought a new motorbike, and I'm going on a road trip through Europe," Casey said.

Annika furrowed her brows. "A road trip? Yourself? Why?"

Casey drank the last of her no-alcohol lager. "To clear my head."

But the real reason was much more complicated. It was to find out who she was. She was lost. Casey had been going from story to story since she was eighteen years old, and now she felt like she had left a piece of her light in every story. She had plunged deeper and deeper into the darkness the people she was investigating surrounded themselves in.

Could she climb back out, or was evil really, deep down, what she was in her soul?

She had to find out.

"If that's what you want, but can I leave you with this?" Annika pulled a brown paper folder out of her bag.

"Where did you get that? A museum of communication?" Casey joked.

"Nowadays, Casey, people often find paper folders more secure than computer systems. You might leave this on a train for a few people to read, but a computer can be hacked, and potentially billions would know."

Annika placed the folder on the bar, but Casey didn't take it. "Where did you get this?"

"Through a third party. I don't know who originally leaked it, but it's either a pack of lies…"

"Or?" Casey prompted Annika.

"Or someone at the very top of government is trying to warn us about unconstitutional activities happening in our government system. Take a look?"

Casey stared at the brown paper file and felt a tiny ripple of excitement, the kind she always get when a lead presented itself. She felt the impulse to reach out and take it but resisted.

"No, that's not what I want any more. You've had plenty of stories out of me, Annika," Casey said.

"But this one? Just one last one for me?"

Casey looked at her with derision. "I think I've given you back more than one favour. You've had exclusive rights over my stories since I started working for you."

Annika sighed. "I know. It's just that this story is important to me. If you ever change your mind, then you know how to get hold of me. I have another appointment. Speak to you soon."

Casey turned away from Annika and picked up her motorcycle helmet and jacket. "Don't hold your breath." She put on her well-worn leather jacket and watched Annika leave the bar. After Annika exited,

Casey caught sight of something on the stool where Annika had been sitting. It was the folder.

Casey grabbed it and her helmet and ran to the door, trying to catch Annika up. But as she burst through the doors, Annika's limo was already driving away.

She looked down at the folder. "Well played, Annika." Annika knew Casey wouldn't leave an important document behind. She'd left it on purpose.

Casey walked to the parking area where her motorcycle was and gazed at the folder, and she experienced that tingle again.

I'm not going to look at it.

She placed it inside her leather jacket, next to her chest, and zipped up, keeping it safe. She'd drop it off at Annika's office tomorrow.

Casey pulled her fringe into a small bun at the back of her head. The back and sides were undercut and short. She then pulled on her helmet and climbed on her bike. When she powered it on, she hesitated and put her hand to her chest. There could be something inside the folder that was important, essential for Casey to bring to the public's attention. Maybe a quick look wouldn't hurt?

She closed her eyes. Movies in her head began to play. Selling Thea's drugs around the prison, the violence she witnessed when inmates didn't pay up. It went against everything she believed in or used to believe it.

Because she didn't know if she was that principled a person any more. The more violence you were involved in, the more you became deadened inside to it.

The tingle Casey got for a new story was replaced by anger.

No, I'm not doing it.

She revved her engine and drove off.

CHAPTER TWO

Chief Bohr led Poppy onto the plane, with Mattius following behind. Jess had arranged for Poppy to be seated first, so there weren't lots of people around her.

Poppy felt embarrassed walking past the other passengers, as if she was special. She wasn't. She just happened to have a really famous sister-in-law, although the notoriety had been useful when she needed to bring some attention to her UNICEF campaign.

Poppy was welcomed aboard by the cabin staff, and one of the crew led Jess and Poppy to first class. "Why first class, Chief Bohr? I don't need special treatment."

"It's not about the luxury of the surroundings, Ms. King. It's simply easier to keep you safe. We're in the cabins at the end."

"Okay, and it's Poppy."

"Sorry, Poppy."

They were led to a section of the plane that had small cabins, with doors. "You're in here, Ms. King," the member of the cabin crew said.

Jess opened the door and indicated for Poppy to step in. The booth was incredible. It was a self-contained room with two seats, a minibar fridge, holo screens to any and every kind of TV or film or game you wanted. The seat could be opened into beds.

Poppy had been on the Denbourg royal plane with her sister, and it had rooms for dressing and such, but this commercial flight really showed how the other half lived. Even if she had all the money in the world, Poppy wouldn't travel this way. That money could be much better spent helping others.

Not that Poppy worried about money. She understood her privilege. Her father, now retired, had been a surgeon, and her mum ran her own catering business. Growing up, she'd never worried about where things she needed were coming from. Neither had Lennox.

They were well-educated and able to go through school without worrying about student loans. When each of them reached twenty-one, they inherited money left to them by their grandmother. Poppy had used some of hers to buy a flat in Battendorf, where she went to fashion school.

When they were settled, a second crew member came to the door and offered them a glass of champagne.

"No thanks," Poppy said.

Jess waved him off.

Poppy groaned. "I don't think I want to drink ever again after last night."

Jess smiled. "You did look like you were letting off a lot of steam."

Mattius popped his head in. "Chief? The rest of the passengers are boarding now."

"Okay. On guard."

"Are you going to tell me what this is about now?" Poppy asked.

"When we're airborne. I need to use some blocking equipment to keep our conversations private, and it would be better if we took off first."

"Really?" Poppy said with annoyance. She couldn't imagine what had required all this fuss but sat back and waited until the plane took off.

Once they were in the air, Poppy reached into the cooler and took out a bottle of fresh orange juice. She really needed it after last night. As she began to twist the cap off, Jess blocked her hand.

"May I check this first?"

Poppy frowned in surprise. "You want to check my juice?"

"Please? I will explain."

She handed it over and Bohr swept her palm over it. The tips of her fingers had a soft red glow. She then tapped her finger against her temple, and a small holo screen popped down from her eyebrow, covering her eye. Her retina appeared to be reading information that was displayed there.

"Yes, it's simple orange juice. You may go ahead," Jess said.

"You thought I could be poisoned?"

"You can't be too careful."

"Hey, wait! Are those tech implants you're using?"

Jess didn't reply but tapped the side of her nose and winked.

"Oh, it's secret agent stuff?"

The plane was soon boarded and they were in the air. "So, Chief? Explanation?"

"Of course."

On the screen in Poppy's booth, Jess called up a picture of Denbourg and, some might say, the world's most notorious criminal, Thea Brandt.

"Do you know who this is?" Jess asked.

"Of course I do. She was my sister-in-law's ex-girlfriend, and she had Roza's father and brother assassinated, changing the destiny of Roza's and my sister's lives."

Jess nodded. "As you know, she was a criminal kingpin who sold arms to unfriendly countries. After Thea was arrested, the Denbourg, British, and US forces used intel to destroy her network of criminal cells and weapons stores. We thought we had destroyed her power base and, thus, Thea herself."

"But you didn't, I take it?" Poppy said.

"No," Jess said, "turns out that Thea had been building up her power base again slowly, over her time in jail." She switched the screen to a news story with the headline *Kill List*, written by the investigative journalist Lucian.

"Is that *the* Lucian?"

"If you mean the prize-winning undercover journalist, then yes. The Denbourg secret service received information that Lucian had broken a story about how Thea was still running her weapons and drugs empire from her jail cell and has prepared a kill list to wreak havoc on our country."

Poppy was shocked. "Are Roza, Lex, and children okay?"

"Yes, we have reviewed and enhanced security around them, and options are being considered as to what to do with Thea."

Poppy's heart raced with panic. The thought of losing her sister and her family was terrifying. "Lock her up in a box and ship her off to Antarctica or something," Poppy said angrily.

"It's not as simple as that. I wish it was, but the layers of her organization run so deep that you cut off one head, another appears elsewhere. It's how she has been able to run her business from prison. We don't know the mechanism exactly, but she has friends and worker bees everywhere."

"This kill list. What is it about?"

"Thea seems determined to wipe the House of Ximeno-Bogdanna-de Albert-King from the face of the map."

Poppy began to fear what was coming next. "Who's on the list?"

"The immediate royal family—Queen Rozala, Crown Consort Lennox, and the children, Crown Prince Lennox Augustus George and Princess Maria Rose."

"My God."

"That's not all. Both your parents, and yourself. That is why Mattius and I have been sent here. Queen Rozala sent officers to your parents, and I was tasked with bringing you back safely from India."

Poppy shook her head. "That's why you were checking my drink? I just can't take this in. How did this Lucian get the story?"

"Apparently, she, as we now know, went undercover as a prisoner. Spent a year serving time and used that time to get closer and closer with Thea and her inner circle. This is the headline story, but the news organization will be serializing the story of Lucian's stay in prison."

"The famous Lucian is a woman, then?" Poppy said.

"That's how she presented in jail at least. Her true status, we don't know for certain."

Poppy's mind was racing. Fear for her family overwhelmed her thoughts. "Are you people bringing Mum and Dad over from the UK?"

Jess shook her head. "No, the Queen has been advised that they would be safer for the moment back in the UK. Our officers and the British government's MI5 agents are working together to keep their house protected."

"What about me? I'm starting a new business course at college. I'm not going home. Going to business school is part of my dream."

"At the moment, my only orders are to bring you safely back to Battendorf."

Her sombre mood was matched by the heavy grey clouds she watched through the plane window. She was so full of optimism last night. She'd laughed and drunk with her friends and looked forward to a new challenge, something that could actually make change in the world.

Working with UNICEF had inspired her to try a new way of manufacturing reasonably priced clothing and paying fair wages to those who made them.

Poppy's love of clothes, and her degree in fashion design, gave her the determination to make her dream come true. The last piece of the puzzle was to earn her diploma in business. Maybe she wouldn't be able to do that now?

❖

Casey spooned her Chinese takeaway onto a plate and took it over to the couch. When she was in prison, she'd missed Chinese food so much.

The TV played low in the background, and she started to eat. Each mouthful replenished a little of the energy she had lost over the last year in prison. Physically at least, not emotionally.

Casey's new apartment was in a former mansion in the centre of town that had been split up into separate dwellings. Casey's was a loft apartment, with a balcony that looked out on Battendorf's River Dorian. Annika had secured this place for her, and Casey was pleased with it. The stone architecture was a great aesthetic, and she only needed to walk out of the building and she had a coffee shop, a baker's, and many restaurants. It was an expensive, arty part of town, and only a five-minute walk to Restoration Square and the palace.

The nature of Casey's career had meant moving from place to place, apartment to apartment, never settling or laying down any roots. She had to be careful and maintain anonymity. That made putting down roots a no go. Not that she'd had any roots to start with. As a child she had been moved from place to place, until she came to live with her brother and Goldie. It was a secret wish and dream of hers that she could one day have that kind of life. But the day-to-day existence of an undercover reporter made that impossible.

She ate mouthful after mouthful of the delicious food as she watched the news channel run with the story she had scooped. Casey could imagine Thea's face as she watched the story about her unfold. She could also imagine the people who would pay, with the power of Thea's wrath.

Suddenly, Casey wasn't hungry any more. She pushed her plate onto the coffee table. Thea used violence to make herself feel bigger, more powerful, and nothing made her feel better than to bully the weak. She could see how a young Princess Rozala was a victim of coercive control in their ill-fated relationship.

She got a beer from the fridge, a real beer this time, and dumped her plate at the sink. On her way back her eyes caught the folder on the coffee table. The facts for a fresh new investigation, another wrong to right or people to expose.

"No," Casey said out loud.

This last job had broken her, or that's what she feared. Casey couldn't risk exposing herself again to the underworld. She sat and took a big gulp of beer and watched the news—well, pretended to watch, while all the time thinking about the folder on the table.

Casey crossed her legs and willed herself not to look, but it called to her like a siren. These stories always did. She had been chasing news since she was in charge of her high school newspaper. It was ingrained in her, and despite the trauma of the year she had just endured, the need for the chase was still strong inside her.

Maybe she could just scan it quickly. It might not even be her kind of story, or worthwhile doing. Then her brain couldn't annoy her about it any more.

"No." Casey slammed her bottle on the table. She leaned over and held her head in her hands. "No. I'm leaving in a few days for my drive across Europe. That's my next project."

Casey swept her hands back over her hair and pulled her small topknot tight. Her nerves were jangling like she needed a fix. She looked up again at the table. Could she hand back the folder and never know what was inside it?

She reached out her hand towards the folder and stopped. This could be nothing, a disinteresting case, or it could be the one that sent her back down the rabbit hole. But would she ever come out again?

Casey couldn't fight her instincts. She grasped the folder and opened it quickly. The first thing she saw was a picture of Queen Rozala and Crown Consort Lennox. It was clearly a paparazzi picture and showed Lennox striding ahead of the Queen, who was behind holding the hands of their son and daughter.

Above the picture was written, *The House of King now rules?*

"What is this all about?"

A second picture showed the Queen up against a wall in the palace garden, looking stressed or fearful. Lennox had her hands holding the Queen's shoulders tightly. These pictures were either unfortunately timed, or Lennox King had control issues, which surprised Casey.

She wasn't a royalist by any means but always had the impression that the royal couple had a reasonably happy marriage.

Casey put the pictures to the side and started to read through the pages of information. She just scanned it, but there apparently was testimony from former staff that the Queen had been battling many mental health issues, since dealing with fertility struggles after the birth of Prince August.

She read on and found allegations that, in fact, the Queen's mental state was being kept a secret from the people of Denbourg, and that Crown Consort Lennox was ruling in her stead.

"This cannot be right, can it?"

Casey had been in prison for a while. So she didn't know all the royal gossip, not that she was interested, but she'd always had the impression that the royal family had been pretty stable in the years since Rozala's father and brother were killed.

There were a few URLs referenced in the file, and Casey decided to dig a little. "Computer, find governmentinsider dot com."

Milliseconds later the webpage was displayed on the holo screen in front of her. A blog titled *Government Conspiracy*.

The blog alleged that former financial sector insider Lennox King had been placed in the royal family by the global elites to control Rozala and to further their agenda. As soon as Casey saw the phrase *global elites* she switched off.

Why would Annika try to interest her in conspiracy theorist shit?

Casey read some of the comments below the article and was even more turned off by the comments. They claimed that the global elites themselves were being run by aliens, as were the royal families across the world.

She threw down the folder in disgust, and said, "Computer, call Annika."

Annika answered, but it sounded like she was at some kind of cocktail party. "Hang on, I'll get some privacy." Annika was now visible in a library. "Yes. I'm now on a secure channel. How can I help you?"

"I want to know why you gave me this folder."

Annika smiled. "You couldn't resist reading it, then. I knew you wouldn't be able to last."

"You clearly have lost all respect for me if you're giving me royal conspiracy theories about aliens."

Annika sighed. "That's just the fringe, the introduction, if you will. You have to read on. I had the same reaction when this info was passed to me, but conspiracies often have a grain of truth in them that grows arms and legs, and that's what I want you to investigate."

"So what is this grain of truth?" Casey asked.

"I don't know if it is true or not, but look at the rest of the articles that I've included, small columns from respected newspapers and journalists, all insinuating that King isn't just the consort's surname, but that she is king in all but name. That they are keeping the Queen's mental health issues secret."

"How could that be true?"

"That would be for you to find out, but if any of this is true, it is an affront to our constitution and must be brought into the open for the sake of our democracy."

What Annika said was true, but the story seemed so improbable. "Do you believe this?" Casey asked.

"Ninety-five percent, no, I don't, but if there's just that five percent chance, it's our duty as a responsible news outlet to find out for sure."

Casey tapped her fingers on the coffee table and then looked up at the TV. The news was showing footage of Queen Rozala, walking amongst a crowd, shaking hands, with Lennox holding a hand at the small of her back.

"I suppose if she was having mental health issues before, then my story about Thea having her family on a kill list won't help. How would I get close enough to find out?"

"Will you do it?" Annika asked.

Casey rubbed her forehead. It was now or never. She did owe Annika her career, the awards that she had been given, and her financial position. All were dependent on Annika having given an eighteen-year-old a chance. "I'll do it. You'll set up my usual backstory?"

Since Casey first went undercover for Annika's newspaper, she had been listed as an employee of one of Annika's media company's many subsidiaries. This gave her a plausible backstory. If anyone took the trouble to investigate her background, then Casey was on the payroll of a minor company owned by Athena Media Corporation.

With each name came a new company she worked for.

"Yes, I'll email the details. What name do you want to use this time?"

Casey thought about it. When she had taken off her disguise in the motel room, it had been a promise to herself that she would be Casey James from now on, and she intended to stick by that.

"Casey James."

"What? You can't use your real name," Annika said.

"No one apart from my family and you knows my real name. I only worked in the newsroom for six months before my name disappeared off payroll. Besides, I promised myself that I'd be true to myself from now on, and this is my last job."

"You said that before."

"I truly mean it this time. I need to find a way into the royal family."

"I have your way in. You're going back to school."

CHAPTER THREE

"Y ou know what to do?" Thea asked her second in command.

"I do. It will be no problem."

Thea was sitting on her bed in a large jail cell at the end of the first floor. She liked this position. She had rebuilt an empire from here, and the castle walls were the prison door with lieutenants and foot soldiers stationed up and down the corridor.

Even the prison officers didn't like coming up to her castle, and many were in her pay, but she had put her trust in someone and was betrayed.

One of her people put their head around the door. "They're on their way, boss."

Regi, her second, said, "Everything will be done as you ask, boss. This won't be for long."

A prison officer walked into the cell, and Thea's people stood, circling her.

"Stand down," Thea said. "Officer Bastie is just doing his job."

They took a step back, and then the deputy prison governor entered, followed by a couple more officers.

"Deputy Governor Vastas, or will it be Governor? I see your superior has been replaced."

"Because of you, Thea," she said forcefully.

Thea just responded to her by laughing. "And you're going to escort me? I am honoured."

The deputy governor turned to Officer Bastie and said, "Chain her."

Officer Bastie brought forward the chains and said, "Stand."

Thea stood slowly and held her wrists out. The other prison guards locked wrist cuffs and ankle restraints on.

"Follow me," Vastas said.

Thea walked out onto the landing and saw that the other women had been locked down in their cells, but as she shuffled in her chains, she heard a rhythm being beaten out the cell doors. The women were with her.

When she had arrived in this jail, Thea had nothing but her reputation. A few inmates tested her reputation and regretted that decision as they lay at her feet, blood streaming down their faces.

The others soon fell in line, and the beginnings of her prison empire took root, and her syndicate began rebuilding her empire on the outside. Her enemies thought they had broken Thea's international crime syndicate, but she had too many well-placed people all over the world for it to be destroyed. They picked up the pieces, and Thea controlled it from her prison cell.

She was led down two levels below the first floor to a basement level of the prison. She'd had no idea this even existed. The guards stopped at a large heavy door. The beat of the women's voices from upstairs was well gone. This level was deserted, and eerily quiet.

"I thought solitary confinement was on the west side of the prison, Deputy Vastas."

Vastas stared her out and then said smugly. "No, this isn't solitary, Brandt. This is where we house special category prisoners. Serial killers, abusers…people that caused very special kinds of harm to those on the outside. Someone like you who threatens the life of our Queen and her family—our very democracy."

Thea smiled. "Oh my. Our democracy? What a monster."

"Get in," Vastas said firmly.

The officers escorted her into the cell. It was probably twice the size of her other cell, but with far fewer amenities. There was a hard-looking bed, one wooden chair, and a toilet.

"Welcome to your new home, until the Queen's government decides what to do with you."

"Well, at least I'll get some peace and quiet." Thea was determined not to show weakness or give the impression this was getting to her.

"You'll have lots of peace and quiet, no doubt. Take her restraints off."

Once Thea was free, she took a step closer to Vastas and whispered, "Perhaps you could send one of my women down, now and then. I have very particular needs."

Thea was sure she could see a blush of pink on the Deputy

Governor's cheeks. She simply turned around and walked out of the cell.

The guards followed her, and the door was locked, leaving Thea with nothing except her thoughts.

❖

"Are you all right? Lund told me you were upset, and you didn't let the children go to school."

Roza wiped away her tears and turned away from the window.

Lex was there, offering her reassuring presence. Roza slipped into her arms.

"Just having a wobble, pathetic, huh?"

Lex frowned. "Don't ever say that. You are a strong woman. You've been through so much, but you're here, still standing."

"I wouldn't be without you," Roza said.

Lex held her tight in her arms. "We are a team."

"Every time I think I'm mostly over the trauma of Thea, something happens, and it all comes flooding back."

"Don't beat yourself up. The scars that woman has caused run deep, but you always conquer those fears," Lex said.

Roza pushed away from Lex. "But she's threatened our children now, and Poppy, and your parents."

"August and Maria will be perfectly safe. They are surrounded by security."

"My father and brother were surrounded by security, but they were still shot in the head," Roza said.

Lex took her hand and led her over to the couch. "How about we leave off sending them to school for the rest of the week and see how things are. We can't keep them locked away forever."

"I—we've lost too much already, Lex."

Lex felt a stab of pain cut through her. With the grief of losing her father and brother, both Roza and Lex had thrown themselves into making a big family. That's what Roza had wanted. A big family with lots of children and noise to drown out what she'd lost.

But since the difficult birth of their first child, Prince Lennox Augustus George, Roza and Lex had struggled terribly with fertility issues. The worst thing was the constant public speculation about more children. The heir and a spare was what the country wanted, and Roza had wrongly felt herself a failure for not providing that.

Of course Lex would have loved more children, but if it wasn't to be, she was quite happy with their beautiful boy August.

Roza was particularly affected. Then one day Maria came into their life. Roza was visiting a refugee camp near the border of Turkey and met women and girls who had fled from the civil war in neighbouring Mourd.

Maria's mother had just given birth when Roza met her, and her story of fear and the sexual violence that she had run from stuck in her head. Roza had to see her again, but when she enquired, she found out the young mother had passed away that morning.

To Lex's surprise, Roza asked if they could adopt Maria and bring her back to Battendorf. She was fully behind the plan as they both desperately wanted another child. The Palace officials and government advisors were very much against it, but at Roza's and Lex's insistence, the government eventually agreed.

They brought home Princess Maria Rose, and they and the world fell in love with the sweet little girl. Maria completed their family, and her adoption helped to shine a light on the devastating war in Mourd.

"What time is Poppy arriving?" Roza asked.

"She should be here in a few hours. I've asked her to stay here tonight so we can have a proper chat—"

"And keep her safe," Roza said.

"Yes."

Lennox cursed Thea Brandt. After a tough couple of years, Roza was finally getting back to being the enthusiastic, funny, high maintenance woman she loved. Depression and anxiety had taken their toll on her during their fertility problems, but together they'd gotten through it.

Now Thea had raised her ugly head, and Roza's anxiety came thundering back.

"She'll probably push to go back to her flat tomorrow, after we tell her what's happening next."

"How do you think she'll take it?" Roza asked.

Lennox hated being the bad guy, especially with her sister, but needs must. "About as well as when I accidentally threw her favourite toy in the bin with the other rubbish, and it was taken away by the bin men."

Roza snorted with laughter. "You didn't."

"I did. Recycling and taking out the rubbish was my job at home, and I didn't know Mr. Ted was inside a box in the kitchen. So I gathered up all the recycling, and Mr. Ted was—"

"Recycled?" Roza smiled.

"You could say that. Poppy screamed and cried for three hours, until she cried herself to sleep."

"Let's hope she doesn't scream for three hours tonight."

❖

When Poppy's plane landed in Denbourg, her head had settled after a sleep and painkillers. Chief Bohr had instructions to bring her to the palace, not to Poppy's flat. Poppy couldn't wait to see her family.

It had been three months since Poppy had last been home, and she had missed all the family so much, especially her niece and nephew. Maria was at an age when three months might as well be five years, but Lex and Roza always made sure they spoke to her frequently via video call.

A waiting royal car had picked them up on the tarmac as soon as they exited from the plane and driven them directly to the city centre of Battendorf. The main square, where the public and tourists flocked to, sat in front of her destination—Ximeno Palace, where the royal family lived, for a large part of the year.

Poppy loved going to Restoration Square when she was visiting. It had all the requisite statues—great army commanders on horseback, former kings and queens—but it was the buzz of the people Poppy enjoyed.

The streets that surrounded the square had a very cosmopolitan feel, lined with cafes, small boutiques, art galleries, and some high-end clothes shops. Poppy loved coming to visit Lex and spending a whole day window shopping. The square itself and its benches were Poppy's favourite place to eat lunch as street performers and entertainers moved around the office workers and families of tourists. There was an ice-cream booth in the north corner of the square that Poppy just had to go to every time she visited.

But instead of dropping Poppy off at the square, the car drove on and up to the gates of Ximeno Palace. The grand palace had gone through a big refurb when Roza became Queen.

She was led through the palace to the family wing. Poppy had a regular room she used that was near her sister, sister-in-law, and the children. She gazed around the rich paintings and gold cornicing and felt a stab of guilt.

The grand surroundings always jarred her when she came back from her work with UNICEF. Only two days ago, she was helping some women use some new equipment in the clothing factory where they worked. UNICEF was working, at Denbourg's urging, to improve the working conditions, but those women would probably think they had come to a different planet if they came here to Denbourg.

When she arrived at her room, the footman said, "Your bags will be brought up shortly, ma'am."

"Are the Queen and Crown Consort at home?"

"No, miss. They have an afternoon engagement but will see you at dinner," the footman said.

"What about the kids? Are they home from school soon?"

"No. They weren't sent to school today, Prince August is playing in his bedroom, I believe, and Princess Maria is in the nursery."

"Okay, thanks."

Once he left, Poppy collapsed onto the bed. She had forgotten what a proper comfortable bed felt like. She lay and let herself sink in. *I'll just close my eyes for a second.*

Poppy felt herself start to drift, and she snapped open her eyes. "No I need to wash this journey off me—and my hangover."

She got undressed and went into the bathroom. It was beautiful, exactly like you'd expect in a palace—no gold toilets, though. That's what Lex had told her as a gullible teenager on her first visit to the palace—that the sinks were gold, the toilets were gold, the cutlery and plates were gold. To be fair, Poppy chuckled to herself, there was gold cutlery.

She got into the large shower and allowed herself to luxuriate in the never-ending warm water. It was bliss. Poppy thought through what she would do next. Get dressed, go and find the kids, maybe have something to eat.

She shut off the shower and wrapped herself in the most amazingly soft white towels. The dressing gown was just the same. "How do they get these things so soft?" When she walked out of the bathroom, she felt so comfortable, warm, and cosy, that a little voice started to whisper, *Just a small nap would be okay. Thirty minutes tops.*

Poppy was just about to give in when she caught sight of her nephew, August. He was hitting a ball against a wall in the palace back courtyard. He was surrounded by more security than she had ever seen before. Poor Gus. He looked so dejected.

"I think his favourite aunt needs to come to his rescue."

She towel-dried her hair, pulled it into a ponytail, and dressed quickly. Poppy hurried as best she could, but this palace was like an overwhelming labyrinth at times.

Eventually she found her way to a door that would lead out to the back courtyard. One of the protection officers, whom she didn't recognize, put her arm out to stop Poppy and said in her Bourgian tongue, "What is your business here?"

That was what she heard anyway. Poppy wasn't exactly a natural with foreign languages, but she had picked up what she needed since she'd come here to visit as a teenager, and to live as a student. She didn't always get much practice. Roza and most of her officials tended to speak in English most of the time because of Lex, so it was easy to be lazy about learning it.

An officer came striding over. "This is the Crown Consort's sister. You were briefed this morning she would be arriving. Sorry, Ms. King."

The younger woman looked horrified. "So sorry, Ms. King."

"Don't worry about it." Poppy smiled. "I wanted to come and see August. He looks a bit sad."

The man said, "Yes, ma'am. He's not been in his happiest mood today."

Poppy walked across the courtyard. August must be lost in a dreamworld. When she got nearer she said, "Gus?"

He turned around, and the frown he was sporting turned into a huge smile. "Aunt Pops." He launched himself into her arms, and she squeezed him tightly.

"Hi, Gus, I've missed you and your sister so much."

"We've missed you too."

Gus was so cute. He'd picked up on Lex calling her *Pops* as a nickname. It was even cuter coming from Gus's mouth with his Bourgian accented English.

He didn't seem to want to let the hug go, so Poppy stayed holding him until she heard him crying.

"Hey, hey, what's wrong?"

She pulled back and wiped his tears with her thumb.

"Everything."

Poppy took his hand and led him over to a set of stone stairs and sat down. She rubbed his back and said, "You tell your aunt Pops what's worrying you."

August wiped his eyes on his jumper sleeve. "Mari and I missed school today."

"Yeah, I heard."

"Mama says that there was a security thing," he said sadly.

"I know, I had a couple of protection people escort me home from India. Your mama and mum are just trying to protect you and your sister."

Gus hung his head low and kicked the stones by his feet. "I missed my presentation today."

"What presentation?"

"My group at school, we've been working on a big project on the rainforests. I loved it, and it was my group's turn to give our talk to the class. We worked so hard on it."

Poppy put her arm around August's shoulders. "Aw, that's such a shame, Gus."

"It's always the same. Royal stuff always gets in the way. I just wish I was like the other kids. They can do what they want. Ride their bikes all day, go to each other's houses, have sleepovers. I've got to go everywhere with the suits."

August indicated to his protection officers spread throughout the courtyard. Poppy felt so sorry for him. As much as the Queen and Lex tried to make the children's lives as normal as possible, they were never really going to be like every other kid.

"I'm sorry, Gussy—you have your cousins to talk to, don't you?" Poppy knew how close the whole family was to the Buckinghams in the UK. The children loved to be in each other's company because no one could understand the particular pressures of royal life better than family across the sea.

August was really good friends with Teddy, the eldest of the British royal children. Teddy, now twelve, was heir to George's throne, as August was to Roza's. Although there were a few years between them, they were close. Poppy knew that August looked up to Teddy. Teddy was confident and full of personality, and August was quiet and not so sure of himself, so his friendship with her was a good thing.

"Yeah, I'm playing some online games with Teddy tonight."

"That's good. Listen, why don't we go and get Mari and go swimming this afternoon?"

August's face lit up. "I'd love that."

"Let's go, then," Poppy said, then turned to August's guard and told him.

He nodded stiffly. *He doesn't have much of a personality.*

She held August's hand as they walked back to the palace back door.

"Aunt Pops?"

"Yeah?"

"Why does this person have Mama on a kill list, and what is a kill list?" August asked.

Bloody hell. How could she explain that one? She took the easy way out. "I think that's best for your mama to answer that for you. Let's get Mari."

Casey was old school. She didn't use the countless different apps to organize her projects—she liked to use an old-fashioned pinboard and whiteboard. The biggest wall in her office displayed both. There was something about holding a printed picture or document that made things clearer in Casey's mind.

Annika had her PA send over all the information they had on the new investigation. As she had done with Thea, the first thing to do was place a picture of her target on the board. She couldn't help but be excited about this new case.

Casey pinned a picture of Poppy to the middle of the board. Although she was investigating Queen Rozala and Crown Consort Lennox, Poppy was her way in, and she had to find out everything about her.

She stood back and admired the beautiful young woman. She looked carefree with a gorgeous smile. Her information said that Poppy King was a lesbian or certainly had only been seen at events with a female date.

I wonder what her type is? "Computer, show me pictures of Poppy King at any formal events or with a partner."

Casey saw very few pictures that could be described as Poppy with a date. She was mostly in groups of friends. Casey was intrigued.

"Computer, search for all information on Poppy King."

There was a lot, mainly news stories and interviews on her

UNICEF work, her campaigns with Queen Rozala about the ethical clothing industry, and many magazine articles showing her playing with her niece and nephew.

Casey held her chin and felt a grin form on her face. "A quiet family girl, not a party girl, Poppy King? I can use that as an advantage."

Others would have seen this as cynical, and it was. But when it came to a story, she would use every advantage she could. Casey was pretty confident with women and was sure she could turn on the charm and chat Poppy up.

One thing was for sure. It was going to be a lot easier than spending time in jail, befriending one of the world's biggest crime bosses.

Yeah maybe it would be fun.

"Computer, call Goldie."

The phone started to ring and was quickly answered. She could hear the sound of classic pop in the background as his face filled the screen.

"Where were you this morning? I hope you haven't left without saying goodbye to me."

"I wouldn't do that. I'm not leaving, so you'll have to put up with me for a while longer," Casey said.

"What's changed?"

"A new story. I know you think it's a bad idea and you worry about me, but I think I owe Annika this one. It's not my usual take-your-life-in-your-hands kind of story. It's a royal investigation. Not too much danger in that."

Goldie shook his head. "Better not speak too soon. There's danger everywhere, but if anything happens to you, I'll kill you myself. Got it, treasure?"

Casey grinned. "Got it."

❖

The pool water churned as Poppy helped Maria splash her brother. It was such a luxury for Poppy to use the palace pool, and bringing her niece and nephew was the best part. August adored his little sister and simply loved playing with her. Poppy and her parents adored her just as much. She was a beautiful girl with warm brown skin, dark brown hair, and deep brown eyes.

Maria was a contented child most of the time, but still her nanny was happy to have Poppy take her down to the pool. It gave her a chance to catch up on a few tasks.

Maria giggled and squirmed in Poppy's arms. She gave her a big kiss. "Will we do big swims to your big brother?"

"Gus." Maria slapped the water.

"Okay then, kick your legs." Poppy supported her around the waist, while she wore water wings on her arms as she kicked her way over to August's open arms. "You can do it, Mari."

Maria giggled and kicked as hard as she could until she was lifted into August's arms.

Just then a breeze entered the pool room as someone walked in through the door. Poppy looked up when Maria shouted, "Mama, Mum."

It was her sister and Queen Rozala.

"Causing chaos as usual, little sister?" Lex said.

"As always."

Maria was reaching to get to her mama, so Poppy helped her over to the side of the pool. Rozala was waiting with one of the towels Poppy had brought.

Poppy bowed her head to Roza and held Maria up for her mother to take.

"Hi, Poppy. Thanks for entertaining these two," Roza said.

"I'm always happy to spend time with my favourite niece and nephew."

Roza wrapped Maria up in her big fluffy towel and hugged her close. "Hi, my little sweetheart."

Lex gave Maria a kiss and knelt down to speak to August and Poppy. "Gus? Everything okay?"

"Yeah, Aunt Pops surprised us and took us swimming," August said.

"Your aunt Poppy is always surprising. You better get a shower before dinner."

"Can I do some gaming with Teddy after dinner? I said I'd meet her online later."

"We'll see later. Go and get showered," Lex said.

When August swam off, Lex asked, "Was he okay?"

"He was down in the dumps and worried when I arrived, so I thought distracting him might help," Poppy said.

"It seems to have worked."

"He's a sensitive boy," Roza said, "and this...situation is just making it worse."

Lex took Maria from Roza's arms and gave her a kiss. "We can talk about everything at dinner. Are you getting out or swimming with the shark I've had installed?"

"Oh, shut up," Poppy replied. She climbed out of the pool and put on her dressing gown, which she had left on one of the loungers around the pool.

Roza kissed Poppy. "We're so happy to see you."

"Thanks. It's nice to be home. Was your appointment okay today?"

Roza walked on, and Lex said, "Can we talk later?"

"Sure."

When they walked out of the pool room, Roza's head of security was walking towards them with a few of her team.

"Ravn," Poppy called out and walked quickly over to her and kissed her cheek. Ravn went quite red. "It's good to see you."

Ravn cleared her throat. "You too, Ms. Poppy."

When Poppy had first met Ravn as a teenager, she had such a big crush on her, and it was Ravn that made her realize she was gay.

Not only was she good *looking*, but she was even more because of the way she lived her life. She was loyal to Roza and Lex and to her wife and children. She adored them, and Poppy dreamed of having that in the person she fell in love with.

Satisfied she had embarrassed Ravn enough, Poppy went upstairs to get changed and rest a bit before dinner.

CHAPTER FOUR

Thea sat cross-legged on her bed with her eyes closed. She had nothing, no stimulation, not a pen, a piece of paper, or a computer console, but she did have her own mind. It was sharp and clear, and one of the reasons she could carry on her business after being sent to prison.

Her mind was like a computer monitor. Thea could see each of her underground cells, and the people of influence who pledged or owed her loyalty. Her mum had said she could do anything with her brain, be a doctor, a lawyer, an astrophysicist, but things changed when her mother was killed by her boyfriend.

Any thoughts of using her brain power for good had disintegrated. After finding her mother's murderer and killing him, Thea wanted to taste more power and control, and from small beginnings she built a criminal empire, selling drugs and arms to whoever wanted them, and still moved to the very top of society.

Thea remembered what a kick it gave her to seduce then-Princess Rozala. The novelty soon wore off, but keeping Roza under her control angered the establishment, so it was sweet to carry on with their romance, until King Christian forced them apart, and then his forces took part in destroying what she built.

She banished those thoughts back to her memories and concentrated on the here and now.

In her mind's eye she saw a much healthier network of underground cells than she had when she entered prison, nine years ago. Her network was a spiderweb that spread across Europe, and if one cell went down, there was always another to pop up and continue their essential work.

Thea's eyes sprang open when she heard the lock on the door open. A prison guard walked in with a tray of food.

"Dinner, Brandt."

She stared at him with steady eyes as he approached the bed with the tray. When he set the tray down, she saw a tremble in his hand.

"Tell your boss I want a word with her," Thea said flatly.

He gave a quick nod and left the cell.

She gazed down at the tray. The food looked awful, but it wasn't the food that she was interested in. Thea lifted up the plate, and stuck underneath was a computer access device. Thea placed it on her knee and activated it. A holo screen appeared, and all at once she was connected to her world again because that's what this was going to be about—making the world out there Thea Brandt's.

As she moved around the net, she saw story after story about the journalist Lucian, who had exposed her regrouping of her organization and her precious kill list. When the story had come out, Thea had been incandescent with rage. The woman she knew as Luca Connell had wormed her way in her trust.

Thea had thought of her as a protégé, someone who could join her business outside, but she had been tricked, and Thea despised disloyalty. After Luca disappeared from the prison, Thea had her people trying to find out who Luca Connell was, but of course that name and person didn't exist.

But whoever she was, Thea would find out and show her what disloyalty brought you in the Brandt organization. After the dust had settled a few hours later, and it was mooted that Thea would be sent to another, more secure prison, she realized this was an opportunity to bring her plans forward.

She started to contact her people and set some wheels in motion.

Every cloud…Thea thought.

❖

Roza loved watching Lex and Poppy argue about childhood fights and laugh at the stories they were telling August. He was laughing away with them while eating his pizza. It was so good to see him laugh, and Lex too. Lex could be too serious at times as she took the weight of the world on her shoulders.

As a treat for August they decided to have an informal dinner and send out for pizzas. Chef wouldn't be too pleased, but she liked August to get some normality from time to time.

"Mama?"

Roza held Maria in her arms after she finished her food. She rubbed her eyes and looked tired, but no doubt it would still be a fight to get her to bed with all the excitement. She kissed Maria's head and pulled her to her chest. Maria put her arms around her neck and cuddled into her mama's neck.

Roza sighed and closed her eyes. Maria had brought so much joy to their family. Roza had been nervous the day she brought up the subject of adopting to Lex. She was sure there would be some objection, but instead Roza got unstinting support, from both Lex and August. Then she just had to tell her government officials.

They weren't greatly enamoured with the idea, but that was the good thing about being Queen. Your wishes usually won out. Roza had been Queen for ten years now, and the years felt like they had flown.

She looked over to Poppy, who was fighting with Lex over the last piece of pizza. Poppy had been sixteen years old when she met her, and now she was a beautiful young woman, despite Lex still thinking she was a teenager.

Roza felt sorry for the first really serious girlfriend Poppy would bring home. She'd had girlfriends here and there but nothing at all serious, and still, each time Lex got tense.

Lex liked it when Poppy chose to study in Denbourg, because it meant she could keep a beady eye on her. Roza laughed when she saw August steal the last piece of pizza that the two siblings were fighting over.

"Well done, Gus."

Poppy patted him on the back. "I'm glad you got it, Gussy."

"It's like that, is it?" Lex gave them a mock glare.

August ate his pizza quickly and downed his drink. "Mama? Mum? Can I meet Teddy online to play games? She said to meet her at six."

Lex looked at Roza and she nodded. "Yes, you can. Tell Teddy hi from us."

"I will."

Roza was delighted August had Teddy. It was going to be a good few years before Maria could catch up and be able to take part in the kind of activities August enjoyed.

August quickly kissed his aunt, then hugged Lex, and then kissed Roza and Maria.

Once he was gone, Roza said, "I suppose I better get this one bathed and off to bed."

Normally both she and Lex did this together. They needed a full-time nanny and missed a lot of Maria's day, with all the engagements they had, but they always tried to bathe and put her to bed, Lex reading her a story as she dozed off to sleep.

It was a special time. It always warmed Roza's heart to see Maria sleeping soundly, all warm and safe, and fulfilling her birth mother's plea to give her newborn a better life. And a better life is what she had, two parents and a brother that couldn't love her more.

Tonight would be different. Roza was going to leave to allow Lex to speak with Poppy about what had happened with Thea Brandt, and the new security measures. Poppy would not be happy.

She was just about to excuse herself when a footman came in and bowed. "Your Majesty, the prime minister is on the phone for you."

Roza's stomach clenched. She hoped it wasn't more security concerns about Thea. "Of course. I'll take it in the study." Roza stood up and handed a sleepy Maria to Lex. "Would you mind taking Mari?"

"Of course not. Come here, my little honey pie," Lex said.

Lex was so sweet with her, but of course when Maria got into her mum's arms, her tiredness seemed to vanish. Lex meant fun and rough and tumble to Maria.

Roza headed to the study she used in their living quarters, put a light on, and sat at her desk. Before she lifted the phone, she looked up at the picture of Queen Maria and King Christian, her mother and father. Roza hoped she hadn't let them down, and they were pleased with how she had dedicated herself to the job.

Roza never knew her mother. She died in childbirth. Her father had never recovered from the loss, and as Roza grew, she felt he resented her for surviving. Others said no, but he did push her away, probably because she was the image of her mother.

She, of course, rebelled to get the attention she craved, and that drove an even deeper wedge between them. When King Christian and her beloved brother Gussy died, her life was changed overnight. She went from the spare to the heir, to being Queen at a much younger age than should have been the case. But with Lex's help, Roza got rid of her party girl past and dedicated herself to Denbourg and the job of being its Queen.

"I haven't done too badly, have I, Father?" Roza asked sincerely.

The only noise in the study was the tick-tock of the clock on the fireside mantelpiece. Roza shook off her memories and became Queen Rozala before saying, "Open call."

Prime Minister Justin Larcohn appeared on the screen. She quite liked Justin. He was young, with fresh ideas, unlike the last person in his position. He had only been prime minister for a year, but so far she was pleased with him.

"Prime Minister, how can I help you?" Roza said.

Justin bowed his head. "Your Majesty. Thank you for talking to me. I won't take up too much of your time."

"Please, carry on."

"My ministers and I have been locked in a meeting about Thea Brandt all afternoon, and I'd like to tell you our plans and get your approval, if I may?"

Roza became tense at the very mention of Thea's name. To think that at one time, she'd thought she'd loved her. But Roza had come to realize over the years that it wasn't love, it was dependency.

Thea made her believe that she couldn't survive without her. It was an emotionally abusive relationship, and even though she had moved on, life had moved on, and she had discovered what real love felt like with Lex, there would always be some tiny part of her that feared her.

"We have agreed in principle to send Thea to Blestch Island Prison."

"The last prisoners left Blestch Island five years ago," Roza said.

Blestch was a prison that was more than a hundred years old. In its time it had been used for the worst prisoners to be convicted in the Denbourg courts. One of the shooters in her father's and brother's murders was the last to be transferred out of Blestch, as it was mothballed.

The island, just off the Denbourg coast, was surrounded by extremely treacherous seas, and even the most hardened open-water swimmer would be taking their life in their hands to swim across to the mainland. In fact most smaller boats avoided the waters around the island.

It was the perfect location.

"I see, and will the facilities be up to scratch? We don't want to commit human rights violations."

"Considering what she was convicted of, Your Majesty, that's very magnanimous of you."

If only he knew the thoughts and dreams she'd had of all the ways to punish Thea for killing her family, but she was Queen, for better or worse, and she had to be seen to be following the rule of law.

"Everything must be done correctly, Prime Minister. We don't want any mistakes that could give our detractors an excuse to criticize."

In Roza's case, that was her distant cousin, and if it wasn't for her, and the change in law seventy years ago, he would be king, as the closest male heir to her father. He couldn't help himself—he gave quotes and opinions to the news media, to make himself feel more relevant.

"I quite agree, ma'am. If you remember, the last inmates to leave did so in order that the power systems could be upgraded. The upgrades to the facility were expensive, and at the time it was felt that the price couldn't be justified, but the hard work was done. With that head start we think we can have it up and running well enough to transfer Thea there."

"I see."

"Do we have your approval, ma'am?"

"Of course, Prime Minister. I will follow your advice."

"Thank you, ma'am."

Roza felt uneasy as she ended the phone call, and she didn't know why. This plan would keep Thea even further away from her family, but she couldn't help the unease.

❖

Lex led Poppy into the drawing room of their palace apartments. This was going to be difficult, especially after Roza's news about Thea. Poppy would probably argue that things would be safer now, but she would have to contradict her.

Poppy put her coffee down on the side table and flopped onto the couch, sitting cross-legged.

Before Lex got the chance to speak, Poppy said, "Gus was upset today. When I got here, he was outside, looking sad."

"He wasn't happy to be missing school," Lex said.

"No, he was to present a project, he told me, and he was sad he missed it," Poppy said.

"I know," Lex said with a sigh. "Roza didn't want them to go to school today. She was too frightened."

"I can understand why, but you can't lock them up forever, Lex. I think he feels a lot of pressure being Roza's heir and having to have so much security around him."

"I know. He's at an age that he's starting to understand a little of what's ahead. I feel guilty all the time, Pops. He can't have sleepovers like the other kids…" Lex snapped her fingers. "Maybe we *could* have one here. We've got the pool, the games and cinema room, and that would make sure he was safe but give him some normalcy. I'll talk to Roza."

Poppy smiled. "That's a great idea. Oh, and if you could get him a new security agent, that one he's got has no personality."

"I'll try. You see—it's good having you here with us. Gives Gus someone else to confide in."

"I love them to bits."

"You're the best aunty, and by the way, you did good work with UNICEF, Pops. We're all very proud of you," Lex said. This was Lex's segue into discussing Poppy's course.

"Thanks, but it's never enough. As much as I and the team tried to teach the clothing companies the harm that they do by buying off these sweatshops, more needs to be done. As long as people are willing to buy a cheap T-shirt, there will always be some unscrupulous company ready to fill that order. That's why opening my own clothing brand means so much."

Lex loved her sister's passion and how much she had changed her thinking. As a teenager, Poppy was all about the brands, the latest lines from every fashion label. She adored fashion but didn't see any deeper until she began to study the field, and since then her interest and compassion had grown and grown.

"Yes, that's true—"

Poppy squinted. "Wait, I feel a *but* coming."

"No, no but."

Realization began to dawn on Poppy. She had been manoeuvred here for a chat for a reason. She knew Lex always helped with Maria's bedtime routine.

"There's something, Lex, I know. It's to do with Thea Brandt and the protection people you sent me, isn't it?"

Lex cleared her throat. "Yes, the situation with Thea has changed a few things. Your business course—"

Poppy jumped up. "No, no way."

"Please listen, Pops. This is important."

She started to pace. "Go on, then."

"The advice we have been given by the security services is that it would be unsafe for you to start your business course."

Poppy squeezed her eyes shut, trying to control her anger. "You see, this was the *no, no way* I was talking about. This is the next stage of my life, Lex. I need to do this."

Lex leaned forward, resting her forearms on her thighs. "You won't get a next stage of life, Pops, if you don't listen. You are on a kill list."

"Why would Thea want to kill me? I don't matter to her."

Lex stood up angrily. "You matter to me, you matter to Roza, to my son and daughter, to Mum and Dad."

Poppy lost some of her anger at the comment, but none of the resolve. "I know that, but I can't stop living, Lex. I can't stop my life."

Lex crossed over to her position. "I'm sorry that my life has to change yours, but Roza is my life and—"

Poppy held her hand up. "No, I'd never complain about who you are now and who you love, but how long should I stop living my life? Thea Brandt is always going to be in the background."

"Maybe just delay for a year? Till things settle?"

"No, I need to do this. This is my dream. I want my clothing company to give people a choice and show the other clothing companies that there is a market for slightly higher priced goods, and how to make it cost effective. I want the customer to walk into a shop and see two T-shirts, one priced at one euro and one more ethically made and only slightly higher priced, to give them the choice and make them think about how those two T-shirts are being manufactured. I need my college course to help me do that," Poppy said.

Lex walked up to the fireplace and leaned on the mantel with a sigh. "Do you know how I would blame myself if anything happened to you? How devastated Mum and Dad would be?"

Poppy could feel she was getting to Lex and pushed her further. "I'm a bit part player on that kill list. She'll not be worried about me. As long as you, Roza, the kids, and Mum and Dad are safe."

Lex rubbed her forehead. She was clearly wavering.

"How about you get those two guards to stay with me at school… Jess and Mattius."

Her sister looked up sharply. "You've never liked having a guard assigned."

That was very true. When Poppy'd announced she was going to work with UNICEF in both the Far East and Southeast Asia, Lex had been uneasy about it and wanted to send a guard with her, but Poppy had won that argument in the end. She was good at that, especially with her sister.

These were different times, and if Poppy had to give up some freedoms she would. "I won't say a word against having guards. I quite like Jess anyway."

Lex pinched her sister's cheek. "You have amazing powers of persuasion, Pops."

"I can go?" Poppy said excitedly.

"I'll speak to Roza about it. The Queen's word is law."

Poppy launched herself into Lex's arms. "Thank you. Everything will be fine."

"I haven't okayed it with Roza yet," Lex warned.

"She won't mind. Roza always encourages me in all dreams."

Now to convince the Queen.

Not long after Thea's dinner was delivered, she heard the door unlock again. This time she didn't open her eyes because she knew who it would be. She heard the door shut and lock. "I assumed you'd be here sooner, Deputy Vastas."

The sound of stilettos on the hard floor of the cell made Thea open her eyes.

"I came as soon as I could. I did have to shut down a few security measures before I could come and see you—unofficially."

Thea was a great observer of human nature. It was how and why she'd been so successful in her criminal career. It had taken time to set up her control base from prison when she first arrived. Once she did, Thea turned her attention to the prison guards who watched everything she did.

Some were hers with a bribe, some were controlled by her knowledge of their secrets, and just a few were incorruptible. The last governor was one of them and had slowed down her plans, but then Vastas came along. She could read Vastas from the first glance, and the way her eyes caressed Thea's body.

Deputy Governor Daria Vastas was intoxicated with Thea's power and, as it turned out, money.

Thea stood and stalked over to Vastas. When Thea was inches from her, she threaded her fingers through Daria's hair and saw her shiver. "When I ask you to come, I expect you to come quickly."

Thea walked her back up against the wall, and Daria said, "I have some news for you."

"Oh? Tell me." Thea let her fingers and nails graze Daria's neck, where she knew she was particularly sensitive.

"The prime minster has decided you are to be moved to Blestch Island."

Thea laughed. "That bastard wants to maroon me and hopes I die there. When is this supposed to happen?"

"Friday—you are to picked up and transported to the harbour, where you'll be taken by boat to Blestch," Daria said.

Thea's mind whirred with the instructions she would need to give her people on the outside. Her plan had always been to make a break when she was taken for her court date at the end of the year. The Denbourg authorities were charging her with new financial violations, and it would be the perfect time to make a break. But inadvertently Lucian, whoever she was, had given her a perfect cover to go sooner.

"Perfect," Thea said.

"You'll get what you want," Daria replied.

Thea grasped her hair more roughly. "I always get what I want."

Daria leaned in for a kiss, but Thea didn't move. The uneasy, needy look in her eyes was what she was waiting on. Thea kissed her hard. Daria moaned, and their kiss became frenzied.

Thea ran her hand roughly up Daria's thigh, and she held Thea's neck and wrapped her legs around Thea's waist. Thea grasped her sex roughly.

"Yes, I've been thinking about you fucking me all day," Daria said.

This confirmed the fact that she owned Daria. "Yes, and I bet you were fantasizing about it last night."

Daria nodded.

Thea pushed into her underwear and felt how much she wanted Thea. She squeezed, then slipped her fingers around Daria's clit.

"Yes, yes, please, Thea."

Thea stroked her a few times and said, "You're going to do everything you can to make this work?"

"Yes, I will."

Thea teased her opening with her fingers. "You'll work with my people on the outside to make it work?"

"Yes, yes, I promise. Please fuck me."

Thea knew how much Daria loved her touch, but also to be denied. She pulled her fingers from her and said, "Get down on your knees and earn it."

There was disappointment and then a ripple of excitement. Daria dropped down to the dirty floor and pulled down Thea's trousers enough so she could put her face between Thea's legs.

Thea grunted with pleasure as Daria sucked her into her wet mouth. She grasped Daria's hair tightly and moved her hips along with Daria's pace. She looked down and groaned with pleasure. The governor of the prison, on her knees for her.

There was no one and nowhere Thea went that she couldn't bend to her will, her control. Even the fucking Queen of Denbourg had been down on her knees for Thea. She thought about the pathetic Queen Rozala. She had been so easy to control.

Thea could see Roza's face as she fucked her body and her mind. She'd had her exactly where she wanted her until King Christian got in the way. But he soon paid for his interference with her business and her life.

She pictured the scene she'd seen so many times on-screen, the hit she had ordered on the King and his heir, and her orgasm built quickly. Thea placed one hand against the cell wall and said, "Faster, bitch."

If only she'd thought about killing them sooner. Thea would be in Lennox King's position with her way clear to control the Queen. It would have been beautiful. But she would have to make do with killing off Roza and her family one by one. Thea wished she could meet Lennox King before she was killed, to remind her who fucked her wife first.

The thought sent Thea over the edge, and she felt her orgasm rush hot and powerful from her sex and down to her feet.

"Fuck," Thea roared.

She then pushed Daria away from her in disgust. "Get up."

Daria rose on shaky legs and said, "You are still taking me with you?"

Thea cupped her cheek. "Of course I am. You are central to my plan, my dear Daria."

CHAPTER FIVE

"What do you think?" Poppy asked Roza.

She and the Queen were walking back from the nursery after successfully getting Maria to sleep.

"I don't know, Pops—it's too dangerous."

"But Roza, I'll be the last on her list. I won't even merit a hit on my life. I'm only your sister-in-law."

Roza stopped walking and turned around to face Poppy. She grasped her by the shoulders and said, "Poppy, you are not my sister-in-law. I've known you since you were sixteen years old, and you have been with me through thick and thin. Becoming Queen, our difficulties conceiving," Roza said with a shaky voice, "you are my sister and always will be."

Roza pulled her into a hug. Poppy was so touched. "Yes, that's how I feel too. I love you, Roza. There's no one better in the world Lex could have married."

Roza nodded and brought her emotions back under control. "Thank you. Now, if I grant permission, you'll promise to do what your secret service agents say?"

Yes! "Cross my heart."

"Have you talked to Lex about this?" Roza asked.

"Yes, she said as long as you were okay about it. The Queen's word is law, she said."

Roza smiled. "Okay, you can start, but we'll revisit it after a few weeks."

"Can I have Jess and Mattius? We got on well."

"If you like. Just do what they say, Pops."

Poppy used her finger to cross her heart. "I'll be on my best behaviour."

Roza chuckled. "I doubt that. Come on, let's tell Lex."

❖

Poppy spent one more night at the palace, then went back home to her flat, along with Jess and Mattius. It wasn't ideal, but they were nice people and had a lot more personality than most of the agents—well, Jess did.

She was sitting on the couch doodling some T-shirt designs on her drawing pad when a call came through on her TV. It was her mum.

"Answer call." Faith King's face popped up on the screen. "Hi, Mum."

"Hi, sweetie. How's things?"

"Strange. Having two guards follow me about," Poppy said.

"I've set ours to work, helping me with the garden."

Poppy laughed. "You would. Poor guards."

Faith furrowed her brow. "Well, if you have access to four strapping MI5 officers guarding you, it would be silly to waste them. I am feeding them well for it."

Poppy smiled. Her mum used to own a successful catering business until she retired. She was an amazing cook, and Poppy knew the officers would be appreciating it. "How are you, Mum, and where's Dad?"

"I'm fine, and he's just gone out to the supermarket for a few things. You know what he's like." Her mum shook her head.

"It's that time, is it?"

Her mum did all the cooking at home. It wasn't a chore, she loved it, but once a month her Dad insisted on making his wife a romantic dinner, after which the kitchen looked like a bomb had hit it.

"I hope it's not curry, for your sake, Mum." Poppy winked.

There had been many disastrous recipes over the years. One meal stood out. That particular month her dad decided to make a curry from scratch. No jars or tins of premade sauce, nothing. He worked on it for three days, marinated everything, and took the best care. To be fair, it probably would have been delicious if he hadn't dropped the casserole lid.

Glass smashed all through his precious curried dish, and they ended up getting a takeaway instead.

"Don't worry," her mum said. "He's not allowed to use my casserole dishes anymore. He has to make do with the pots and pans."

"I hope it's safe to eat, at least," Poppy said.

Her mum rolled her eyes. "Anyway I wanted to make sure you were okay."

"I'm fine."

"You're okay with putting your business course on hold?"

"Ugh, I'm not. I talked it over with Lex and Roza, and they said I could go as long as I took bodyguards."

Her mum frowned. "It's too dangerous, Poppy. That horrible woman Thea Brandt wants to hurt Roza's family."

"Mum, I'll be okay. I can't put my life on hold. As long as Roza, Lex, and the kids are safe. That's who Thea wants."

"I don't like it. If anything were to happen to you—" Her mum's voice cracked.

"Mum, nothing will happen. I'm going to be well guarded. Jess and Mattius are good at their job."

Her mum pointed at the screen and said in mock anger, "You better be, Miss Poppy King."

Poppy laughed. "Promise, Mum."

❖

Casey was in her office, working on her backstory. She liked to have everything covered in case her target asked the most obscure questions about her life. Casey enjoyed this part. It was a challenge making the history of her character, similar to what an actor would do to play a role.

She often thought she would have been a good actor if she'd been that way inclined. But bringing criminals and their practices to light was more important than adulation or prizes—although she had won two Pulitzer Prizes, awarded pseudonymously, of course.

Or bringing criminals to justice used to be the point. Her assignments had been getting darker and darker. Before Thea Brandt's story, she had infiltrated a right-wing motorcycle gang in Belgium. It was the way she had got into motorcycles, but she had seen some dark things, and after her time in jail with Thea, Casey worried she was getting a kick out of the dark underworld, instead of the story.

At least this royal story should be straightforward and, at its worst, might be a story of a Queen incapable of ruling. Casey's phone rang.

"Answer phone."

"Casey, it's me."

She recognized Annika's voice straight away. "What's wrong?"

"Turn on the TV, and go to our news channel."

Casey hurried through to the living room and said, "TV on."

The TV was already on the news channel, and she saw a smoking mass being shown from above.

"What happened?"

"That is the high security van that was transporting Thea Brandt to her new jail."

Casey's heart started to pound. Was this an escape attempt? Could she be out on the streets? "Any survivors?"

"The police aren't saying officially to the public until the autopsies have happened, but I got a tip-off that there were five people on that truck, including Thea and the prison governor Daria Vastas, and five bodies are left."

"I can understand the police waiting till the autopsies. Thea is capable of anything," Casey said.

"By the state of the truck, they'll be relying on dental records I would think. Thea's terror could finally be at an end."

Casey let out a breath. "I'll wait for the official word. Where Thea is concerned, anything is possible. How did it happen?"

"It was hit by a weapon coming from the hills surrounding the main road towards the harbour," Annika said.

Could it be true? Casey's story had brought about this change of plans and the accident. One thing she was certain of—no one would be weeping for Thea.

❖

"Hang on, Mum. I think Jess is knocking at the door."

Poppy went to answer the door and said to Jess, "Don't knock, Jess. Just come in whenever you need to."

"Have you seen the news?"

"No, I'm on a call with my mum."

"May I show you?" Jess asked.

"Yes, go ahead." Poppy followed Jess to the living room.

"Excuse me, Mrs. King." Jess asked the TV to switch to one of the main news channels. Her mum's video went to the side of the screen.

"Look," Jess said.

Poppy was gobsmacked when she saw the breaking news banner along the bottom of the screen.

"Mum? Go and turn on the news."

"Why?"

"Just do it, Mum."

There was silence while her mother caught up with the breaking news. Poppy looked up at Jess.

"She's gone? She's truly gone?"

"It's too early to say for sure, but it's looking like it."

"My God," her mum said, "Roza can finally have some peace, and Gus, Mari, Lex, and you would be safe."

"You're right. She could finally let go of the pain she's been carrying since her dad and brother died."

❖

Roza sipped the last of her coffee and then got up to pace the floor. This had been the pattern since she and Lex had found out about the explosion of the prison truck. She had tried to get on with her day for the children's sake, but once they were safely in bed, Roza's fears and worry couldn't be suppressed.

"Maybe we should just go to bed," Lex said. "It could be hours until the post-mortems are finished."

"I can't. This woman has lived in my head for well over a decade. I need to know," Roza said. Roza kept staring at the computer access point, willing it to ring. Her head was full of old memories, insecurities, and the utter depths of grief. If Thea was dead, it would bring the closure she'd always been searching for.

At last the phone rang. "Computer, answer as a voice only call." She didn't exactly want to see the prime minister dressed in her dressing gown.

"Your Majesty," he said.

"Yes, Prime Minister. Have you heard anything yet?"

"Yes, ma'am, but we aren't releasing these results to the media till tomorrow."

"Is it her?" Roza said more firmly.

She felt Lex stand behind her and gently stroke her back in support.

"According to results from her dental records, this body is Thea Brandt."

Roza clasped her hand to her mouth fell back against Lex. The emotion was too much, too confusing. She heard Lex take over.

"Thank you for your call, Prime Minister."

Once he was gone, Lex lifted her into her arms and carried her through to their bedroom. She let Roza down and pulled back the bedcovers. Lex encouraged her to lie down.

Roza was silent and appeared as if she was in shock. Lex got in behind her and held her close, so that Roza would feel her strength and comfort. Roza grasped tightly to Lex's hand on her chest.

Lex knew how difficult this would be for Roza to process. She had suffered her fair share of mental health issues throughout their marriage, making Lex feel even more protective of her. Even though this was good news, especially after the news of the kill list and their places on it, it would be difficult to come to terms with. Thea's death would bring back Roza's grief for her brother and father, and the rocky relationship she had with him.

And Thea's mental abuse, her coercive control, was something Roza hadn't ever truly dealt with. Lex sometimes felt Roza was always on alert for Lex's first abusive move, which of course never came.

"Is it really over? Do you think anyone else in her organization will come for us?" Roza asked in a shaky voice.

"I doubt it. She had a personal vendetta against our family—that's why she put so much energy into it. Anyone who takes the top job in her criminal organization won't have the same reasons or energy to come after us."

"I hope you're right. Maybe we can send the children back to school on Monday, as long as their protection stay close," Roza said.

"I think that's a good idea, sweetheart. Gus is at an age where he needs the input of his peers."

Roza nodded. "I know he's starting to understand what his future will be. It's a lot to come to terms with when you are so young. I don't even understand the pressure. I lived my life knowing I'd be just the spare to the heir. It was my brother who had to live with that pressure. I wish he could talk to him."

Roza's voice cracked, and Lex squeezed her harder into a hug.

Roza continued, "Gussy was everything you would want in an heir. Strong, upstanding, honourable military career, loved by the people. What was I doing while he was doing all these things? Going to questionable parties with Thea and drinking too much."

Lex had spoken to Roza on this subject so many times before, but it was something Roza just couldn't seem to let go. Nobody had believed in her. Her father and brother had loved her, but from what Roza had told her, they were constantly cleaning up Roza's messes. It was only Lex, George, and Bea, and her former lady-in-waiting, Perri, who had believed there was so much more inside Roza.

"Darling, turn around and look at me," Lex said.

Roza turned over, and Lex saw tears falling from her eyes. Lex wiped them away with her thumb.

"You didn't have the expectation or the training, but I've told you before, that makes the job you're doing even more remarkable. You learned on the job and learned quickly, with support from the people that love you, what this job is all about. Your people love you. Support for the monarchy has never been higher. You work hard for charities, causes, big and small, and make a difference to people's lives. There are few who could have done so well."

Roza was silent for a few moments and then said, "I couldn't provide a spare to the heir, though, could I? Not like Beatrice. She has had children so easily."

Lex was angry. Roza had said similar things before and was just looking for something to beat herself up over. But she did understand how much the constant trying for more children had affected their mental health. It was something they were continually working on.

"Don't ever say that. Gus will grow up to be an excellent king, when the time comes, and Mari will support him."

Roza covered her face with her hands. "I know that logically, but my father and Thea both loom large in my mind, taking shots at me."

Lex cupped her face and said, "Look at me. Now Thea is gone. She can't hurt you any longer, physically or mentally."

Roza nodded. "I should send a message of condolence to the prison governor's family."

"Tomorrow we can do that. Now you just have to rest."

"I don't know where I would be if I didn't have you, Lexie. I don't know where the country would be either."

"Is that not what a crown consort's role is? Supporting the monarch?" Lex said.

Roza trailed her fingers across Lex's cheek. "You do too much. I love you so deeply. I'm the luckiest woman in the world."

"No, I think others would say that I'm the lucky one, and they'd be right."

Roza kissed her, hard at first, then slowly she fell into deep languid kisses. She was so full of emotion that she had to express it to the person who was everything to her.

She rolled on top on Lex, who tried to turn the tables on her, but Roza said, "No, let me love you."

Roza sat up and pulled her nightdress off. Lex's hands immediately went to her hips, then swept up her ribs, and lightly cupped her breasts.

"You are beautiful and strong, and no matter what life throws at you, you get through it," Lex said.

Roza leaned over, and her brown hair cascaded onto the sides of Lex's face. As she moved down Lex's body, her hair caressed her chest and stomach, and Lex groaned when it teasingly caressed her sex and thighs.

Lex cried out when Roza's tongue touched her and kissed and sucked until Roza felt Lex's fingers grasp onto her hair. This was what mattered, Lex, their love, their family. She only prayed she could keep the hurt Thea caused her out of her mind and out of her life.

But Roza worried in dark spaces of her mind that she would never be free of her.

CHAPTER SIX

Monday morning came and Poppy was super excited to be starting her course this morning. It had been a number of years since she had graduated from fashion school, and she enjoyed learning.

This would be the start of a new chapter of her life. Poppy's new fashion brand would be made ethically overseas and do a good job of highlighting the industry's hidden use of low paid, underaged labour.

Things had also improved since Friday. Thea Brandt's death made her extended family's lives safer. Hopefully she would have the freedom to enjoy student life now.

Poppy filled her rucksack with all the things she would need for the day and walked to her front door. Lex told her she would still be driven to school in the meantime, while Thea's death and organization were assessed for further threat.

It could be worse. She liked Mattius and Jess, at least, and it was only transportation. Everything was ready, so she walked to the door. Jess was waiting outside.

"Good morning, Poppy," Jess said, "Mattius is waiting in the car."

Jess surprised her at the door. She assumed that they'd both be down in the car. She didn't know how Lex had gotten used to this level of security.

"Morning, Jess. I hope I haven't kept you waiting."

"Don't worry about that. We're here when you need us."

Thank God security wasn't going to be as tight now that Thea was dead. Poppy would have hated to be under watch constantly. She was a private, quiet soul, somewhat introverted, and being watched constantly wouldn't sit well with her.

Jess accompanied her down to a waiting car. It was one of those armoured cars that drove Roza and Lex around. But who was going to bomb a car she was in?

But she said nothing and got in the back seat. Mattius greeted her from the front seat.

"Morning, Mattius, thanks for picking me up."

He looked a little surprised about her greeting. "It's our duty to keep you safe, Ms. King. Please call me Matt."

"Thanks."

Jess got in the back seat with her and said, "Let's get going, Mattius." She called up a computer screen, and a document containing her timetable filled the window.

"Why have you got that?" Poppy asked.

"To plan the security for your day," Jess said matter-of-factly.

"But I thought you were just dropping me at college."

"No, we'll be with you on the campus throughout the day and take you home."

Poppy was not expecting that. "But there's no need for that. Thea's dead, and I wasn't exactly top of the kill list anyway."

"We've been instructed to give you a high level of protection until further notice. The security services want to assess the changes to Thea Brandt's organization first."

Poppy sighed. "My classmates are not going to treat me normally if I've got security constantly."

"Those are my orders, Poppy. There may be one of Thea's associates who wants to carry on her plans, and any one of your classmates could be one of the people sent to take care of that job."

"Bloody hell. Right, okay, what will you be doing?"

"Mattius will patrol the hallway leading to each class you have, and I will be sitting in class with you, near the door, so I can get between you and anyone coming through the door."

"That's a bit over the top, isn't it? Sitting in class with me? I mean, I really like you, Jess, but you're going to look intimidating to the other students. Black secret service suit, at least two guns under your jacket. Nobody's going to talk to me."

Jess sighed. "Those were my orders, but I understand your concerns. Perhaps rather than inside your classroom, I could stand at the door, and Mattius can position himself at the reception area."

It wasn't what she expected or wanted, but it looked like she was going to have to live with it if she wanted to take her course.

"Okay, but please try not to frighten anyone."

Jess cocked an eyebrow. "That's kind of my job, but I'll try to tone it down with your classmates. Let's go, Mattius."

They drove off and made good time. Poppy got increasingly nervous as the journey went on. She already dreaded their first impression of her. The whispers behind her back, the looks and nervousness. The royal thing was like an elephant in the room, and she wasn't even royal. It normally took some time before people started to relax and get to know her. And there were always people who were fake just to try to get close to her.

"Sit far away from the door," Jess advised. "Then if anyone gets past me, you'll be closest to the window at the other side of the room."

Poppy had all sorts of replies in her head, but what would be the point? She had to live with this overbearing security, for the time being anyway. So Poppy just nodded. God knew how Lex lived with this kind of thing.

By the time Jess had finished with the instructions, the rest of the students had filed in. She would be one of the last, and no doubt all eyes would be on her.

"I better get going. Speak to you later," Poppy said.

"Anything you need, or if something or someone is bothering you—just call me or Mattius."

It's just a class, Poppy wanted to say, but instead she nodded and walked into the classroom. Everyone, including the lecturer, turned to stare at her. This was worse than she thought. Where would she choose to sit? She looked around all the empty seats until she saw one near a man and a woman who were looking at her, but had big, open smiles on their faces. She chose the seat next to them.

Once she was seated and activated the computer at her desk, the lecturer looked at the clock on the wall and said, "Okay, everyone. I think we have everyone here except one. Let's make a start. Could you input your name on your computer, so we all know who everyone is?"

All around her people were whispering and pointing and staring at her. She hoped the novelty of having the Queen's sister-in-law in class would wear off as they saw how normal and boring she was.

Beside her the man with short red hair who had smiled so warmly at her with his female companion said, "Hi, you're Poppy, the Queen's sister-in-law, aren't you?"

Poppy smiled. At least he was upfront about his interest. "Yes, that's me."

"Didn't I tell you, Brit?" He offered his hand across the desks. "I'm Joe, and this is my sister, Britta."

Going by their accents, they were native to Denbourg, but spoke English seamlessly.

"Hi, nice to meet you both. I'm Poppy, as you know."

"I'm sorry," Britta said. "I told him not to bother you so soon."

Britta had the most gorgeous black hair, which faded into a bright pink a few inches from the ends, tied up in a ponytail.

"Don't worry about it. I'm glad you've spoken to me. I—"

"Excuse me?" The lecturer was looking right at them. "This isn't a tea party. I'm trying to explain what classes you have this year, and what assessments you will be expected to complete."

Poppy glanced at the holo board behind them and saw his name. "Sorry, Mr. Anderson. Please continue."

"Thank you for allowing me," he said sarcastically. "Now, as I was saying, your exams over the year will take up forty percent of your overall mark. I'll assign you to your groups very soon."

Great. He likes me then, thought Poppy with an inward sigh.

Poppy heard the roar of a retro engine outside. She followed the sound to the window at the side of the of the classroom. Poppy was surprised to see a traditional looking silver and black motorcycle pull into one of the staff car parking spots right outside the front of the building.

The rider got off the bike and pulled off their black helmet. A tumble of collar length blonde and brown hair fell out. The rider put down the helmet and turned around. It was a woman.

Poppy felt a tightness in her chest and stomach, especially when the rider pulled her hair into a topknot and revealed the undercut back.

I wonder what she's professor of, Poppy thought as she smiled. This school was largely attended by mature students and by those seeking a more vocational education path. Poppy remembered from the school information that there were joinery and art departments.

It had been a long time since she'd felt that kind of instant attraction. There had been two people in the UNICEF team that had been attractive to her, but they had an unhealthy interest in who her family was. That was a complete turn-off.

Poppy found her mind wandering into a few different scenes. In one, the woman she glimpsed was sawing a plank of wood with a tool belt hanging sexily from her slim waist. In the other she was running her hands over a big hunk of wet clay.

"Ms. King? Are you with us at all?"

Poppy jumped in fright and realized she had been caught up in her lusty thoughts for far too long. "Sorry. Could you repeat the question?" Poppy asked.

She could feel the rest of the class staring. Honestly, she had gone to so much trouble to keep Jess and Mattius from making her stand out, and here she was, making a spectacle of herself without any help.

Mr. Anderson's stare bored right into her. "The rest of your colleagues have explained their reason for taking this course. Would you like to share?"

Poppy was angry at herself. She had always been the studious good girl at school and then art college, never a problem to anyone, a team player who took her education very seriously. But today, because of a sexy woman on a motorcycle and her libido, Poppy was in the bad books already.

There was a long silence before her new friend Joe jumped in. "Professor, may we jump in first and let Poppy go after us?"

He nodded.

Joe looked at Poppy and winked. "I hope you don't mind, Poppy."

Poppy mouthed, *Thank you.* What a great guy Joe was.

"My sister and I were lucky enough to inherit a beautiful retail space on Restoration Square outside the palace. We are both passionate about conservation, fair trade to farmers, and…coffee."

Wow, they couldn't be more in tune with what she believed in, and their business was in her favourite shopping area.

Britta backed him up. "We've got big plans and think this course will really help set us up for the future."

"Thank you, now, Ms. King?"

Poppy opened her mouth to speak when she heard voices outside the door. Then, embarrassingly, Jess walked into the classroom and said, "Professor? Do you have a Casey James on your class list?"

Mr. Anderson looked up to the ceiling in dismay and then went to his computer screen, then said with an edge to his voice, "Casey James? Yes."

Jess waved her hand and said, "Ms. James, you may come in."

To Poppy's surprise, her sexy motorcycle rider walked into the classroom, then promptly walked backwards, saying to Jess, "God, all this because some jumped up sister-in-law of the Queen is in the class."

Jess glared at the new arrival and shut the door. Poppy felt embarrassment and anger all at the same time. The professor in the staff car park was no more than a student chancing their arm.

Poppy watched as the newcomer strode to the other side of the classroom. She could tell this Casey James was cocky and overconfident just by the way she walked over to the free desk and chair.

Casey then sat back in the chair, balancing on the back legs, and said, "On you go, Prof."

"Why thank you, Casey," he said in a similar tone to the one he'd used with Poppy. Then he went back to addressing the class. "Now as Ms. King has dominated most of our time so far, I hope we can forgo both her and Casey's introductions to the class."

Poppy wished a hole would open up below her and swallow her up. This first morning couldn't have gone much worse. She could hear the whispers and laughs coming from behind her.

This was so embarrassing, and the cocky Casey James had made things ten times worse.

❖

Casey was hardly listening to the professor rambling on about essays, group projects, and exams. She was looking dead ahead, but all her thoughts and attention were on the young woman sitting on the other side of the classroom.

Everything had gone to plan. She'd walked into the classroom nearly exactly as she had rehearsed in her head a million times over. Well, almost according to plan. The bodyguard at the classroom door wasn't expected, but in the end, that worked out well for her.

She made more of an entrance, that was sure. The plan was not to engage with her target at all. Casey had guessed that her target, the middle class daughter of a surgeon, would be partial to a bad-boy type. She was playing that role to the full.

Instead of sitting at her desk and taking notes on her computer, Casey sat languidly, rocking on the back legs of the chair.

Without even looking, she could feel eyes burning into the side of her face. She had to know if her little fish had taken the bait. Casey turned her head slowly and was met by the eyes of her target, Poppy. She made a game-time decision and winked at her.

Poppy looked immediately embarrassed and turned away, pulling her hair across her face.

Gotcha.

Now that her bait was attracted to her, the next stage was to get her on the hook and keep her there. That would take some time, but Casey could be patient. Very patient.

Mattius escorted her back to the car while Jess contacted Ravn, head of palace security, but Poppy wanted to think before she got in the car. There was a bench overlooking a large pond in front of the college building. She sat down to try to make sense of her thoughts.

She didn't even know if she wanted to attend any more if the whole year was going to be like this. Poppy felt despondent, angry, and guilty at feeling angry.

Poppy heard Jess's voice beside her. "May I sit down?"

She nodded and lifted her head.

"It's nice here, isn't it?" Jess said.

The bench overlooked a large pond with ducks and geese going about their business, swimming along while some students fed them.

"Yes."

"Mattius said you were upset. Not a good first day?"

"The day couldn't have gone worse," Poppy said. Her eyes welled up, and she wiped the tears before they could develop any further. "I've been planning this for so long. Coming back from my travels, starting my own sustainable fair-trade fashion line, and taking my business course. There should be none of this drama. I shouldn't have security, I shouldn't get special treatment. I'm not a princess, a queen, a consort."

"I know—"

But Poppy was on a roll, and she had to get this off her chest. "In that class today, I was the centre of attention, like I was someone special. I'm not. I'm an ordinary doctor's daughter. I worked hard for UNICEF, and I suppose my family, the royal part of it, did get the campaigns publicity, but I was only part of a team. Mr. Anderson clearly thinks I'm a disrupting influence—"

Jess put her hand up and stopped her. "Wait. Take a breath."

Poppy closed her eyes and inhaled deeply, then let it out.

"Don't worry about Professor Anderson. He's an antimonarchist, but harmless."

"How do you know?"

"Everyone on the staff who you would have contact with was security checked. The professor is all talk, but no threat."

"It made the class so uncomfortable, and then the arrogant motorcycle woman came in and made things worse. Did you see the way she walked to her seat as if she owned the place?"

"She was fairly annoyed with me at the door. I had to check her with the professor because she didn't fit the typical student profile. But yes, quite confident in herself."

Casey James had completely ignored her after making such a fuss and had the audacity to wink when she caught Poppy looking.

"The whole experience made me feel like there was a huge spotlight on me, and it's going to be like this for the duration, no doubt."

"Poppy, look around you."

The front of the building was filled with students, a lot of them new and trying to find their way to the next class.

"All of these people have felt like the other in the room at one or many times in their lives—I know I have," Jess said.

"You?" Poppy said with surprise. "But you're a special forces officer. You command respect wherever you go, and you're a beautiful woman."

"Thank you. Yes, I have felt like that a few times in my life. Everybody has troubles that lie hidden behind masks and false smiles. Yours might be an extreme kind of situation, but I'm sure some students today would take your embarrassment in a heartbeat, as long as they could leave their troubles behind," Jess said.

That was so true. In all actuality, what did she have to worry about? A little extra attention, and a professor she had to win over. Plus, it wouldn't be forever, like it was for Roza and Lex.

Poppy smiled at Jess. "You're very insightful, you know that?"

Jess chuckled. "That's the way they breed us in special forces."

"Thank you, Jess." Poppy put her hand on Jess's, which Jess seemed surprised by, because she stiffened up. "You've really helped me put things in perspective."

Jess stared down at their hands nervously. "Of course, Poppy. Anytime."

Poor Jess. She obviously wasn't used to her charges being so open with her.

Poppy looked up in time to see Joe and Britta walking out of the building. They waved, and Poppy waved back.

"Poppy," Joe shouted, "would you like to get a coffee? The bar is just over the road."

She immediately smiled and shouted back, "I'd love to."

Then she quickly realized she had Jess and Mattius with her. "Is it okay if I go with them, or do you have to get back to your headquarters?"

Jess stood. "Where you go, we go. The only stipulation I'd make is that we drive you over there, so that I can do a quick security check on your new friends."

Poppy was about to complain when she remembered the conversation she'd just had with Jess. In the grand scheme of things, it wasn't too much to ask.

"Can I meet you over there in a few minutes?" she called to Joe and Britta.

Britta grinned happily. It looked as though she was surprised she'd accepted. "No problem, see you there."

Joe and Britta walked off arm in arm, smiling and giggling. Why anyone would be that happy to have coffee with her, she'd never know. But Poppy wanted friends in her course.

She got up from the bench and turned towards the carpark, where she heard some overexcited voices. Her fellow student, Casey James, the one with the arrogant attitude, was helping one of her classmates onto her motorcycle.

When she had put her guest on the bike and given her a helmet, she lifted her own. Casey pulled the band holding her topknot and let her hair loose. She ran her hand through her floppy dark blonde hair, and Poppy felt her stomach tighten.

Casey then put her helmet on, and once her new friend was on, she kick-started the bike and drove. The girl wrapped her arms tightly around Casey's waist, while her friends clapped and whooped as the bike drove off.

"Doesn't look as if arrogant biker is going to be short of friends," Poppy said in a superior fashion.

"We'll do a background check on her, but I'm sure she's okay. Just a bit of a show-off, I'm sure."

Poppy shook off the confusing reaction she was having and said, "Let's go, Jess."

❖

Poppy was having a wonderful time with her new friends Joe and Britta. She didn't have many friends outside of the UK, and after today at least some people were on her side in class.

Joe was funny and, from what she'd gathered, an extremely happy-go-lucky person. Her gaydar had pinged that he was gay, but he told her he was in fact pansexual.

Britta was a quirky funny person who loved goth fashion and music, from her black and pink tinged hair to her toes. She was a lesbian and so much on Poppy's wavelength.

A few drinks had turned into dinner at the bar they were in, and then on to cocktails, which led to even more laughter. Jess and Mattius each shared lookout duties at the door and covered for each other while they ate dinner.

Earlier in the evening, Poppy had checked with Jess that it was okay to stay on. Jess assured Poppy that they were both on shift until Poppy went home, and besides neither had family to get home to.

The waiter brought three margaritas to the table. "Now we're talking," Britta said.

Joe took a quick sip and declared, "Hmm, these are delicious."

Poppy took a sip and couldn't agree more. "They are so good. But I don't know why I'm drinking—I had the hangover from hell just a few days ago."

"Big night out?" Joe asked.

"It was like a going away party, with my UNICEF team in India."

Britta clicked her fingers and said, "That's right, you worked for UNICEF. I remember seeing some adverts on social media for your campaign."

"Was it child workers?" Joe asked.

"That was part of it, but more broadly about the unethical side of the clothing industry. After I studied at fashion school, I learned more about it, and I just couldn't work in the industry as it was. I had to do something about it." It might have been the alcohol loosening her tongue, but she found herself hitting her hand on the table and rhyming off some of the evils she had been fighting against. "Low pay, poor conditions, child labour, it's so wrong. If we don't save the world, then who will?"

As soon as she said that last line, she had to laugh at herself, and Joe and Britta laughed along with her.

"What do I sound like?" Poppy said.

Britta reached over and squeezed her shoulder. "You sound like someone who cares. There should be more people like that. That's what Joe and I want to do. Take the money away from the huge coffee brands and give it to the farmers."

Joe piped up, "My sister is the bean and the blend specialist. I'm the one with the flair for numbers"—he snapped his fingers—"and hospitality."

Poppy laughed. "You two are like a breath of fresh air after today. I'm so glad we met."

Joe raised a glass. "Here's to saving the world."

Both Poppy and Britta joined him. "Saving the world."

Poppy saw some of the other bar patrons turning their heads and whispering. "I think I've been spotted."

Mattius and Jess moved closer.

"Is her name Jess?" Joe asked.

"Yes. Chief Bohr, or Jess. These guards will only be with me a little while. Just until my overanxious sister calms down about the whole...security threat thing."

"Yeah," Britta said, "it must have been a worrying time for your family."

"Brit," Joe said in indignation, "you lectured me about not asking anything about Poppy's family."

Britta shrugged. "It just felt like I should." She turned to Poppy and said, "I'm sorry if I was intruding where I shouldn't."

"Don't be. I can tell, straight off the bat, you two are genuine. Believe me, I've gotten used to spotting people trying to befriend me because of who I am related to," Poppy said.

Joe looked Jess as she walked past the table, patrolling the area. "As interesting and gorgeous as your sister-in-law is, at this moment I'm more interested in your security guard, Jess. She is so"—Joe twirled his hand, searching for the right words—"powerful and beautiful at the same time."

Poppy smiled. "Yes, she is." She looked at the time and said, "I better get home. I've kept Mattius and Jess out long enough. I had such a great time, guys."

All three stood and Britta said, "Us too."

Poppy hugged them both and said, "I'll get the bill."

"No you won't—gentleman always pays," Joe said with a flourish.

He jumped when Jess came walking up behind with Poppy's coat and said, "It's already taken care of, Joe."

Jess smiled and winked at him. Poppy and Britta stifled laughter when Joe just about melted.

"I'll see you two tomorrow."

"We might get our group projects in the afternoon, Mr. Anderson said," Britta reminded them.

"I hope I get you both. We'd have so much fun." Poppy waved goodbye and followed Mattius out the door.

CHAPTER SEVEN

A t first she felt the cold seeping deep into her bones and started to shiver. Her mind was muddled, cloudy. She could hear explosions that made her body jump in fright. Then a man's voice slowly filled her ears.

"Doctor, is she waking?"

"Give her a few minutes."

She tried to force her thoughts to stop swirling and become more ordered. The noise of explosions and screams rattled through her mind. Fire and heat scorched at her body. In the distance she saw her mother smile and use her soothing voice to slow down her thoughts.

"Mother?"

"Open your eyes, Thea," a male voice said.

Thea...that name meant something. It was her name, she was sure of it. Then seconds later her mind and memories slotted into place with a bang. She gasped, opened her eyes, and sat up too quickly.

Her head went dizzy, she felt sick, and burning pain spread over her body.

"Thea? Doctor, help her."

She felt a cool sensation in her arm, and the pain started to recede, and as it did she calmed.

"Relax, Thea."

She knew that voice. It was her only other family in the world. Thea opened her eyes and saw her brother Morten's face.

He smiled. "Good to have you back, Thea."

"Morten—" Thea tried to sit up again, but she had no strength.

"Try to stay still. You were badly injured."

Thea lifted her arm and saw bright pink skin, red, raw, and angry looking. "What happened?"

"We couldn't get you out of the prison truck as quickly as we hoped, so you caught some of the blast, but the doctor is going to fix everything." Morten looked to the doctor at the other side of her. "Aren't you, Doctor?"

"Of course, Mr. Brandt."

"The doctor has placed a neural link in your brain, and it's busy knitting your skin back together."

"Was there any permanent damage?"

"Your arm, but it has been replaced with an artificial one, which will be even better than the original," Morten said.

Thea moved her arm and flexed her fist. It felt astonishing. Quick, powerful. It was just like a normal arm, controlled by her brain. She grabbed for the doctor's white coat and pulled him down to her.

He looked terrified, which was like a shot of energy to Thea. This arm was faster, stronger—yes, this would do nicely. She let him go and turned back to her brother.

"What about changing my appearance?"

Morten looked to the doctor who said, "We have to wait until your skin heals some more, and then we can use the Intelliflesh to change your appearance."

"Just like you planned." Morten smiled.

"The DNA?" Thea asked.

Morten nodded. "We placed the body in the truck, and what was left of it after the fire was identified as you. You are free and clear, Thea."

Thea smiled as best she could. "Well done, little brother. I'm very pleased."

"Nine years was far too long. I missed you."

Morten didn't have the mental strength that she had. Thea supposed it was partly his natural character, and the rest her and her mother's treatment of him. He was spoiled by them.

"I'm back now, Morten, and we are going to destroy our enemies one by one. First, I need the prisoner named Luca."

The betrayal was deep. Luca, as she'd called herself, reminded Thea of a younger version of herself. Thea thought that was why she trusted her so quickly. But she would have her tortured and killed before her eyes.

"Find her."

❖

After dropping off her new friend Inger, Casey doubled back to the college building and waited for Professor Anderson to leave. She followed him a few cars behind and pulled up round the corner from his home.

Casey's research into him had shown her that she might be able to get what she wanted. She left her bike parked up and walked along to his door. According to the names on the buzzers, the professor lived on the third floor.

She didn't ring for him, as she was sure a new student calling at his home on the first day would seem a little suspicious. Fortunately, with the right tools, a lock was no problem to Casey. She pressed her watch face to the panel, and her personal computer disrupted the signal.

The door clicked, and she was in. She took the stairs instead of the lift. She wouldn't cross paths with many residents that way. It wasn't long until Casey was approaching his door. There would certainly be cameras around the door, and if she was seen it could cause problems.

Casey called up the holo screen from her watch and hacked into the camera's system and switched it offline. She knocked, and she heard footsteps come to the door. Then she heard Professor Anderson swear.

"Bloody cameras. Who is it?"

"Casey James, sir."

"Casey who?"

"The student who came in late and disturbed your class."

The door creaked open, and the professor's face popped out. "Did you follow me? This is highly irregular—what do you want?"

Casey smiled. "Yes, I did follow you, I'm sure it is irregular, and I want to ask a favour."

"What could I help you with? Extra tuition is chargeable."

"I don't want extra tuition, but what I need may be to your benefit. Can I come in?" Casey asked.

Professor Anderson popped his head out further and looked side to side. "You better not try anything."

Casey held up her hands. "I come in peace. I promise."

"Get in then, before my neighbours think I'm *entertaining*."

Casey said under her breath, "I'd doubt they'd be expecting someone like me."

He took her through to the living room of the flat and everything she could see was beyond neat. Magazines on the coffee table were neatly fanned out in alphabetical order, his couch had a clear plastic cover over it, and strangely, the shades of the light fixtures still had the shop's coverings on them.

This guy has issues, thought Casey.

Since she wasn't invited to sit down, Casey came right out with it. "I want you to put me in Poppy King's project group."

Professor Anderson snorted. "So would half the class. I was simply going to allocate groups based on the class seating arrangements. That would take you right out of the group."

Casey thought it was time to unnerve him a bit, and from what she'd picked up from his flat, he clearly had neatness issues. She put her helmet down on the coffee table, then plonked down on the couch as if she owned the place.

Her professor was squirming in his highly polished brown brogues.

"I could make it worth your while," Casey said.

He couldn't take his eyes off her helmet on the coffee table and then her. "Please, I've already got the secret service on my back. They've already done a background search on three people she sat next to."

Then to add insult to injury, she put her boots up on his table. "But you're in charge, Professor."

He panicked, rushed to her side, and said, "Please, could you not do that."

Casey, acting innocently, pointed to her feet. "What, this?"

"Yes, please," he said frantically.

Casey didn't want to disturb him too much, just unnerve him a little. He ran to the kitchen, brought back a disinfectant spray, and cleansed the whole area.

After he let out a sigh of relief, Casey said, "Look, Professor. I know you have difficulties."

He frowned. "What difficulties?"

"Gambling. You're heavily in debt, aren't you? The debt is with some nasty people."

"How did you find out?"

Casey smiled confidently. "I can't give up my sources."

In fact it was quite easy to find out from a simple background check. "I can take the stress away in a second—if you put me in Poppy King's group."

Professor Anderson rubbed his forehead. "What about her secret service people? What if they object?"

"You let me worry about that." Casey took out her phone. "You've got your phone on you?"

He pulled out his slightly larger, more old-fashioned phone and said, "I need forty thousand."

"I know, I'll give you forty thousand, but I've also prepaid for a counsellor to help you control this addiction. Take the help, and don't end up in this dark place again."

Tears came to his eyes. "You're not one of bad guys, then."

Casey had a flash of grabbing one of Thea's rivals and binding her to a chair, so Thea could give her a fierce warning. The woman wasn't an innocent, but just being involved in the violence brought darkness and shame to her soul.

"I try not to be. Here, open your bank app."

He did and she touched her device to his. "Thank you, Professor. Just remember my favour."

"I will. You won't tell anyone about my problem, will you?"

"You have my word, if I have yours?" Casey held out her hand and Professor Anderson took it.

"Thank you, Casey."

"See you in class."

❖

The next afternoon, their first lecture was on the culture of customer care. Their lecturer was an energetic younger man called Grant, who insisted on a less formal approach. He did seem to focus a lot of his enthusiasm on Poppy and came to sit on the side of her desk at one point.

Poppy saw a message from Joe pop up on her computer screen as she took notes.

I think Grant has a thing for you…

Poppy looked to her side and chuckled with Joe and Britta. His *thing*, if he did have it, was probably centred around who he thought she was, rather than who she really was. It had happened time and time again.

People expected someone like Roza and were slightly disappointed that she wasn't. Towards the end of the lecture, Professor Anderson came in to inform them that their groups would be emailed to them shortly, and that they would use his next class time to make their plans.

Joe, Britta, and Poppy sat in the canteen with some cold drinks and snacks, while Jess and Mattius were stationed at different points in the large hall. They were waiting on the message about their group projects.

Poppy hoped that she would get teamed with her new friends. Most everyone else was quite quiet, quite reserved, except the two women who had been giggly around the not-so-friendly arrogant biker, Ingrid and Mardy, Ingrid being the one who went away on the back of said arrogant biker's bike. They were sitting at the table laughing and being extremely loud. They reminded Poppy of some of the women she had worked with in the fashion magazine business.

She got an apprenticeship after college to one of the country's top magazines, but soon realized she was not a good fit. Poppy adored fashion but came to hate the needless consumption and the unfair trade the fashion world had with the countries it bought materials from.

That world was full of Ingrids and Mardys, with the false laughs and insincere reactions and looks. Arrogant biker probably lapped that stuff up.

The three friends jumped when they all got an email message at the same moment. "Okay, ladies. Fingers crossed," Joe said.

Poppy scanned the email quickly and saw Joe's and Britta's names. "Yes, we're a team. We'll have a lot of fun."

Joe clapped his hands, and then Britta, who hadn't said anything yet, cautioned them. "Do you see who makes up the fourth?"

Poppy read the email carefully and found one more name, just as a figure appeared at her side. Arrogant biker Casey James.

"Hi, groupmates," Casey said.

They were less enthusiastic to the news, but Joe was very polite and held out a chair.

"Hi, I'm Joe, my sister Britta, and you probably know who Poppy is."

"Vaguely."

Poppy snorted. "You seemed very well aware of who I was when you came late into class yesterday."

"Oh, touched a nerve, did I?" Casey said.

Casey was so cocky and arrogant. It was bloody annoying. Poppy remembered the wink she had given her yesterday and how it annoyed her and…flustered her. That was the only way she could describe it.

From behind Casey, Ingrid said, "Casey? I saved you a seat."

Casey sat next to Joe and said to her, "Sorry, ladies. My new group needs me."

Ingrid's face fell, and Poppy said to Casey, "You're so popular. That bike ride must have been good."

"Always is." Casey winked as she said it.

Again Poppy felt *flustered*. There was that wink again. Just stop.

"Okay," Joe said slowly, trying to cover over the awkwardness, "we better get to class. The prof will be waiting for us."

As they stood, Jess appeared at her side. "Everything all right, Poppy?"

"Of course, Jess. We've just acquired a wonderfully modest new group member."

❖

"I don't like to let the St. Steven's people down."

Lex was going over her diary with her secretary, Patrice Everard. There had been a clash in her diary, and they were trying to work around it.

"What about morning of the fifteenth?" Patrice asked.

Lex scanned the screen and pondered the different dates in her diary. "No, the morning's clear because I'm travelling with Roza to Paris for the energy summit. On the twentieth, if I don't take lunch, I could visit the centre for maybe an hour."

"Are you sure, Your Majesty?"

"Yes, they are too important." They both heard a knock. "Come in," Lex said.

Roza's private secretary popped her head in the door. "Could I have a word, Your Majesty?"

"Of course." She turned to Patrice and said, "Could you give us a few minutes?"

"Yes, ma'am."

Once he was gone, Lady Olympia came in and stood in front of her desk. She had become Roza's private secretary five years ago. The daughter of a viscount, Olly, as she was known to her friends, had been at school with Roza but was three years below her.

They ran in different circles since school, Roza explained to Lex, mainly because Lady Olympia's father and mother weren't exactly rich, in terms of the aristocracy, and their children had to make their own mark on the world.

Olly did just that by being her year's top graduate and opening her own public relations firm, which she sold for a lot of money just before coming to work for Roza. Olly came to become her private secretary and head up their media team.

Olly was beautiful, blonde with an elfin haircut, and you could usually hear her before you saw her, as she was famous for her extremely fast walking pace around the palace.

"How can I help you?" Lex asked.

Olly looked uncomfortable with the information she was about to convey, and Lex felt tension in the room.

"Ma'am, I should be telling the Queen this information first, but I wanted to seek your advice on the best thing to do."

Lex sat forward in her seat. "Of course. Sit down, Olly."

Olly sat and let out a breath. "It's come to our attention that a film is being made about the Queen and yourself meeting and falling in love, and the assassination by Thea Brandt. They have kept production very much under wraps, but there will be pictures and trailers coming out about it soon, and in the run-up to release, the marketing will be wall-to-wall."

Lex closed her eyes and let her head fall back. "Jesus Christ. Especially after Thea's death."

"Exactly, ma'am. I know how much anxiety that time in the Queen's life causes her, and right now everything has been churned up by Thea's death, as you say. I didn't know how to approach it."

God. This was all they needed. The death of Roza's father and brother had a profound effect on Roza, not only the normal grief a daughter and a sister would have, but an event that changed both their lives forever.

Lex didn't want to upset the apple cart just now. "Thank you for coming to see me about it. Would you leave it in my hands? I'll tell the Queen at the right time."

Olly looked worried. "As Her Majesty's private secretary, I'm duty bound to give her all information first-hand. I just wanted your advice on how to do it."

Lex stood up and walked around the desk. "I appreciate the duty you have to the Queen, but I'm asking as a favour to me. I will take full responsibility."

She extended her hand to Olly to shake. Olly still looked reluctant but finally took her hand and said, "As you wish, ma'am."

CHAPTER EIGHT

Two weeks into Poppy's new business course, she was starting to settle into student life. It was strange being a student again. This time was a new experience for Poppy. Travelling the world, and mixing with a lot of different cultures, had made her confident.

She certainly wouldn't have handled the interactions with other students as well as a younger student, sussing out which ones wanted gossip about her family, and who was being insincere.

Poppy was sitting on a bench in Restoration Square, facing the premises that Joe and Britta had in mind for their coffee shop. Today was to be their first meeting on the project. The shop space was in a prime location, right next to the palace. When she'd left fashion school, Poppy would have bitten your hand off if you'd offered her a space for her fashion business in this location.

She was glad they had decided to base their group project on Joe and Britta's business idea. In an unlikely pairing, Poppy and the annoyingly full of herself Casey James had persuaded Joe and Britta that they should go with their business idea. At least she didn't have to worry about Casey James befriending her because of who her family was. Casey made it quite clear that she couldn't care less.

Jess and Mattius were nearby, giving her space to eat a sandwich for lunch, while keeping a close eye on her. She spotted Joe and Britta arriving and unlocking the shop. Poppy was so lucky to have met them and become friends. Poppy had good antennae now for people, and those two were great.

Then there was Casey James. She saw Casey's motorbike pull up across the street near the shop. She was a hard one to work out, and Poppy had tried. In their first two weeks Casey hadn't followed the pattern of trying to get too close, or to ingratiate herself. She flitted between groups in the class, but mostly kept apart from the class the vast majority of the time. Poppy noticed her, though. She didn't try to keep track of her whereabouts, but her eyes always seemed to zoom in on her whenever she was around.

Poppy noticed Casey would often leave the campus at lunchtimes and breaks when most would head to the canteen there. In class she never really looked as if she was paying much attention, but when a question was asked, Casey was always there with the correct answer.

Casey did join Joe, Britta, and her for break or lunch in the canteen, when they wanted to discuss their group project. She usually spent the time being annoying and cracking jokes. One thing was for certain. When Poppy was in fashion school, she wouldn't have had the confidence to deal with Casey's snarky comments or bad jokes.

Poppy finished her sandwich and dabbed her mouth with a napkin, then dropped the remains of the packaging into the bin.

"You ready to walk over, Poppy?" Jess asked.

"Yes. They've all arrived now."

Both Jess and Mattius stepped behind her and followed her across the square. She was hoping that she wouldn't need protection for very long. Not that she didn't like them. They were kind and friendly, but she would like her private life back.

They reached the building and Jess said, "We'll wait outside."

"Thank you, Jess," Poppy said.

When Poppy turned back, Joe was there with the door open and a huge smile.

"Hi, Poppy, Mattius, Jess."

His voice lingered on Jess's name, and Poppy smiled. He had such a crush on her it was funny.

"Jess, Mattius—would you like to come in and sit? We have drinks and snacks."

Jess appeared oblivious to his crush. Poppy thought so anyway. "That's very kind, Joe, but we need to guard the front door."

Joe tried, not very successfully, to hide his disappointment. "Okay, well the offer's there. Come in, Poppy."

She walked in to find Britta and Casey sitting at a table in the middle of a large open space. It was a stunning room, high ceilings and beautiful plaster mouldings. It was like stepping into the past.

"What do you think?" Britta asked.

"Just beautiful, Brit."

Joe led her over to the table, where there were cake boxes and stay-warm flasks.

"Good afternoon, Casey. You found a moment in your busy schedule to join us," Poppy said.

"Yeah, I had to cancel a few important dates, but here I am."

Casey stood up and helped Poppy off with her jacket and silky scarf. She shivered when Casey's fingers brushed against her neck. She got a flash of soft lips brushing the curve of her shoulder.

"Thank you, Casey."

She rubbed her forearms, trying to reverse the effect of the goosebumps on her arm. That would be embarrassing if Casey spotted it. She would see it as a badge of honour, and she didn't want to give Casey the satisfaction.

Why her body was reacting like this, betraying her, Poppy had no idea. She hadn't felt the intimacy of another woman's body in a long time. She wasn't a womanizer by any stretch of the imagination. She had only had a few lovers in her life, no great love, though. She wanted to find that great love. Poppy was a romantic at heart, and she was holding out for someone special.

She sat down and saw pens and notepads were provided, old school style. "This is a really special place."

"And there's so much potential," Joe said. "There's a whole other level downstairs, so that might be a good place for the bar in the evening."

"I know, it's going to be so much fun working on this project," Poppy said.

"*Such* fun." Casey imitated her polite, posh voice.

"Very funny. Is that meant to be me?"

Casey just laughed. It was a lot of fun needling Poppy—not too hard, just enough to see those annoyed looks upon her face. It was simply fun. Normally on a big job she was extremely serious and careful. Casey might have genuine reasons for taking her undercover job, but no matter how hard she tried, she couldn't stay neutral and balanced. Poppy was beautiful, genuine, and kind, and that's what made her feel guilty, lying in the darkness at night.

Brit, sensing the tension no doubt, took hold of one of the stay-warm cups and said, "Would you try some of our coffee? Just to give you an idea of the quality and what we're trying to do here."

"I'd love some," Poppy said.

"Casey?" Brit asked.

"Yeah, I'll take some."

Casey was going to stand up to reach the coffee cup but remembered that she had Poppy's scarf in her back pocket, and just in case there was still some poking out of the pocket, she remained seated and reached awkwardly across the table, making Poppy sigh with disapproval. She had swiped the scarf while helping Poppy with her coat. The scarf was her ticket to seeing Poppy alone at some later date.

Joe picked up his coffee cup. "Now this is my favourite. It's called Deep Mountain. This bean is from Colombia, one hundred percent Arabica beans. Have a taste."

Coffee wasn't Casey favourite drink, but she didn't mind it. The hot liquid hit her tongue, and with the sugar she'd added tasted intense. "Wow. That's strong," Casey said.

Britta turned to Poppy. "Do you like it?"

Poppy hummed. "Hmm. Delicious. I think it may be the best I've tasted."

"What about you, Casey? Do you like it, even though it's strong?"

Casey took another sip and smacked her lips together. "Yeah, nice."

"Nice?" Joe said dramatically. "You can't describe this liquid nectar as *nice*."

"Calm down, Joe. Not everyone is a coffee snob like you."

Brit said to Poppy and Casey, "We have a contact in the Colombian coffee confederation. They're a non-profit who protect the rights of local farmers. We plan to work with them and have our own special blends roasted, and we're hoping to make similar deals with other coffee growers in Brazil, Jamaica, and Thailand."

"Impressive," Poppy said. "Our two businesses are so well attuned. That's exactly what I want to do with my clothing company."

"You all think it's possible to change the world, don't you," Casey said.

"Of course, you don't?" Poppy said pointedly.

"No, human beings are selfish and power-hungry. Always have been. Little will change while self-interest is mainly what shapes people's wants and desires."

Poppy squinted at her. "You're a glass half empty kind of person, then?"

"Not in general, but I'm realistic."

"Realistic?" Poppy said in a disgusted voice. "That word is just an excuse not to try."

That really annoyed Casey. Joe put his hand up and said, "Can anyone join this argument?"

"No," Casey said immediately. "An *excuse*? I've tried all my life, time after time, to make the world a better place, but if anything, it gets worse. Humans are humans, and they don't change." Casey just blurted that out without thinking. Lucian had tried to make things better by exposing cons, drug dealers, murderers, and all kinds of criminality. But that didn't mesh with this character she was playing.

Poppy stared at her pointedly. Casey begged her silently not to ask any more questions.

"How have you done that?"

How did she get out of this? "Brit, wasn't this supposed to be a meeting?"

"Well, yes. We wanted to show you the space, get your ideas on our general plan. Joe and I can get the prices and availability of stock and machines. Then maybe next time we meet, we can talk about themes. Classic or modern? What do you think, Casey?"

Casey was delighted the subject had changed. "Sure, I can do that."

"But," Brit said, "we both thought that Poppy could draw up some floor plans for the space. I know you're a designer."

"I'd be happy to give it a go."

"Then we can reconvene and look over what you've come up with."

"I'll need some measurements," Poppy said.

"I can do that." Casey got straight up. She didn't want to sit in this tension any longer. Maybe it was just her, but she had never broken character like that on a job before.

That was the problem. She was too often forgetting this was a job.

CHAPTER NINE

Poppy sat on her couch doing some homework while the TV played in the background. She was waiting on a news item about Roza and Lex. It was nice when she could keep up with her sister and sister-in-law on TV. It made her feel closer to them.

She read the same paragraph for what felt like the hundredth time and let her head fall back in exasperation. Poppy was intelligent, but business law was so dry. It would be a struggle to get through this class.

Poppy decided to take a break and picked up a sketch pad. Drawing always lifted her mood. Earlier she had jotted down the measurements of the first floor and basement that Casey had taken for her.

Casey. She was a strange one to read. Poppy thought she had put her in the arrogant, full of her own importance category, and that was that. But she actually felt bad about their heated discussion at the coffee shop.

When Casey had talked about trying to change the world over and over again, she'd heard genuine pain and frustration there. The rest of the time Casey was so quiet, and as they left the shop, Poppy felt the needed to build bridges. But when she tried, Casey dismissed her overtures and zoomed off on her bike.

Poppy started to sketch some outlines. She kept looking up from her work to make sure she didn't miss Lex on TV, and then her phone buzzed. It was Jess. "Hello?"

"We've got Casey James down at the main door."

"Casey?" That was strange. What on earth did she want?

"Yes, she's brought the scarf you left at the cafe space the other day. Shall I just take it, or send it up?"

Poppy had forgotten about her missing scarf. She'd assumed it slipped under the table they were sitting at.

She heard Casey in the background say, "Oh for God's sake, I'm bringing a scarf, not a bomb."

Poppy couldn't help but chuckle. Casey's irreverent attitude didn't sit well with Jess or Mattius. This might be a chance to kiss and make up. That thought made her stomach tingle with excitement.

"Send arrogant biker up. Computer, pause TV."

Poppy jumped with a surge of excitement, weirdly, and ran her fingers through her long blonde hair. She was about to pull off her comfortable oversized jumper when she stopped.

"What am I doing? I don't need to look nicer for her," she chastised herself.

They didn't know much about Casey, except that she'd been employed by the same company since she was eighteen. She was originally from the United States but moved to Denbourg aged seventeen.

Jess wasn't completely happy with the background intel but was reasonably assured that she wasn't too much of a threat. Besides, all Poppy had to do was discreetly touch her computer or any of the touchpoints in the living room, kitchen, and bedroom, and Jess and Mattius would be here within moments.

"Poppy?" Jess's voice came over the intercom.

"Yes?"

"Did you give Casey James your address?"

"I gave Joe, Brit, and Casey my phone number and address, so we can group chat about our project and study together."

Jess was so careful. What harm would Casey do?

"That's not a great idea, but we can talk about it later."

Poppy sighed. "Okay, fine."

There was a knock, and Poppy hurried over and opened the door wide. There standing braced against the door was Casey. Her hair was hanging loose and floppy today, and she was wearing black jeans, a black T-shirt with white distressed lettering, and a black canvas jacket. In her hand she held Poppy's scarf. "Who is this arrogant biker you were talking about?"

"You, who do you think?"

Annoyingly Poppy's tingle turned into a wave of excitement, just as when she'd first seen Casey. She never went for women like her classmate. Women like Casey were the kind of butch or masculine-of-centre women who stood in a gay bar, and confidence and surety radiated off them.

That usually made Poppy run in the opposite direction, when she made her head rule her heart, and she would be letting none of those flutters affect her.

Casey held up her scarf. "Do you want this back?"

Poppy reached out to grab the scarf, but Casey pulled it back. "I didn't come here to be insulted, you know."

Poppy smiled. "Okay, you better come in."

"Oh, you are so kind," Casey said, handing Poppy her scarf.

"Thank you. It was kind of you to bring it."

Casey gave a little flourishing bow. "You're quite welcome."

"Where did you find it?" Poppy asked.

"On the floor. I think it must have fallen off your chair. I saw it on floor on the way out, but you were talking to Brit, and I got talking to Joe. I forgot I had it in my pocket."

Poppy wiggled her nose in the cutest way when she smiled. At least she was getting the occasional smile now.

"Can I get you coffee, tea, a drink?"

"Yeah, a tea would be nice, herbal or fruit tea if you have it."

Poppy put her hands on her hips. "Herbal tea? Really?"

"Yeah, why?"

"Doesn't really suit your biker image."

"I'm not a biker and"—Casey pointed to Poppy—"even if I was, there's nothing wrong with herbal tea if I was a biker."

"Quite right. You just be you. No judgement here."

"I'm sure. May I sit? Or will Jess leap through the door to tackle me to the ground?"

"You'll be okay. Please sit."

Casey took off her jacket and sat down. She looked around the warm, cosy apartment to pick up any extra sense of who Poppy really was. Normally she'd have a whole raft of information after meeting her target, but when she got home after the meeting at the coffee space, all she could list was *annoying*, *sweet*, and *funny*.

Not the usual sort of words she'd put in her background info. Casey noticed the TV was paused on an image of the Queen and Lennox King. She would need to find out more about that.

There were pictures of Poppy's family everywhere. A lot of her nephew and niece. She could just imagine Poppy was that kind of person who loved family above all. It was strange. Seeing Poppy in her own environment made this feel more like meeting a friend, not a means to an end.

Her brief was to get close to Poppy to get closer to the royal family. She was supposed to be charming her and had to keep that firmly in the front of her mind.

Poppy walked through with a tray of tea and some biscuits. "Here we are. Raspberry fruit infusions and biscuits. Raspberry all right for you?"

"Perfect."

While Poppy put the tray on the table, Casey said, "I don't know where you get this idea that I'm arrogant—I'm neither arrogant nor a biker."

Poppy sat down beside her and lifted her teacup. "You ride a bike."

"Yeah," Casey replied.

"So that makes you a biker, and the arrogant part is pretty close to the mark."

"Just because I have a bike doesn't mean I'm a biker. I only bought it a couple of weeks ago."

"You did? I had you down as having a motorcycle as soon as you could go on the roads."

"No, I've ridden bikes before, but never owned one."

That was half true. The newspaper had provided one for her investigation into the far-right biker gangs. But that wasn't something Casey James had chosen. This time, it was for her.

"So what changed a few weeks ago? To make you want one, I mean," Poppy asked.

Before she had the chance to censor herself, Casey found herself telling the truth. "I wanted to take a break from the world, my job, and my life, so I was going to take a road trip, find out who I am and want to be."

Casey could have slapped herself. Why was she telling Poppy this?

"What changed your mind, and what brought you to our business course?"

Casey tried to take a moment before she answered this time, so she took a sip of the raspberry tea. "Hmm. That's delicious. I don't think I've tried that one before."

"No, you probably haven't. I got it at a little tea boutique I go to, over in the south side of Battendorf."

"Well, it's delicious."

There was silence for a minute then Poppy asked, "So, what changed your mind?"

How did she answer that? Why not try for something close to the truth, because Casey was finding it was difficult to lie or fabricate to Poppy.

"My boss didn't want me to leave the company, so she offered me the chance to do this course for six months as part of their staff advancement programme. Give me a chance to have a break and reassess."

Please don't ask why.

She could see it in Poppy's eyes. Poppy wanted to ask why, and Casey had no idea what she would say. Her instinct was to say a death in the family, but she didn't want to have to lie about things like that.

Fabrication was her stock-in-trade. Why was she faltering now?

Luckily Jess called up to check if Poppy was okay, and that line of questioning was halted for the time being.

When Poppy was finished with the call, Casey said, "She's not coming up to bundle me out the door, is she?"

Poppy smiled. "No, I told her you were harmless."

Casey quirked her eyebrow. "I don't know if I would like to describe myself as *harmless*."

"You do like that bad-boy image. I can see that."

"Where do you get that from?"

"Wearing all black, the silver-studded leather bracelet around your wrist, the motorcycle."

She liked to wear black because it suited her mood better, and it was easier just to fade into the crowd that way.

"I think you read way too much into things, Poppy. Is that why Jess thinks I'm sent to bring about your downfall?" Casey asked.

Poppy laughed, and Casey felt her chest tighten. That was not good. *She's just a tool for the story. Remember that.* But she felt such a shit for even thinking that way. Poppy didn't deserve it.

"What were you doing tonight, before I disturbed you," Casey asked.

When Poppy laughed she did that cute little thing with her nose, the twitching like a little bunny rabbit thing that Casey found so cute.

"I was working on our group project and my own work. Plus watching my sister on TV," Poppy said.

Casey sensed mentioning her sister was a test as to her true intentions, so she ignored that and spoke about something else.

"You're really passionate about your project, aren't you?" Casey said.

That question seemed to take Poppy by surprise. "It's my life's work. I can't do much, but I want to make a small difference."

"You were in UNICEF, weren't you?"

"Yes, I'm trying to make the garment industry better. I thought, by making my own line, I could publicize the problems, and it might encourage other companies to do the same. I've been working on designs for a while now," Poppy said.

"Can I see some?" Casey asked.

Poppy hesitated.

"Oh, I'm sorry—if you're not comfortable…"

"No, it's okay. I just haven't shown anyone before, apart from my sister and sister-in-law."

Casey sat back and crossed her legs. "Honestly, don't feel you have to."

Poppy picked up her sketch pad and pencil. "I like to sketch old school."

Poppy flicked back some pages on her sketch pad. Casey took the pad from her, and Poppy scooted closer. That was nice.

"This page is some designs of the label. I wanted the sentiment to say there are no boundaries in my designs. No men's, women's, rich, or poor. Simply human."

"That's a nice brand name."

"Thanks." Poppy blushed and pushed her hair behind her ear bashfully. "I've never told anyone that yet, not even my family."

Casey loved the sweet bashfulness. Her stomach tightened again, and Poppy's closeness was making her body react. She gulped and turned back to the sketches.

"I want people to link the T-shirt, the jacket, whatever, back to a human at the beginning of production."

"Yeah, it's easy to forget that there's a real person at the beginning of this process, even if they're just operating a machine."

"You've got it," Poppy said.

Casey could hear the excitement in her voice. She admired that and wished her own job could give her that sense of excitement and will to save others. When she first started working as a journalist, she did get that buzz.

A young Casey was full of energy—wanted to right wrongs, as she helped a more senior reporter expose cons and scams and bring those bad guys to justice—but as her career developed, she began to lose a piece of herself with each job.

Poppy continued. "*Simple* is going to be the main watchword. Simple styles, simply line of clothing. I want the customer to think *I want a Simply Human T-shirt*. It's not flashy but it displays your support for those garment workers. Fashion with a conscience. If I can get it off the ground, of course."

Casey smiled and shook her head. "I wish I had voted for your business as our group project now."

"I don't—Brit and Joe deserve our full attention. My business might not work in the long term, but I know I'll get some media coverage because of my family."

"That's very nice of you," Casey said.

"Not nice, it's just the right thing to do."

Poppy's smile and goodness made Casey feel shame. Casey hadn't known her long, but she was so obviously a good person. Poppy was even giving her a chance after she'd behaved like a dick to her. It turned out Poppy didn't fall for the bad boy. It turned out that both times Casey spoke the truth, at the cafe and here, she got the best response.

She suddenly stood. She had to get out of here.

"I better get going."

"Oh..." Poppy appeared to be caught off guard. "Have you finished your tea?"

Casey picked it up and downed the rest. "It was really nice."

Poppy followed her to the door. "Busy evening planned, with Ingrid perhaps?"

Casey felt embarrassed at the stunt she'd pulled. "Nothing like that."

"Well, thanks for bringing my scarf. I'll see you in class tomorrow," Poppy said.

"Yeah, 'night."

Casey walked downstairs still feeling deep guilt at what she was doing. She came to the main exit where Jess and Mattius were standing.

"Ms. James?" Jess crooked her finger, beckoning Casey to her.

Jess definitely didn't like her. "Yeah?"

"Be careful," she said flatly.

"I don't know what you mean, Chief Bohr."

"We both know the return of the scarf was not urgent, especially when you will see her tomorrow."

Casey looked over to Agent Mattius, who was also staring hard. "I just thought while I was passing..."

"If you are anything other than someone trying to ingratiate yourself with her, then think again. You will be dealt with," Jess said menacingly.

Casey held her hands up. "Hey, I'm neither trying to ingratiate myself or anything else. I'm sure you've done a background check on me anyway."

"Naturally. You seem familiar with that way of working," Jess said.

Casey shrugged. "I just assumed that's how it would work. I mean Poppy no harm."

"Let's hope that's true. Mattius, see Ms. James out."

"It's Casey," she snapped back.

Jess didn't really deserve that. Casey was just trying to project her anger. As she stepped outside into the night, she realized the anger was at herself, because she was trying to do those things that Jess insinuated.

She walked dejectedly down the street. Things weren't turning out as she planned or as Annika said they would. This was supposed to be a lighter piece of investigative journalism. Nothing like infiltrating right-wing motorcycle gangs, or becoming a major player in Thea's criminal jail network.

Casey had met many corrupt people, but it was a whole different ballgame to deceive an honest, good-hearted person like this. She should have just gotten on her bike and driven away from Annika's story.

Maybe I still should.

❖

The next morning Poppy woke up full of energy and was looking forward to class today, even though it was all day in business law. She was enjoying the camaraderie of her new friends, and even arrogant biker was growing on her.

Poppy packed her bag and thought back to last night. There was so much more going on underneath Casey's skin than first appeared. They were talking and bantering, and then something just changed, and Casey couldn't get out of her flat quick enough.

It was like the moment at Joe and Brit's new building. Casey was fine, talking normally, and then Poppy had pushed a bit too far in their debate. The wounded look came upon her face like last night, and she left the table, eager to get some space.

Poppy wanted to know more about her. She was a sucker for a wounded soul, and those brief glimpses told her there was one underneath Casey's bravado. She grabbed her bag and went downstairs to the waiting car.

"Good morning, Poppy," Mattius said.

"Morning, Mattius. How are you today?"

"I'm doing well, thank you."

Poppy got in and Jess was waiting for her. "Good morning."

"Morning, Jess."

As the car drove off, Poppy said, "Any word on Thea?"

"No, just the same as it has been. Why do you ask?" Jess said.

"I just wondered how long I'd need security."

"I think the Queen would like it to continue for a while longer. Thea may not be a threat any more, but who knows how many of her associates are out there."

Poppy sighed, then felt bad. "Jess?"

"Yes?"

"I don't want you to think that I'm eager to get rid of you both. I like you and Mattius very much. It's just that I long for a life where security isn't necessary."

"Don't worry, Poppy. We understand how difficult it is not having a private life, and we're not here to be liked. But don't worry—we do know that's not the case here."

"Thanks."

They arrived at the campus, and she was soon in class. The class was full except for one notable exception. Casey never turned up. Poppy was sure she'd arrive by lunchtime, but all day there was no sign of her.

Three days later, there was still no sign. Poppy, Joe, and Britta were getting worried.

Poppy had a free period this afternoon, so she thought she'd try to find out if Casey was okay.

Jess met her at the main door to the college. "Jess? Can you tell me where Casey lives?" Poppy immediately saw Jess stiffen.

Jess replied, "You have her phone number—can't you call her?"

"That's the point. She isn't answering. She hasn't been to school in three days, and I just want to make sure she's all right."

"If you have the number, the computer will tell you," Jess replied.

"I've already tried that. She has an unregistered phone, which I'm sure you already knew," Poppy said pointedly.

"Does that not give you caution?"

"Lots of people have unregistered phones, for lots of reasons. Who knows why she has."

Jess sighed. "I'll find an address, but you're not going alone."

"Of course not. I wouldn't dream of it," Poppy said sweetly.

"Okay, let's go. Mattius, we're taking a detour."

Poppy slipped into the car and said, "Can we make one short stop first?"

❖

Casey sat on a dining room chair, elbows on her knees, hands clasped, staring at her two bags sitting by the front door.

She had waited three days to decide whether to lift those bags and leave, and the time was drawing near. Casey had called Annika on Monday and asked her to return that call as soon as possible.

But nothing. So Casey sent a text asking Annika one last time to contact her, or she was gone.

Casey had given her thirty minutes, and the time was trickling away. The night Casey had left Poppy's flat, she had walked and walked, trying to get a handle on what she was doing to Poppy.

It wasn't fair, it wasn't right. Poppy was an innocent in the world and trying to do her best in it. Casey didn't want this life any more. She should have never been lured into it again. She would drop the investigation unless Annika could come up with a good reason not to.

To make matters worse, Poppy, Joe, and Brit had been calling her phone, no doubt to ask where she was. They had group work to do, and she'd been missing in action. Poppy, Brit, and Joe. All three were earnest young people, trying to make a positive impact in the world, and Casey was a fraud.

The phone rang just as Casey was about to get up and leave.

"Computer, answer."

"Casey, you left me a message."

"Annika, I can't do this story."

"What? It's an easy job for you. Stick on your butch charm, and Poppy King will be eating out of your hand."

"That's the point," Casey said. "I don't want to do that. For one thing, she sees right through it. She might have been brought up in a comfortable middle-class life, but she's not stupid. She's got a good head on her shoulders and is a really kind person."

"I'm sure you can adapt to the situation, Casey."

"I don't want to lie to her. She doesn't deserve it."

Annika sighed. "This has never been a problem for you before, and it's not lying, it's undercover work."

Casey could feel her frustration and anger building at being put in this position, so soon after her jail time with Thea.

"Annika, you have no clue what I have to do to get a story. I lie, I cheat, I've hurt people, and I've just had enough. I tried to tell you that I didn't have it in me any more. It was one thing lying to people who didn't deserve any better, but this is different. Poppy is different."

"Why is she different? Of all the things you've done in the past to get stories, why is this one different?"

Casey didn't want to say it was how Poppy made her feel, so she just replied, "Call it the straw that broke the camel's back. I just want to leave, Annika."

She heard another big sigh on the other end of the line. "Casey, I didn't want to do this but—"

"But what?"

"I want to be the first reputable media outlet that either proves or disproves this story. To be frank, you owe me."

"What?" Casey said in disbelief. "My stories have made your media network the best there is."

"I've made your life very comfortable in return, Casey. You have money, and crucially, you have protection," Annika said.

Was that a thinly veiled threat? After all she had done for her?

"You're not hurting Poppy King directly—she is a means to an end."

A means to an end. Is that how she had sounded all these years? Had Casey suddenly woken up from Annika's world?

"It doesn't feel right," Casey said.

"I want this story, Casey."

Before she could respond, there was a knock at the door. "I need to go. There's someone at the door."

"Just remember what I said. I'll talk to you soon."

Casey didn't say anything in reply. She was too angry. "End call."

She got up and looked on the screen beside the door. It was Poppy. Casey couldn't believe it. What the hell was she doing here? Casey locked the doors to her study, where all the research on Poppy and her family was.

She then hurried back to the door, ran her fingers through her hair, and opened the door. Instead of the hello she was expecting, Poppy said with annoyance in her voice, "Where have you been?"

"Here, why? And how did you get my address?"

"May I come in?" Poppy asked. Before Casey had a chance to reply, Poppy pushed past her into the flat. "Why is because Brit, Joe and I were worried about you. I tried to call you but there was no answer."

Casey had seen missed calls on her phone, but they were from a withheld number. No doubt all of Poppy's family had the same setup, so their privacy could be kept safe.

"I haven't been feeling well." Casey shut the door.

"Are you okay? What was wrong?" Poppy said with concern.

"Just a virus kind of thing."

"How are you feeling now?" Poppy asked.

"Much better."

Casey saw Poppy's eyes flit down to her bags by the door. *Shit.*

"Going somewhere?"

"No, no. Just getting rid of some old clothes," Casey said.

"Donating them, I hope?"

"Yeah, yeah. I will do. You never told me how you found out where I live."

Poppy smiled. "I walk around with two palace security agents all day."

"I see."

Poppy's smile suddenly disappeared. "That didn't sound good, did it? I mean, I asked them to find out because we were all worried about you. I hope you don't mind."

Casey's guilt twisted in her stomach again. Even when Poppy was intruding on Casey's privacy, it was to make sure Casey was safe. All the time Casey was doing the same for her own gain.

"Of course not. It's nice to have you three thinking of me," Casey said truthfully.

"Oh, I brought you something that might make you feel better." Poppy rummaged in her canvas bag and pulled out a metal dish with a lid.

Casey walked closer and read the label. "It's your raspberry tea."

"Yes." Poppy smiled. "I thought I'd pick some up for you."

"You didn't have to do that," Casey said.

"I know I didn't, but I did. It's nice to be nice," Poppy said.

❖

It's nice to be nice.

Those words and Poppy's kind actions made the next two weeks at college difficult. Casey was frustrated and angry at her situation. The best way to deal with that was to be the arrogant and annoying person Poppy thought she was, and the glare she caught Poppy giving her was exactly what she wanted.

They hadn't talked a great deal or done any group work over the last two weeks. Her class had a lot of coursework to do, so any other projects were put on the back burner.

Poppy waved her over, and Casey waited about ten seconds, so she didn't look too eager.

It was Joe that greeted Casey this time. "Can you make it to our flat on Friday? We're having a cocktails and canapés night, or as my boring friends put it, a group meeting."

Joe rolled his eyes and Casey couldn't help but smile. "Yeah, I'll be there. Sounds fun."

Poppy gave her a good stare, and Casey winked right back, making Poppy blush.

I've still got it.

They'd been studying for month, and the cynic in Casey or Annika would say she'd done a good job of getting into Poppy's inner circle. It was just her sense of right and wrong that was taking a beating.

CHAPTER TEN

R oza only had a morning royal visit today, so she was catching up with government business and correspondence in her office this afternoon. She was signing some paperwork, documents that needed royal assent, while the TV news played in the background.

She was in a sombre mood. That morning, she had opened a new children's hospice in the city. She was extremely proud that parents and the local community had banded together to create such a wonderful organization. Roza had such great admiration for the staff who chose to work with sick children coming to the end of their lives. It was truly a vocation. But even braver were the parents who'd lost children. They continued to work hard, raising money, with the hope other children would have this centre to care for them closer to home.

Roza put her pen down and tried to control the emotion that was welling up inside her. When she was talking to the parents, all she was thinking about were her babies, Gussy and Maria, and having to deal with losing either one of them. She had no idea how the parents got through every day.

She looked at the picture on her desk of Gus holding his sister up in his arms. "I love you both."

For a second she imagined not being able to touch or hug them ever again. Tears started to fall. Roza quickly got a tissue and dabbed her eyes. She had to know if they were okay.

"Computer, put me through to the nursery."

"Your Majesty?"

"Nanny Joan, I just wanted to check in with Mari."

"Prince August took her down to the play park, ma'am."

"Okay, thank you, Joan."

She was disappointed not to speak to Mari but happy that she was spending time with her brother. Adopting Mari couldn't have gone any better. Gus could have been jealous of another child getting attention, but no. He'd taken her straight to his heart the minute he met her.

Gus was such a good boy. A mother couldn't have dreamed of having such a wonderful son. She was sure the parents she met this morning thought that about their children.

She thought of the stress and pain of trying to conceive again after Gus. Roza's heart rate started to quicken, and her chest tightened. She grasped the edge of the desk and closed her eyes. Anxiety was making her breath shorten.

"Take deep breaths."

Lex usually talked her through this if she was with her. The deep breaths, whilst concentrating on air going in and out, started to calm her heart. As her muscles lost their tension, her ears picked up a few words from the TV news.

"*The house of King now rules Denbourg.*"

Roza's eyes snapped open. The news had finished, and the channel had ran on to a tabloid-style celebrity gossip show. The presenter was talking to two so-called royal experts.

"*Amanda, these sorts of rumours have been circulating quietly for a month or so now. Is it true or trash?*"

"*Well, Stephan, it depends on which rumours you're talking about. If you mean the conspiracy theorists' claim that Lennox King, former banking industry expert, was placed in her role by global elites to control Queen Rozala, then probably not.*"

"You think?" Roza said sarcastically.

"*I hear a but coming,*" the presenter said.

"*You're right. My Palace sources tell me that Queen Rozala is debilitated by anxiety and depression, and the extent of it is being kept from us. The Queen isn't…let's just say she isn't functioning properly, and Crown Consort Lennox is acting as head of state, not Rozala.*"

Roza couldn't believe what she was hearing. It was a stupid gossip show, but still, how could anyone tell such lies?

"*That is frightening, if true. Could you tell us more about your Palace source?*"

"*Let's just say a close family member.*"

Roza felt anger rush through her. "We can guess who that is."

When Roza took the throne, the only other heir was her second cousin, Prince Bernard. He had despised the fact that she was the heir and lobbied the media against her through the years. When Gus was born, he got even further away from the crown, which doubtless made him angrier.

Bernard was part of European far right organizations, and so no one wanted him anywhere near the throne.

"TV off. Idiots," Roza growled.

She saw something scroll across the top of her screen. Roza had been scrolling through the palace social media accounts, and one of top trending items was *Royal movie project nears release.*

"What now?" Roza said with exasperation.

She touched the holo screen to open up the story, which teased the first pictures from the upcoming release *I Believe in You.*

Roza saw two publicity photos from the film. One showed the two actors playing her and Lex. Lex was played by actor Story St John, and she was played by Lula Deniau.

The second picture was an image of the actors playing her father and her older brother, seen through the eye of a sniper's scope.

Roza's hands started to shake as her mind flashed back to the horror of the moment she found out about her father's and brother's deaths.

The Privy Councillor took a large gold and jewelled sovereign ring and held it before Roza.

"It is with a heavy heart that I must tell you that His Majesty King Christian and His Royal Highness Crown Prince Augustus were killed yesterday afternoon in a terrorist assassination. It falls on me as chief privy councillor to bring you your father's ring. The King is dead, long live the Queen."

The bodyguards and officials repeated the phrase, while she pushed the ring onto Roza's finger, and then Roza collapsed. Lex caught her and cradled her in her arms. "They can't be gone. Tell me it's not real, Lex. Please, please, please."

Roza pinched the bridge of her nose and squeezed the fountain pen she held in her hand until her knuckles were white.

How could she not have known about this?

"Computer, put me through to Olly."

"Yes, Your Majesty?"

"Come to my office now," Roza said with anger in her voice.

After becoming Roza's private secretary five years ago, Olly became Roza's trusted friend very quickly, and Roza didn't know what she'd do without her. Which was why it so surprised her that this film came out of nowhere. She and Olly talked about everything.

Roza's anger was simmering by the time she heard a knock at the door. "Come."

Olly entered and gave her a curtsy. "Your Majesty?"

Roza spun round the screen with the pictures from the new film. "How did we not know about this? Why did I have to find out about it by chance? Our media team are the best. There's no way they wouldn't have known about this."

As soon as Olly understood what Roza was saying, she immediately looked downcast.

"I—yes, we did." Olly was struggling to get her words out.

Roza walked around to the front of desk. "What is going on here, Olly?"

"This is very awkward, ma'am."

"Just tell me. I'm your friend as well as your Queen."

"When we found out about the movie, Crown Consort Lennox—"

Roza stiffened. What had Lex done?

"What did she do?" Roza asked.

"You were going through some difficulties at the time, with anxiety and stress, and Consort Lennox thought it would be too much for you. She asked that we didn't talk about it until she could break the news to you, ma'am."

Roza couldn't believe it. She felt anger, betrayal, and disappointment that Lennox would do this.

"Olly, if this kind of thing ever happens again, you must come to me, no matter what my consort says. I am your Queen. Do you understand?"

"Of course, ma'am. I'm truly sorry."

"We'll say no more about it," Roza said before walking out of her office. She was full of righteous indignation, and her anger multiplied with every step towards Lex's office.

Roza didn't knock but just stormed into the room. Lex was talking to someone on the phone and quickly ended the call.

"What's wrong, darling?"

"Computer, show pictures of the new Denbourg royal film," Roza said.

Lex's eyes flicked closed as the penny finally dropped.

"How could you?"

Lex jumped up from her seat. "Darling, I just—"

Roza stepped back so Lex couldn't touch her. "Don't *darling* me. You put my private secretary in an impossible position. I'm the Queen here, Lex, and you are not the king, despite what your surname might be. Don't forget that."

"How could I forget that? I've been walking four steps behind you ever since we were first married," Lex said with more anger than she should have.

Roza threw her arms up in the air. "Oh, now it's coming out? Your fragile alpha ego can't take your wife being in a superior position?" She was losing control. She thumped her chest with her fist. "I am Queen, I am head of this family, so don't ever, ever give any of the staff orders that keep me out of the loop."

She stormed off out the door. She could hear Lex coming after her saying, "I was just trying to protect you."

But Roza didn't want to hear it.

❖

"So, how does it feel to be played by Story St John?" Queen Georgina asked over the video link.

Lex sat alone in her dressing room when George called. "Awful."

Today hadn't been going too well. After their fight, Roza never came down to dinner with the children. Lex was informed by Nanny that Roza had been in to see the children on her own and then went off to get ready for their engagement tonight.

Lex's instinct was to give her some space, so she came to her dressing room a bit early to get ready. She was sitting in her dinner suit with her shirt open and bow tie hanging loose around her neck when George called.

"Is Roza very upset by it?" George asked.

"You could say that. She didn't know about it until she saw the still photos on TV today."

George frowned. "That must have been a great shock. Surely the palace staff knew this was coming up."

Lex cupped her hands over her face and rubbed her forehead. "I asked her private secretary not to tell her, that it would be best coming from me, and"—she rested her clasped fists under her chin and closed her eyes briefly—"it never seemed to be the right time."

George was quiet for a time before saying, "As your friend, I totally understand wanting to protect your wife, especially when Roza's had a difficult time with her mental health."

"But as a sovereign?" Lex asked.

George sighed. "As sovereign I can understand why she would be angry. She must know everything, it's her duty to know all the information the Palace knows, and there should be absolute trust between the monarch and their closest staff."

"I did the wrong thing, overstepped my bounds," Lex said, "but everyone outside sees an institution, a department of government, a head of state, while I see the sometimes fragile woman I go to bed with every night. Sometimes I've had to overstep just to keep her going."

George nodded. "I know you've been such a great support to Roza—she couldn't have done it without you. Over the years there've been times when Bea has kept me following the right path, and times when I've stumbled too."

"Queen Beatrice is the master in the role of consort," Lex said. "It has been a struggle for me. It's natural to me to take the lead and protect my wife, but I have held my tongue and let her take the lead as I feel I should. Especially when I know Roza has had a difficult time."

"I have great sympathy for you. If Bea was the regnant Queen, and I the consort, I would have trouble taking a step back and letting Bea step into unknown situations first."

"I'm playing into my detractors' hands, though, aren't I," Lex said.

"What detractors?"

"Had you not heard? The conspiracy theorists that think I was placed with Roza by the banking global elites, to control Denbourg."

George rolled her eyes. "Of course they did. What utter nonsense. Ignore it and concentrate on Roza."

"I'll apologize, but as fate would have it, we're both going to come face to face with my new alter ego tonight."

"How so?" George asked.

"It's the annual charity performance for the Entertainers' Guild. Story St John is one of the performers."

"Typical good timing. I'm sure they invited her to take part knowing there would be a slight tension in the room."

"No doubt."

Normally at royal events, etiquette would save any blushes or awkward moments, but it had become a tradition over the years for the stars of TV and film and comedians to gently needle those in the royal box.

She was sure there would be jokes, ones that would make both her and Roza squirm, and they'd have to keep smiling. Not easy when you've had a huge fight.

"Thanks for calling, George. I better try and talk to Roza. Send our love to Bea and the kids."

"Will do. Good luck."

She was going to need it.

"Are you sure this is the best idea, Thea?" Morten asked his sister.

Thea gazed at her new image in the mirror. Intelliflesh had come a long way in nine years, and Thea was reaping the benefits. She touched her new male appearance, squarer jaw, stubble, heavier brow, which along with short hair made her unquestionably male in looks.

She rubbed her stubbled face and quite enjoyed the rough feeling. Along with her well-cut suit, Thea would look like any male businessman. She could have made this look permanent with the doctor's help, but Thea would have to change appearance often, so that her surviving the attack on the prison van would never be questioned.

"Yes, Morten. It will be fine. Stop worrying and let me do the thinking." Thea straightened her bow tie. "I want to see Roza in the flesh before we begin our plans."

"But the charity show is so public," Morten said.

She turned to Morten and put her hand on his shoulder. "Nobody will question my appearance. Relax, okay."

"I've lost out on nine years with you. I don't want to go through that again."

Morten had always been a sensitive boy and needed Thea. She knew that.

"You are not going to lose me again. Believe me. Now, any word on our elusive Luca?"

"I've put the word out with our usual people on the street, and our computer guys are hacking into the street-level camera systems to see if there's anything that can help us. We have her leaving the prison, but after that the cameras failed, and she disappeared."

Thea walked over to the bar in her hotel suite and poured a brandy. That was the frustrating thing. How Luca could just walk out of the jail, she didn't know. Her good friend, the late Deputy Vastas, had no idea. The order to open security doors and gates came from somewhere on high. She was determined to find out.

She poured a drink for her brother and said, "We must find the former governor. He knows something."

"He is being protected in a safe house somewhere. They think we'll come for him," Morten said.

"The longer they think I am dead, the more they will relax their guard. We'll get him and make him talk."

That was why faking her death was so important. She needed her enemies to drop their guard, and when that happened, she would pick them off one by one.

Her date for the evening came out of the dressing room looking gorgeous. Long dark hair, silky silver cocktail dress, cut to the thigh. Thea felt herself throb inside and her Intelliflesh dildo start to harden.

Tonight was going to be a lot of fun, Thea thought with a grin.

❖

Roza was struggling. Her heart raced, and she was shaking inside. Lex had tried to talk to her, but she'd met her with only silence. Rage mixed with pain had taken hold of her, and Lex was the target.

If she'd known about this film earlier, she could have prepared for it. But Lex had taken that away from her and caused trouble between them. Of all the events they had to go to, tonight's just couldn't have been timed more perfectly for the media company.

Tonight's charity performance included a sketch starring Story St John. The media would have a field day, zooming on to her, trying to see if they could catch a reaction on her face.

Roza would try her best, but she was dreading this evening. Lex came through from her dressing room, dressed in her dinner suit. She had avoided her all day, but there was no choice tonight.

"Are you ready?"

Before she could answer, there was a knock at the door. "Come," Roza said.

A footman popped in and said, "The car is ready for you, Your Majesty."

"Thank you."

Roza draped her silk shawl over her shoulders.

"Roza, let me—" Lex said. She normally helped Roza with her jacket or shawl. Lex hurried to the catch up with Roza since she had had just walked away. "Roza, wait. We can't go to this event and not speak."

But Roza just marched on. Ravn opened the door for the Queen, and she got in carefully. Lex got in at the other side.

"Roza, we can't go to a public event not speaking to each other, especially when Story St John is going to be there. It'll upset you."

Roza felt her anger bubbling inside her. She didn't turn around and look at Lex, just stared out front. "Something I would have been more prepared for if you hadn't interfered with the Queen's staff and business."

Lex never replied this time, and a heavy silence filled the car.

Thea knew all of Roza's facial expressions and emotions. She had been a master at manipulating her, as she was with most people. That's how she had become the head of the most successful criminal organization in the world.

As she gazed across the theatre full of people to the royal box directly across from her own, she could tell how uncomfortable Roza was. Her forced smile as each performer came on was evident to see.

Thea, in her male persona for the evening, shared a box with her lady escort for the night and had guards behind her. Being disguised had given her so much freedom. Her freedom had taken many years of planning, but Thea had been patient, knowing this day would come.

Here she was, sitting so close to her former lover. She lost count of how many times she had watched the footage of the assassinations of Roza's father and brother. Thea had always meant to finish the job by taking Roza out, but first she'd have to build her business and her networks back to a position of strength. But time had only given her more ways to hurt Roza.

Now she was married to Lennox King and had a son and heir, and a daughter. This was Thea's time, and it was coming soon. It was inconvenient that Luca had found out about her kill list, but even though there would be more security around them, Thea would get them.

If she did assassinate everyone on her list, there would be a cousin of Roza's who would be exceptionally grateful, and forever in her debt, as he was next in line to the throne. Debt and favours would open doors for her.

For this evening, Thea would be content with watching her former lover squirm. Over the course of the evening she could tell there was an atmosphere in the royal box. Roza hadn't even looked at Lennox King so far this evening.

Then came the best bit. Story St John came on-stage to take part in a comedy sketch. She watched as Lennox tried to take Roza's hand, only to have Roza pull her hand back with anger. Lennox tried to cover it, but Thea wondered if the cameras caught it.

Roza put her false smile back on, but Thea could read the turmoil going on in Roza's head. She always was mentally weak. Thea knew Roza wouldn't have lasted this long on the throne if Lennox hadn't been there.

So she would start picking off those around the periphery of the royal household, ending with Roza alone. Roza would crumble to dust.

❖

The royal car stopped outside the private palace entrance. Roza was out sharply and walked at a fast pace through the entrance hall. So fast that Lennox was hardly out of the car.

She called after her, "Roza, wait."

But she never stopped. Lex let out a sigh and looked up to the starry sky. Ravn asked her, "Is everything all right, ma'am?"

"*Lex*, Ravn. I've told you before. We've known each other too long, and been through too much to be so formal."

"I need to be respectful when we are outside and with the younger members of staff. They need to see a positive role model."

Lex nodded. They were so lucky to have Ravn as head of Palace security.

"Is there anything wrong?" Ravn repeated.

"I made a mistake, overstepped my bounds, and Roza is furious with me."

Lex wouldn't talk like this to anyone other than family. Ravn was completely trusted.

"I'd heard a few murmurings," Ravn said.

Lex looked at Ravn with surprise. "You did?"

"Gossip spreads around the palace like wildfire, I'm sorry to say."

With a heavy sigh Lex started to walk into the palace, followed by Ravn. "I was just trying to protect her. You know how delicate she's been over the last few years. This and the full media hype around the film will be so hard on her."

"I know. It must have been difficult for her meeting Story St John tonight."

"You are not kidding," Lex said. A footman took her outdoor coat, and she and Ravn walked into the entrance hall. "Especially when Story cracked a few jokes about filling my shoes, and the whole theatre chortled with laughter. I had to put a smile on my face and shake my head, as if it was just cheeky banter. All the time knowing how much it all was hurting Roza." Lex stopped at the bottom of the grand staircase.

"I'm sorry, Lex. She will come around. I know you always do your best for her."

Lex nodded. "I better go and start making my apologies. Goodnight, Ravn."

"Goodnight, Lex."

Lex trudged upstairs, trying to rehearse what she would say when she got to the bedroom. When she did arrive upstairs, Roza's dresser, Tilda, was waiting outside the door looking nervous.

She curtsied to Lex and said, "Your Royal Highness, the Queen asked me to tell you that your night things are in the consort's room."

Lex couldn't believe what she was hearing. "Excuse me?"

"The Queen has had your things put in the consort's room."

She was shocked. The consort's room was next door to the Queen's bedchamber. Lex used the dressing room and the bathroom to get ready, but she had never slept in there apart from Roza before. That room with its connecting door was from a time when a king and queen slept apart. A bygone age.

Lex could see how uncomfortable Tilda was, so she nodded and said, "Thank you."

Once Tilda walked out of sight, Lex walked further up the hall to peek into Maria's room, and then Gus's. They were both sound asleep. She walked back to their bedroom and walked in.

The lights were all off, and Roza was in bed facing away from her.

"Roza? Sweetheart? I am truly sorry, and I know tonight has been a really emotional evening, but—"

"Your night things are in the consort's room," Roza said flatly.

"Please, Roza. This is silly."

"That's right. I'm a silly, weak woman who has to be protected. I couldn't possibly do my duties as Queen without you deciding everything for me."

"I didn't mean that. Roza—"

"I want to be left alone." Roza still had her back turned on Lex.

Lex couldn't hold her temper any more. "You're totally blowing this out of proportion."

"Of course I am. You're obviously the more capable and sensible monarch. I'll send my official papers and private secretary to you in the morning. I'll just paint my nails and shop for gowns like a good little wife, while King Lex takes care of government business."

"Is that what you really think? Have you been reading all that nonsense in the media?"

Lex waited a moment for Roza to respond. Silence filled the room, and Lex felt it cut very deep. It must be Roza's anxiety and PTSD from the murders that was talking, but it still hurt.

She walked out of the bedroom and into the consort's room. Lex took off her dinner jacket and threw it down on the bed, and her bow tie soon followed. She then sat down on the edge of the bed and held her head in her hands.

Lex heard her phone beep with a text. She prayed it was Roza messaging from the other room. "Computer, read message."

"Hi, big sis. I just wanted to make sure you two were all right. I was watching the theatre show on TV, and Roza looked a bit upset. Did Story being there upset her? I know she'll be sad about the film she's made."

"Send message, *We'll be okay. I'll call you tomorrow.*"

The room was big, echoey, and lonely. Roza and Lex had only slept apart on very rare occasions, when they had to be in different parts of the country or the world for an engagement, or when Roza had to be rushed to hospital after her late-term miscarriage.

Lex hated being apart from Roza. Roza always had this idea that Lex was the capable one, the tower of strength, but Lex needed Roza just as much. In the past Lex would have attempted to cope with an emotional time like this at the bottom of a bottle of vodka and with cocaine.

As a recovering addict she had to find different ways to deal with negative emotions. She hurried to her dressing room, got changed, and made her way down to the palace gym. She needed to run, to lift weights, to push her body to its limits.

❖

Lex was woken abruptly as Gus jumped into bed with her. "Mum?"

Lex pushed herself up to lean against the headboard. She put her arm around Gus and kissed the top of his head. "Morning, my boy. How are you today?"

"I'm okay. Why aren't you sleeping in bed with Mama?"

The question she had been dreading. She didn't want Gus or Maria to know that their parents were going through a difficult time.

"I...I couldn't sleep, so I went down to the gym to tire myself out. I didn't want to disturb your mama, so I just slept in here."

"Oh, okay. Mama isn't having breakfast with us this morning," Gus said.

Oh no. Today she thought Roza might understand why she did what she did, even if she couldn't yet forgive her.

"Why? Did she say?" Lex asked in a nonchalant voice.

"She just said she had Queen stuff to do."

She's avoiding me, Lex thought. "Okay, let's go and get your sister, and we'll have breakfast together."

Lex didn't know how she was going to make this right. But she had to. Somehow.

CHAPTER ELEVEN

Poppy was really looking forward to tonight at Joe and Britta's. It was her first night out with her new friends, and her first time since she got back from India that she didn't have secret service agents.

She really liked Jess and Mattius, and they tried their best to fit in with whatever she was doing, but she wanted freedom. After a call first to Lex, then to Roza, both had given permission to stop the security, because everything appeared to have calmed now that Thea was dead.

Poppy could now enjoy school and her friends without standing out any more. Her taxi stopped outside Joe and Brit's apartment. She paid the driver and then heard the rumbling engine of a motorcycle behind her.

A wave of excitement ran through her body. She turned around to find Casey turning off her throbbing engine, then pulling off her helmet. A tumble of blonde-highlighted brown hair fell out.

She is so sexy.

Then Poppy reminded herself—no bad boys on motorbikes. She liked reliable, safe, and loving, and she didn't think it was possible to have both. Casey set her helmet on the bike and then pulled her unruly hair into a topknot.

When Casey noticed her, she smiled and gave her a wink.

Stop doing the wink thing!

That wink was dangerous. She imagined that wink along with her boundless charm could get Casey anywhere. Although Casey had shown other parts of her personality these last few weeks. Casey had concentrated and taken part in class, instead of just trying to give smart-arse answers.

In the few weeks since Poppy had gone to her flat to check if she was safe, Casey didn't have so many sarcastic replies, and almost none of the bravado she had displayed before. Poppy was reminded of the raspberry tea that Casey had enjoyed, and the feeling that there was something going on just underneath Casey's surface was a total surprise to her.

Casey was a woman of contradictions, and perhaps there was more to Casey James than met the eye.

"Hello?"

Poppy jumped out of her thoughts and realized she had been meditating on Casey's attributes while Casey was saying hi.

"Hi, sorry, I was dreaming."

"A good dream, I hope?" Casey said.

Poppy shrugged and told a small lie, "It was all right, I suppose."

Casey gave a small laugh. "Good, then, shall we?"

Poppy looked at Casey offered arm and was drawn to it. She took it, and she felt her heart pound a little faster.

"So, how did you escape without your scary minders tonight?"

"I persuaded my sister that I would be okay. Thea is dead, so there's no more problem."

The very mention of Thea made Casey's stomach drop and her body tense.

"And Jess and Mattius aren't scary."

They walked up the stone steps to the entrance of the apartment block.

"Not to you, maybe, but I got a deathly stare from Jess anytime I was with you."

Poppy grinned. "They were just making sure you weren't dangerous."

They were buzzed in, and Casey held open the door. "Do you think I'm dangerous?"

Only your wink. "You? No, you're just cocky, arrogant—"

"Okay, you can stop now. I've got the picture." Casey smiled.

They walked in, and Casey looked all around and whistled. "This is an upmarket apartment building Brit and Joe have."

As they made their way over to the elevator Poppy said, "It really is beautiful. Art deco? 1920s? They are lucky."

Casey pressed to call the lift and said, "I thought you'd be used to even grander places than this."

Poppy rolled her eyes. "I'm not royal or used to fancy places—I only visit them. I was brought up in a small English village, in a farmhouse. A nice farmhouse but not a palace."

The lift doors opened, and they went inside. "I should have guessed you came from a small village."

Poppy spun around and narrowed her eyes. "What do you mean by that?"

The lift jerked into action, and Casey had an amused look on her face that really annoyed Poppy.

"Just that you are quite innocent and idealistic, so you probably grew up quite sheltered, like in a little village."

That got Poppy super annoyed. "Innocent and sheltered? You've only known me a month. I've spent time with UNICEF in third world countries, trying to make people's lives better. I've seen slavery, evidence of human trafficking, and if you're referring to"—the lift doors opened—"my love life, you have no idea how innocent or experienced I am."

Poppy heard someone clearing their throat, and Casey smiled smugly. Poppy turned her head slowly, and Brit and Joe were standing outside their door, hearing every word she said.

"Did we interrupt something," Joe asked, smiling.

Brit gave him a dig in the ribs and said, "Welcome to cocktails and canapés. Come in, come in."

As they excited the lift, Joe looked around them.

"No Jess, no Mattius?"

"Sorry, Joe, I don't need security any more," Poppy said.

Joe pouted. "You're kidding. Oh well, maybe if I hang around you long enough, I'll see her again. She was my kind of woman." As they walked inside the flat, Joe said to Casey, "Don't you agree, Casey?"

Casey smiled. She preferred her own women to be a little softer but could certainly see Jess's beauty. "Definitely. Strength and beauty all wrapped up in the same package."

Joe snapped his fingers. "Exactly. Hmm. Beautiful."

Brit came and took their coats. "He's not still going on about Jess, is he?"

"I think he's in love," Poppy said, smiling.

"Shut up, Brit, just because your love life is stalled," he joked. "Just kidding. Take a seat."

Casey looked around at the stunning flat. The large open sitting area had original wooden flooring, and a gorgeous highly polished white piano sat beside floor-to-ceiling windows. Over at the other side of the room was an open kitchen, and behind them were a full-sized pool table and a wet bar.

"This is a great place you have here," Casey said.

"Yes, it's beautiful," Poppy agreed.

Brit brought plates of nibbles and canapés over to the coffee table. "It was one of Grandmother's buildings. She was a bit of a property magnate. The building on Restoration Square was the pinnacle for her. She worked her way up from the bottom, and she didn't let us forget it." Britta sat beside Poppy on the large, comfortable sectional couch. "And she expected the same from us. Ever since we were teenagers, Grandma had us working with her and her staff on weekends, cleaning out properties for renting, helping out at her office, and as we got older, working at her parties. Hence, why Joe thinks he's the king of the cocktail."

Joe bowed extravagantly. "Indeed I am. I always tended bar, and Brit could only manage handing out the canapés. We like to keep up the tradition with our cocktails and canapés get-togethers." He clapped his hands. "So first, I thought we'd start with some martinis, just as a livener, then move on to some more"—Joe hesitated—"interesting drinks."

"I know Casey needs non-alcoholic because she's driving, but Poppy, say at any point if you'd like a non-alcoholic version. My brother has a full repertoire of them."

"I haven't had a drink since that first day we met, but before that, in India, I had the mother of all hangovers. It doesn't take much to get me tipsy."

Casey would have liked to partake in a couple of drinks but felt it was more important to stay alert and pick up any information that might be helpful. After all, she was supposed to be working. *Supposed to be.*

"One dirty martini mocktail and three vodka martinis coming up."

Joe went off to make the drinks, and Brit said, "I'll just get some pens and paper, and we can do this brainstorming session the old-fashioned way."

Once they were both away Poppy leaned over and whispered, "Thanks for letting me know Joe and Brit were there at the lift, hearing every embarrassing word I said, because you made assumptions about me."

It was amusing and kind of cute to see Poppy annoyed. She was genuinely a nice woman, so it kind of gave Casey a buzz, ruffling her feathers.

"You made assumptions about me too," Casey replied.

"I did not," Poppy said firmly.

Casey leaned in close to her face. "Oh really? Womanizer, cocky, arrogant?"

Brit was back with the pads and pens just as Poppy was about to reply. "Here we go."

Then Joe arrived with a tray of drinks. "Okay, have a go at these, my friends. Dirty mock martini for you, Casey, and vodka martinis for the rest of us."

Once everyone had a drink Joe said, "Cheers!"

The drinks were beautifully presented. Joe had clearly worked as a barman before. "Cheers!" they all replied.

Casey had other non-alcoholic martinis before that weren't that great, but she was keen to see how this measured up. The liquid was cloudy, and the glass had perfectly placed olives to add that dash of authenticity.

She took a sip. "Wow."

Joe grinned. "Do you like it?"

Casey was truly surprised at the flavour. "It's amazing. It doesn't have the burn of vodka, but the flavour is right on point. How did you manage that?"

Joe was super excited as he replied, "A barman who worked at some of Grandma's parties taught me. Are you ready for it?"

Casey saw Joe was nearly ready to burst. She loved what an enthusiastic character he was.

"Oh, hurry up. You know how many times I've heard this?" Britta complained.

"Potato water," Joe replied.

"What?" both Casey and Poppy exclaimed at once.

"Yes, potato water. If you think about it, vodka is made from potatoes, so it's only natural, really. It's an old barman's trick."

Casey took another drink and said, "Well, you certainly have a knack, Joe. Maybe it's a bar you should open and not a coffee shop."

Joe snapped his fingers and pointed at Casey. "More on that later."

Poppy held up her glass, "Mine is delicious too, Joe."

"Thank you, Miss Poppy."

"Could we get going now?" Brit asked.

❖

Thea was enjoying dinner in her basement apartment on the outskirts of Battendorf. Her dinner companion was chatting incessantly while playing with her long dark hair, to the point of becoming aggravating.

She had kept her male persona but planned to dispense with it tonight, after her two visitors had fulfilled their purposes.

Morten walked in just as the female guest laughed inanely at her own joke and was making Thea regret having her brought up here.

"We've got him in the other room."

Thea dabbed her mouth with her napkin and stood. "Do excuse me. It's been lovely…chatting."

"How long will you be?" Thea heard as she walked out the door.

"We have everything ready." Morten opened the door the other room, and a man in dirty looking jeans and a T-shirt sat in a chair in the middle of the room.

There were four of Thea's people against the back wall, standing quietly.

"Are you who wants this information? If not, can I just go?"

In front of the man was a bundle of orange clothes and a brown paper bag. On the other side of the room was Thea's computer expert Rhys, working in front of a holo screen.

Morten nodded to one man at the back wall. He walked over and, whilst wearing protective gloves, lifted the orange clothing off the floor. It was the prison uniform she'd worn for nine years.

"You found this?" Thea asked.

"Yeah, stuffed in that bag with some other weird stuff."

Thea's man emptied out the bag, and what looked like the remains of Intelliflesh fell out.

"Where did you find this?" Thea asked.

"At the back of the motel I work at, in the bins."

Morten leaned over and said, "It's not far from the prison."

"Hey, I was promised money for this," the man said.

Thea stepped forward and smiled. "Of course you will get everything you deserve. Did you see this person?"

"Even better," Morten said, "he's got footage from the security cameras at the back. Rhys is working on it."

Thea walked over to Rhys. "What have you got for me?"

Rhys pointed to the screen. "If you watch the second window. A few seconds and…there."

Thea saw a hooded figure jump from a window holding a couple of bags. One they dumped in the bins, and one they took with them.

"Is there no image of their face?"

"That's what I've been working on."

Rhys rolled back the film and put it on super slow motion. "Watch for the flash of blonde hair."

Then Thea saw it. The person turned their head round for the tiniest amount of time. The picture froze on half of a woman's face. Blonde hair covered the other side.

"So this is Luca, or Lucian, as we now know." Thea felt like such a fool for being taken in by this pathetic journalist. She must have gotten soft.

"Any leads on who she truly is?"

Rhys pointed to the corner of the screen, where she could see files whizzing through at a fantastic speed. "I'm running what we have of her through my facial recognition databases, but nothing as yet. She's had some help hiding, I think."

"What about the DNA on the clothes and Intelliflesh?"

Morten walked over to join her. "Wiped clean."

"A professionally done job?" Thea asked.

"Looks like it."

"Hey, are you forgetting I'm here?" their guest said.

"Are we done with him?" Thea asked Morten.

"Yes, we have everything."

Thea pulled out a gun from under her jacket and shot him quickly and cleanly through the head. He fell off the chair to the ground with a thump. "Get someone to clean up the mess, Morten, and my guest in the dining room."

She saw Morten tense at the implication of what she was saying. He was weaker than her. She'd always known that.

"She's seen our set-up, Morten." He nodded, and Thea squeezed his shoulder. "Good. I'm going to take this stuff off," Thea said, pointing to the Intelliflesh. "There's only so long I can enjoy being a man."

CHAPTER TWELVE

Poppy hadn't enjoyed an evening so much in a long time. Joe and Britta were such good company, and she had to admit Casey was too. She was extremely confident, which could come across as arrogant, but she was also funny.

She was so different than when they had first met. Even more of those walls of bravado that she initially had were coming down. Maybe Casey was right, maybe she had made assumptions about her.

Britta helped Joe carry over the next round of drinks. They had graduated from sitting properly on the couch to sitting on the rug that spanned the sitting area, with their backs against the base of the couch.

"Tell them about this one, Joe-Joe," Britta said.

"Ladies first." Joe handed Poppy a highball glass of light brown liquid with a few inches of white bubbly cream on top, making it look like a cappuccino.

"This looks gorgeous," Poppy said. "What is it?"

"It's part of an idea we had for the cafe," Britta said.

Joe handed Casey a glass. "I know you're driving, but could you at least have a few sips? Just to taste it. It's called a Night Cap. Basically a coffee cocktail. Rum, tonic, bitters, cold press coffee, and cream," Joe said.

Britta, who was equally enthused, continued, "We think we can change into a quite chic, mellow evening venue. It can be Joe's baby."

"Sounds like a fab idea to me." Poppy took a sip, hummed with delight, and licked the frothed cream off her lips. She turned around and caught Casey looking at her with soft, smoky eyes. Her gaze gave her a tingly feeling inside. It was only after a few moments that Poppy realized Casey had a cream moustache on her top lip.

She felt a warm smile creep onto her lips. Without hesitation, she leaned forward and wiped Casey's moustache with her thumb while her fingers caressed her cheek. Their eyes locked, and Poppy felt something inside her melt.

Poppy was sure she was imagining it, but Casey's eyes seemed to soften under her gaze, and what she saw beneath was a storm of emotions. Before she could say or do anything, Casey jerked and pulled away abruptly.

"Yeah, it's tasty. If you need to talk to anyone about the bar business, you should talk to my brother-in-law. He owns a small club."

"Does he?"

They began to chat, and Poppy couldn't help but feel angry. There was something, a connection, a moment, that happened there between them, and she'd been mentally, forcibly pushed away from Casey. That she did not like.

Poppy turned to Britta, who raised her eyebrows, obviously having seen the interaction. It annoyed Poppy that she got that brush-off, but it shouldn't, should it?

"Can we get a game of pool, Joe?" Casey asked.

"No way." Poppy lifted her notepad. "We've been here two hours and the square root of nothing. I brought the plans I drew up, but we've got no theme, and so nothing to base our marketing on. No pool for you."

Britta nodded. "I suppose we better. The marketing section of the project is a big part of our mark."

Casey, who had already stood up, said, "The marketing is easy."

That's the arrogance returned. I can't believe I thought there was actually more going on behind those eyes, Poppy thought. "Easy? Oh, do tell us."

Joe and Casey sat back down.

"Your property is in Restoration Square?" Casey looked from Joe to Britta.

"Yeah." They both nodded.

"Use the history of the square."

"I was never very good at history," Joe said.

"The revolution?" Britta offered.

"Exactly. All over Europe, coffee houses used to be the gathering places of free thinkers, political campaigners, and artists. Governments and monarchies hated the coffee houses, as they were where seeds of revolution began."

She was right. Poppy wasn't going to say it out loud, but she knew it was true.

"Yes, that's right," Britta came in to confirm it instead. "In Britain, France, Vospya, and here in Denbourg."

"What happened in Denbourg?" Poppy asked.

"You don't know the history of your own in-laws?" Casey tutted.

If Casey was trying to be annoying, she was surely succeeding. "Please tell us," Poppy said sarcastically. "I know you're dying to."

"Back in the seventeen hundreds, there was a revolution in Denbourg, and it started in coffee houses in and around the square. Your sister-in-law's family was deposed and the monarchy abolished."

"Yeah," Britta said, "it was called The Little Terror."

Poppy hadn't heard that story before. "Roza's family was deposed?"

"Yeah," Casey replied, "the monarch was King Harold V."

Poppy noticed that Casey had lost that arrogant bravado, and her face lit up while telling them about what must be her research. She would never have thought Casey James would come prepared.

Making assumptions again?

"Crops had failed, poverty and disease were rife, and King Harold increased tax after tax, trying to raise money for pointless foreign wars. Eventually taxes began to bite the middle and merchant classes. They met in coffee house, produced and disseminated anti-monarchist newspapers and posters."

Britta joined in. "The people turned on the King and demanded he hand himself in at the palace gates, or they would enter the palace. He did, and the revolutionary leaders arrested him and the rest of the family."

"How come I didn't know about this?" Poppy said.

Joe scratched his head. "I'm from Denbourg, and I didn't even know."

"You never took history, knucklehead," Britta retorted.

"Well, we shouldn't look to the past. The future"—Joe flourished his hands—"is where we should be focussing."

"The past teaches us lessons," Poppy said.

Casey nodded. "Exactly, there's nothing new under the sun. You must always look to the past."

Was she actually agreeing with Casey? "What happened next?" Poppy asked Casey.

"The royal family were meant to be executed. A row of gallows were built out on Restoration Square—or Imperial Square, as it was then. But each time a new date was set, it was retracted, because doubt began to set in."

Casey could tell a good story. She was making it sound like she was a reporter on the ground at the time. Poppy moved further up the couch, right next to her.

"And?"

"A few months into the new regime, the people were growing disgusted. The leader—Protector Holst, as he was styling himself—was using violence and fear to control the population. The ordinary men and women in the street were worse off than under the monarchy."

"What about Roza's family?" Poppy asked.

"They didn't know from one week to the next whether they were going to die. Five and a half months into the new dictatorship, factions of the armed forces turned against Protector Holst. King Harold died of a heart attack while in prison, and that was the turning point. His daughter Catherine, or Queen Catherine as she became when her father died, had been well-liked by the people."

"This is riveting," Poppy said. "Go on."

"Queen Catherine was not like her father. She had a great social conscience. When the guards watching the rest of the family told her of the unrest in Denbourg, she offered them help in any way she could. The army killed Holst, and those who led the revolt came to Catherine with a deal. If they reinstated the monarchy as a constitutional monarchy and not an absolute monarchy, would she accept the crown and a new democratic system. Do you want to finish the story, Brit? She's your countrywoman."

"Yes, I love Queen Catherine," Britta said enthusiastically. "The new Queen and the extended royal family were brought to the square. In front of the crowd she signed the new constitution."

"Wait," Poppy said, "is that what the statue is in the middle of the square?"

Britta nodded. "Uh-huh, Queen Catherine holding up the new signed constitution. The monarchy was restored, Imperial Square became Restoration Square. The Little Terror lasted only six months."

"That's an amazing story. I must ask Roza about it," Poppy said.

"Wait, wait, wait," Joe said. "As fun as this history lesson is, how does it help us with marketing our new coffee bar?"

Poppy was enjoying the conversation so much that she forgot about their project. "Oh yeah?"

"It's simple," Casey said. "The square is surrounded by art and antique shops, restaurants, and overpriced tourist shops. Their customers are exactly the type of people who won't mind paying a premium for ethically sourced coffee. Tourists flock to this square to see the palace, to see all the royal pageantry, to see the history of the square, and to visit the shops there. Find out about historic coffee houses where political unrest began, and use that history as part of the backstory of your cafe bar."

Joe suddenly became engaged. "You mean don't go for a modern look like the other coffee chains. Go for the revolution-era aesthetic, the way some pubs and clubs use American Prohibition?"

Casey snapped her fingers. "Exactly, make the tourists feel they are still part of the history when they come into the cafe for a drink. Have the history on the walls—"

"We could name cocktails and coffees after the historical figures," Joe said.

Everyone was really excited, and all because of Casey. Poppy looked at her and smiled. She really did have hidden depths.

Britta clapped her hands together. "Perfect, you two seem very interested in that side of things, so I propose that Casey and Poppy are in charge of research and marketing."

"What?" Poppy said with surprise.

"Great idea," Joe said. "We'll handle the menu, budget, procurement of the coffee beans, food—things like that."

That sounded like a bad idea to Poppy. As all right as Casey was in small doses when she dropped that arrogant crap, spending extended periods of time with her would be both irritating and confusing, especially as her body seemed to find Casey frustratingly attractive.

Poppy shook her head subtly to Britta. "No, I'm sure it would be better if we all contributed."

Britta smiled and winked at her. "I think it's a great idea. What do you think, Casey?"

"Yeah. Why not," Casey said.

Oh, great, Poppy thought.

"That's decided then." Britta grinned mischievously.

"Now that's all sorted out"—Casey turned to Joe—"can we have a game of pool now?"

❖

Roza stared at the words on her tablet, but none were going in. She was so wound up and tense. Lex would come to bed soon, and Roza couldn't stand the thought of having a confrontation, as they had most nights since Roza had wanted to sleep alone.

Lex always wanted to talk about how she felt, and Roza just didn't or couldn't. She still felt a sense of panic—doom, like a dark cloud had fallen over her. Everything—her mind, her surroundings—was grey and miserable.

But at the same, she was hiding in it, and Lex's attempts to get her out of it made Roza angrier and led her to push Lex away. They talked politely during the day, for the sake of the children, but she just couldn't do any more. She knew she was hurting Lex, but her trust had been shaken.

The gossip columns were full of rumours that Lex was running things here in the palace, and it hurt that there might be a small bit of Lex that didn't believe in her, that thought she was incapable.

Roza put down her tablet and threw back the covers. She walked over to the windows that looked over Restoration Square. She pulled back the curtains a little and saw the night owls still moving around the square. It was a beautiful area, and it brought back some happy memories.

At times of national celebration, she was taken out on the balcony with her family, to wave at the people. Her brother Augustus would lift her up, and people would cheer. She could still remember the smile on her brother's face. She missed that smile so much.

Roza's gaze wandered down to the gates, and her thoughts wandered to a bleaker day. Her father and her brother left through those gates to attend the annual ceremony at the war memorial, King Christian and Crown Prince Augustus in their respective military uniforms.

In the news coverage she had watched and rewatched the next day, repeatedly, they smiled and waved to the crowds. Roza had followed what would be their last journey down to the bottom of the square, and then their left turn to the memorial statue.

Roza felt a few tears start to fall. All the time they travelled, Thea was in a bunker somewhere, waiting to watch their murders. Her mind replayed the images as they exited the carriage. One second they were smiling, and the next they dropped to the ground, lifeless, with blood seeping from their foreheads. At that moment her life was forever changed.

Thea's sneering face leaped into her mind, and she remembered the last thing Thea had said to her over the phone.

Hello, my special girl, do you miss me? Even after everything that's happened, I'll always be in your heart and your head. Won't I?

Roza grasped her head. Nine years and still these intrusive thoughts paralyzed her from time to time, and she didn't know how to stop them.

There was a knock at the connecting door between this bedroom and the consort's room. Roza wiped her eyes quickly.

"Yes, come in."

The door opened slowly, and Lex walked a few inches into the room. "Hi. Are you okay, sweetheart?"

Roza tried her best to seem in control and turned around with folded arms. "I'm fine."

"I didn't know if you wanted me to—" Lex pointed to their bed.

Part of Roza wanted to run into Lex's protective arms, but the bigger part of her needed space. Space to see if she could trust in herself, and in Lex.

"I need time, Lex."

Lex sighed and her voice had a sharper edge to it. "You know I'm leaving tomorrow for my overseas trip."

"Of course I remember. We've been planning it for months."

As part of Lex's substance abuse charity, she was leading her team to meet and publicize recovery programs. The first week she was heading to North America to learn from her US counterparts, but most importantly to talk to those recovering and share their experiences with the world. Then she'd travel on to the UK for the second week to fulfil various engagements. Roza knew how important this charity was to Lex. The original plan had been for them both to go, but the Queen's schedule wouldn't allow it.

They were very rarely away from each other for a few days, let alone two weeks. They had both been dreading it, but now it was making Roza's anxiety even worse, and she was projecting more of her anger onto Lex.

"I've said goodbye to the children. I'll be gone before they waken."

Roza nodded. She was hardly holding it together.

Lex sighed. "I'll call to talk to them every night."

"Okay. I'll make sure they're ready for you," Roza said.

Lex pushed her hands into her pockets. "Remember, Poppy will be over tomorrow for dinner. Look after her for me."

"I always will."

Lex took another step forward. "I'd like to talk to you too."

Roza bit her lip. She was determined not to break. She needed this time to herself to think. Had she been a strong Queen these nine years, or was the truth that she had been emotionally and intellectually held together by Lex? Was Lex the real monarch in this palace? She had to know. Two weeks apart might help her find out.

"I'm tired. Goodnight."

She turned her back and walked to bed. As she slipped under the covers, she heard the connecting doors slam shut. Roza turned onto her side and felt wet tears roll onto the pillow.

I need help.

Casey lined up her shot on the pool table. She and Joe enjoyed a few frames of pool before a giggling Poppy and Britta joined them to watch. It wasn't long until a challenge was issued, and Poppy teamed up with Britta to play.

It was best of five, and there had been a lot of laughter and gentle teasing, if not flirting between Poppy and herself.

Casey was loving it and having so much fun. She felt alive after feeling so much darkness. Poppy was no pushover. She was challenging and knew how to stand up for herself. The banter between them was so easy and fuelled something inside her.

It all came down to this one ball. If she potted it, the other two balls were easy.

"Come on, Case," Joe said. "This is our game."

It was a difficult shot, but all those games she'd played in Goldie's bar as a teenager gave her confidence. "You are never making this, hotshot," Poppy said.

Those words were like music to Casey's ears. There was nothing she liked better than proving someone wrong. Especially if that person was Poppy King.

Casey looked up at Poppy and said, "Keep looking in my eyes, honey."

Poppy narrowed her eyes and pursed her lips.

Without breaking her gaze from Poppy, Casey pulled the cue back and smashed the ball into the top right pocket.

Britta and Poppy gasped, and Casey slowly stood up and blew on the tip of her pool cue like it was a smoking gun.

"And that, honey, is how you play pool."

She winked at Poppy, and Joe pulled her into a hug. "That was freaking amazing." Joe pointed at Poppy—"You lose"—and danced his way around to where she stood with his sister. "Losers…"

Britta playfully pushed her brother away, but Poppy walked over to Casey and grasped her pool cue. "Just where did you learn to play like that?"

Casey looked down at both their hands on the cue. She had the greatest urge to cover Poppy's hand with her own and pull her close. She had felt this magnetic pull to Poppy all night.

Once, Poppy had looked so deeply into her eyes that it felt like she couldn't hide anything from her, and she'd quickly turned away. There was something about this woman that made her hard to hide from.

"Next game's the winner?" Britta suggested.

Casey didn't take her eyes off Poppy, and it was Poppy who blinked first and pulled away from the cue.

"I better get going. I'm spending the day with my niece and nephew tomorrow."

As soon as Poppy said that, Casey came down to earth with a bang. She remembered why she was here. She was undercover, trying to befriend Poppy, to gain access to the palace and the Queen.

The greatest compliment that she could give Poppy was that she forgot she was undercover. She was just having a great time with her new friends. That's what it felt like.

Casey was deceiving Poppy, Britta, and Joe, and she experienced shame. She liked them all. It wasn't supposed to be like this.

Casey heard Poppy say, "I'll call a taxi."

"Poppy, would you like me to give you a run home on the bike?"

Poppy narrowed her eyes and smiled. "I've never been on a motorbike before."

"There's a first time for everything." Casey imagined Poppy holding on to her tightly, and her body reacted.

Poppy appeared to think about it for a second, then said, "Thanks, but no. I think I'd be too scared."

"Oh, go on, Poppy," Joe said. "I'd never turn down a ride. Live a little."

"Yeah, go on." Britta grinned.

It was clear Britta was trying to matchmake. When Joe and Casey went off to play pool, Poppy asked why Britta had thrown them together for this marketing project, and she said, "Did you see the way that you two were looking at each other?"

"No, I couldn't see, could I?" Poppy said.

"Well, I'll tell you what I saw. You were melting into each other," Britta said.

"You're having a laugh, aren't you? Miss too big for her boots fancies herself too much, and for sure has never melted into anyone's eyes," Poppy said.

"I know chemistry when I see it."

Her memory was interrupted by Joe. "Go on, be a devil."

Britta had her arms folded and was mouthing, *Go on.*

She then looked at Casey. She was standing with her hands in her pockets, smiling in an annoying way.

"You scared?"

"Of you or the bike, do you mean?" Poppy bit back.

"You choose."

"Neither."

Joe took a step between them and said, "Okay. Let me cut this sexual tension with a knife before you jump each other. Bike or call a taxi?"

Poppy looked Casey in the eye and said firmly, "Bike."

"Good choice," Casey said. "Let's go, honey."

Poppy put on the jacket that Joe brought her. "That's three or four times you've called me that—don't be so condescending."

Casey just laughed.

Once she got ready to leave, Poppy hugged both of her new friends. "Thank so much for tonight. It was such fun, even though we're meant to be doing serious project work."

"The wonderful Casey James saved the day there," Britta said.

Casey, looking as cocky as ever, bowed. "Thank you."

Poppy sighed. "Let's get this over with, then, hotshot."

❖

Casey enjoyed the look of annoyance she had put on Poppy's face. That pool game really aggravated her. Her whole MO was to not come on too strong and try and get the Queen's sister-in-law on her hook. It quickly became evident that Poppy King would not be jumping onto anyone's hook, and it was more likely to be the other way around.

Even though the evening had turned into a social occasion, with Casey forgetting the fact she was on a job, it had turned out well. Her research into the history of Restoration Square had come in very handy.

It had gotten her a new study partner. So now Casey had Poppy's undivided attention for their part of the project and the chance to flirt with a beautiful woman for most of the evening.

Once they made it down to the reception area of Joe and Britta's apartment building, Casey held open the door for Poppy.

"Ladies first."

Poppy rolled her eyes as she walked out the door. This was just too much fun.

Casey had played the role of the seducer before, in her investigations, most notably when she'd infiltrated the right-wing motorcycle gang, and to a lesser extent in prison with Thea. That was all business, though, as this was meant to be, but it hadn't turned out that way. This evening had made Casey feel alive again. The flirting, the good-natured teasing. It was all so innocent in its own way but made her feel such more excitement than she had felt when she was herself an innocent teenager.

They walked towards Casey's bike, and Poppy came to a sudden stop.

"What's wrong?" Casey asked.

"It's big, isn't it?"

Poppy looked fearful, and Casey felt bad that Poppy had been slightly pressured into this.

"It's really safe, but if you're not comfortable, I'll call you a cab, no problem."

Poppy walked up to the bike as if she was approaching a wild animal. "How do I stay on?"

"All you have to do is hold my waist tightly—I won't let you fall." Casey unlocked the storage box on the back of the bike and pulled out the second helmet. "When you put this on, we can talk to each other, so if you're frightened, just tell me to stop and I will." Casey grinned. "And if you want me to go faster—then just shout out."

Casey saw a blush and a smile come to Poppy's face at her double entendre.

"I don't think I'll be asking you to do that anytime soon."

Casey leaned forward and whispered, "Never say never."

"Do you ever stop?" Poppy asked.

"No, not until a woman asks me to."

Poppy burst out laughing and pushed Casey softly. "You are impossible."

"So, are we going, or am I calling you a cab?" Casey asked.

"I'm going to trust you, as long you promise me you'll let me off if I ask."

"You've got it." Casey grabbed her helmet. "Here, let me help you," Casey said.

"Hang on. I need to check in with my babysitters."

"Who?"

"Jess. It was the only way my sister would agree to not having agents with me. Give me a sec." Poppy took out her phone. "Call Chief Bohr."

Casey nodded and smiled. Jess was a difficulty. She could tell that even though her backstory was well honed, Jess was extremely suspicious about her and made it plain whenever she saw her.

"Hi, Jess," Poppy said, "I'm just checking in."

"Is everything all right?" Jess's voice came over the speakerphone.

"Yes, I'm just leaving Joe and Britta's. I didn't call a taxi because Casey has offered to give me a lift home on her bike."

There was silence, and then after a few seconds Jess said, "Is Casey with you now?"

Before Poppy got a chance to answer, Casey chipped in, "Hey, Jess, I'm right here."

Jess replied but not to Casey. "If you need me at any time, Poppy, I'll be with you in minutes, and remember that we have a lock on your position, so please convey that to your ride home."

Casey laughed silently. That was a warning if ever she'd heard one.

"Yes, I will—bye, Jess." Poppy put her phone back in her pocket. "Sorry about that."

"No, she's right. I'm a stranger, alone with the sister-in-law of the Queen," Casey said.

"The biggest threat to me is this monster of a bike and your silly flirting."

"What do you mean *silly* flirting?"

"Well, you know. The lines you trot out. I'm sure they work on some women, but not me. They're just silly. A game you play."

Casey was meant to be playing a game. A game where she was trying to ingratiate herself with Poppy. But apart from maybe the first week, everything Casey had said to Poppy came from a place of truth. To be told her attempts at flirting were *silly* didn't help her ego.

"Clearly, I'll need to try harder. Let me help you with your helmet." Casey helped pull it on, and then quickly put her own on. "Can you hear me?"

"Yes," Poppy said through the open audio channel. "This is amazing. What's all the information on the screen?"

Around the perimeter, the visor displayed all the critical information a rider needed and gave access to computer systems.

"It has speed, distance, fuel, maps, everything like that."

"Casey? I have been on a bike, sort of," Poppy admitted.

"Oh? When?"

"When I was in India. It was only a moped, but I only lasted a few minutes and demanded the driver stop."

"Don't worry, you'll be safe with me. Ready?"

Poppy nodded. She was ready to try, but her heart was pumping hard.

Casey got on. "You slide on now, and hold on to me, okay?"

Poppy managed to get on, and she heard Casey say, "Now hold on tightly around my waist. I'll go slowly to start."

The bike started and began to thrum underneath her. This was very different from a moped. Casey started to drive, and Poppy closed her eyes, clinging like a limpet to Casey's back.

"Are you all right?" Casey said.

"I don't know. My eyes are closed."

"Keep holding me as tight as you like, but open your eyes. Trust me."

Poppy was breathing hard. She forced herself to open her eyes a tiny bit at a time. It took a little while to get used to, but she started to calm. She could feel how in control Casey was of the bike, and that was kind of exciting.

"How are you doing now?"

"Okay, I think," Poppy shouted.

"Let's go faster then," Casey said.

"Oh God." Poppy held on more tightly as the bike sped up. Poppy felt every turn and how in control Casey was, and her nervousness started to leave her. It was replaced by excitement. "This is amazing, Casey."

"Do you want to take a detour home via the coast road?"

Poppy answered before her sensible mind had a chance to think. "Yes."

Every time Casey moved, her leather jacket rode up, and Poppy's hands touched her bare waist. Touching Casey's skin connected them, and her body thrummed with the same energy as the bike was giving out.

Casey drove them out of the centre of town, down to the coast road, where the river that ran through Battendorf opened out to feed into the sea. This was where Poppy really began to feel the excitement.

"This is exhilarating," Poppy shouted.

"I told you, now hang on tight."

Poppy's fingernails lightly dug into Casey's stomach, and she didn't feel like a passenger any more—it seemed like she was driving, taking part in the experience with Casey.

The bike sped up some more, and the sea air blasted her body. She couldn't hold her excitement in.

"It feels like I'm flying!"

"I'm going to slow down and stop, just past the harbour."

The bike slowed as they rode uphill on a road that led to a lookout point. Casey slowed right down and brought the bike to a halt, and she mourned the loss of Poppy's hands, holding tight around her waist. The thrill of Poppy holding her as she drove made her body come alive. And when Poppy dug her nails into her stomach, it turned her on so much.

Poppy jumped off the bike and yanked off her helmet. Woo-hoo!" Poppy squealed. "That was so good."

Casey loved her reaction. She took her own helmet off and said, "You really liked it?"

Poppy twirled around with delight and then spontaneously threw her arms around Casey. She was not expecting that. Casey slid her arms around Poppy's waist and pressed her nose in her long blonde hair.

She closed her eyes and enjoyed the moment for a few seconds before she felt the urge to slip her hands under the hem of Poppy's little T-shirt.

What are you doing?

Casey broke away from the hug, and there was an awkward silence. She put down both helmets and stuffed her hands in her pocket. "I thought you might want to stop here for a few minutes. It's a nice place at night-time," Casey said.

"Sure."

CHAPTER THIRTEEN

Poppy walked over to the small lookout point, where there were some benches. She took a seat and tried to calm her extremely confusing emotions. The exhilaration of the bike ride had released something inside her, and she'd let go of inhibitions that were normally completely under control.

Lex, Ravn, and the Palace had always been overprotective of her. She was always frightened of embarrassing her family or putting them in an awkward situation, and dampened her natural spontaneity.

But after tonight, a little of that spontaneity had escaped once more. She'd felt a lot more than spontaneity when Casey slipped her hands around her waist. For those few seconds she'd melted into Casey.

Poppy hardly knew her, and even if she had made assumptions about her, she was still brash, overconfident, and cocky. She had to know if there was something more beneath the surface. Poppy thought she had seen it earlier that night when they looked in each other's eyes.

Surely her body didn't come alive just for her looks. She had to know more.

"In all the times I've visited my sister, I've never been here," Poppy said.

Casey sat down beside her. "I come here quite often to think."

"To think?"

Casey looked to the side at Poppy and smiled. "What? Because I take a woman home on the first day of my business course, I can't think?"

Poppy chuckled. "Maybe *think* with a different organ."

"Good one. No, it's this place that has helped me sort out shit inside my head. The waves, the water, it's just peaceful."

"I have a place like that back home in England," Poppy said.

"Is it by the water?"

"Not like this. It's a little glade, with a stone bridge over a small stream that leads to an old wishing well where the fairy folk live."

"The fairy folk?" Casey said with surprise.

"Yes, it's a village legend. The fairy folk live in the well and come up to hunt for food. If you leave them a gift of food or money, they can make your wish come true."

"Sounds adorable," Casey said. "Weren't you afraid of the fairy folk?"

"No, I used to play with my dolls down there. The fairies became part of the game, and then there's the magic tree."

Casey looked surprised. "A magic tree?"

"Yes. The local legend is that if you carved your name in the magic tree, you would find your true love."

"I think that beats a lookout point at the coast," Casey said.

Poppy gave her a gentle nudge. "No, it doesn't. It's just different."

"Do you have your name carved on the tree?" Casey grinned.

"Of course I do." Poppy thought this was a good point to introduce the subject of family. "So does Lex, and the Queen."

To her surprise, Casey simply leaned forward, resting her elbows on her knees, and gazed out at the water.

"Nice," Casey replied.

"You never ask about my sister and the Queen," Poppy said.

Casey's brow furrowed. "Am I supposed to?"

"With most people, that's all they want to talk about."

"I'm not most people, honey." Casey winked as she said it.

Annoyance, anger, and attraction blew up in her at the same time. "Would you not wink—I mean, call me *honey* any more? I'm not anyone's honey."

"Don't get yourself all excited."

Poppy tried to quell the confusing emotions inside. "I'm not getting excited, certainly not by you."

Casey moved up the bench, right up close to Poppy. "Ooh, I think the lady doth protest too much. Just to make you happy, then, what are your sister and the Queen like?"

Poppy crossed her arms and pursed her lips like a toddler in a tantrum. "I'm not telling you now."

"Oh, come on," Casey said.

"No, I'm really protective of my family," Poppy said.

Casey threw up her hand with exasperation. "Well, why ask then?"

"I just thought it was weird. Why don't you tell me about your family?" Poppy asked. That was where she wanted the conversation, but since Casey was making it so difficult, Poppy would need to go straight to it. "Okay, I'll ask."

"What do you want to know?"

"Where do you come from?"

"New York, but I came to live in Denbourg when I was seventeen. My mum was a Denbourgian, father from New York. I was born there, but my mum passed away and my dad had a new family and wasn't too bothered where I went, so my brother and his husband took me in."

"I heard you mention your brother-in-law to Joe."

"Yeah, he owns a bar. It has cabaret, singing, dancing, that kind of thing."

Poppy noticed a faraway look in Casey's eyes. Maybe she would get the truth if she just asked. "Did your brother work there too?"

"No, my brother was in the army. He was killed—" Casey's voice broke, and she got up and walked over to the railing.

Poppy gave her a few seconds. She sensed this was something that Casey rarely talked about. She joined Casey and put her arm on her back. Poppy felt Casey flinch but then relax somewhat.

"Casey? Are you okay?"

"Of course I'm okay. I'm always okay, honey."

There was the bravado back in full force, but she wasn't going to fall for it.

"That's not going to work on me, Casey James," Poppy said.

Casey turned her head to look at her quizzically. Her eyes were red and watery. "What's not going to work?"

"The bravado. You are trying to be obnoxious to push me away and make me be angry with you."

"You don't know what you're talking about," Casey said.

"I know there's more going on behind these eyes than you ever show." Poppy reached up and caressed her cheekbone. "And I'm so sorry you lost your brother."

Casey leaned into her hand and pressed her lips to it tenderly. Before Poppy knew it their lips met in a soft kiss. Poppy didn't want to stop. The feel of Casey's lips set her body on fire.

Poppy wrapped her arms around Casey's neck and pulled her

closer. Casey responded by turning them around and pressing her into the guard rail. The kiss turned more passionate when Casey's tongue teased her lips.

Poppy hadn't been kissed like this since…Had she ever experienced a kiss like this before? She threaded her fingers through Casey's loose blonde locks, and she pulled her hair gently when Casey put her hands underneath her T-shirt and stroked her sides.

Poppy moaned and felt goosebumps erupt all over her body. But as soon as Poppy was losing herself in the kiss, Casey pulled away.

"I'm sorry, I shouldn't have done that." Casey held up her hands defensively.

"Why? I kissed you back."

"People will say I took advantage of you because you've been drinking."

Poppy walked to her and grasped her hands. "I had two cocktails and then switched to Joe's non-alcoholic concoctions. I trust you, and I'm a pretty good judge of character."

"But—"

"But"—Poppy decided to let her off easy—"I suppose we're working together, so best not complicate things."

Casey stuffed her hands in her pockets. "Yeah, I think so, plus your sister and Jess would have me bumped off."

Poppy gave her a soft push and laughed. "Shut up. I am allowed to kiss people. But yes, it's probably not a good idea."

"Let's not let this be awkward between us. Please?" Casey asked.

"No, we won't, don't worry." Poppy took Casey's hand and walked over to her bike. Casey handed Poppy a helmet and said with a grin, "We were good at it, though, weren't we?"

"We sure were. We've got some skills. Take me home, Romeo."

Casey popped on her helmet and said, "Your wish is my command, honey."

❖

As Casey drove home from Poppy's flat, her mood became darker and darker. Why did she do that? She told Poppy things she'd never told anyone on a job before, and then she laughed, she cried, she kissed her.

Casey pulled up and into her garage at her apartment building.

When she took off her helmet, sat on the bike, and stared at the wall. The guilt was slowly eating at the corners of her soul.

I trust you, and I'm a pretty good judge of character.

She rubbed her forehead with her fingers. This was supposed to be an easy last case. A royal story was not like infiltrating a band of hardened criminals or living in jail for months to get close to an international organized crime boss.

Casey thought of the innocent little Poppy playing with the fairies, and her magic tree that she'd carved her name in, hoping for true love. She didn't deserve this deception.

The frustration got harder and louder, until Casey roared and threw her helmet against the wall. Her breathing was heavy, and she tried to take some deep breaths to calm it. Casey closed her eyes and could almost feel Poppy's arms around her waist. She touched her fingertips to her mouth and visualized the unexpected moment that Poppy brushed her fingers against her face, then touched her lips for the first time.

It wasn't just the surprise of the kiss but the way her own desire lit up and her body responded. Poppy's kiss had made her hungry for more. It was then that she heard the sound of a car stopping nearby.

Casey got off her bike and turned around to see a large blacked-out Jeep coming to a stop right outside her garage entrance. It was blocking her in. This couldn't be Thea's people, could it? Had they found out who she was?

She was relieved and confused when she saw Jess getting out of the front seat. Another two agents, big men, got out and one of them opened the back door to let out a tall woman with the bearing of an Amazon. You certainly wouldn't want to mess with her.

Casey walked up to them and said, "Jess? Are you part of the mafia now?"

Jess approached. "This is Major Ravn. Head of royal security."

She looked among the stern faces of all the assembled people and said, "I did deliver Poppy home in one piece."

Major Ravn stepped forward until there were only a few paces between them. "We know that, or you wouldn't be standing upright."

"This is a bit heavy, isn't it? I am a Denbourgian citizen, you know," Casey said.

"Yes. You have dual citizenship, isn't that right?"

Major Ravn was sounding very sure of herself and was truly

menacing. They couldn't have found out who and what she really was, could they?

"Yeah, you know an awful lot about me," Casey said.

Ravn started to pace around the garage, picking things up randomly and putting them back with disinterest.

"Hmm. Do we? I suppose we have a very linear, concise, and ordered security file on you, Casey, if that's your name."

She knew they couldn't know the full truth of who she was, or they wouldn't be tiptoeing around the subject. *Just brazen it out.*

"Casey is my name. Scout's honour." Casey grinned.

"Very amusing."

"Listen, I'm in Poppy's project group at business college, just like Joe and Brit. I offered her a lift home. Is that okay?"

Ravn stood nearly toe to toe with Casey and stared down at her from her superior height. "I've known Poppy King since she was sixteen years old, and I've taken care of her like my little sister. This is a very difficult time for the royal family, and I will not let anything happen to any of them."

Casey was not one to be intimidated. Never had been. She could have been standing in front of Goliath, her heart hammering like mad, but she would never show it. She kept her eyes on Ravn.

"She's just a friend from school. I don't want to do anyone any harm."

Ravn glanced down at her brother's dog tags around her neck. Luckily the tags simply had a code that was scanned for military identification, with his nickname printed on them. Nothing that could identify her.

"Hopefully that's the case—for your sake." Ravn turned on her heel and went back into the car.

Jess locked eyes with her for a few seconds before she too got back in, and they moved off quickly. She'd got away with it…just.

Casey went to pick up her discarded helmet, which she had thrown against the wall. *I don't want to do anyone any harm.*

But she was doing harm, wasn't she? She was deceiving Poppy.

❖

Casey dunked her raspberry teabag in her mug. The phone rang and she answered. "Hello?"

"Casey? It's Annika."

Casey was surprised. "You don't normally call me. I usually have to leave half a dozen messages before you call me back."

"To be honest, Casey, I felt bad about our last conversation."

"Oh, the conversation where you told me I owe you, and my anonymity is in your hands? That conversation?"

"I'm sorry. It was wrong. I just really want this story."

"Why? Is it that important?" Casey asked.

She heard a long sigh. Annika almost sounded desperate. "I have people pressuring me, on my board, and I knew if you did the story, you would handle it sensitively and carefully."

"Who are these people? Do you need help?" Casey asked.

"No, no. I can handle it," Annika said firmly. "But I'm sending you links to tomorrow's headlines. The theatre appearance the other night, added to the fact that Lennox is away on royal tour alone, it's hyped up the rumours."

"Wasn't Lennox supposed to be going alone?" Casey asked.

"Yes, but Roza and the children always go with her to the airport to wave her off. No sign this time."

"Okay, let me take a look."

Casey set down her mug and had the computer display the headlines. Every newspaper had pictures of the Queen and Crown Consort at the theatre the other night. The photographs and film clips had caught them at particularly bad points.

The Queen was looking anxious, almost tearful, and Lennox appeared annoyed, looking as if she was reprimanding the Queen. Body language experts and lip readers were all giving readings of the photos and videos.

The headlines were similar to the ones Casey had read before taking the job: *Does Denbourg now have a King?* Only this time the headlines were in more reputable media outlets. The first thing she thought of was Poppy and how these headlines would upset her.

"Have you seen them?" Annika asked.

Casey sighed. "Yes, I see them."

"Do you see how important this is now? Gossip that I thought had little possibility of being true now is growing in validity. People are openly talking about the Queen's mental state and Lennox King's coercive control."

Casey rubbed her forehead. She was so tense. "If Lennox King is anything like her sister, then this can't be true."

"That might be so, Casey, but we must know. The Queen appoints prime ministers, writes new laws, is the head of the Church, sees each top-secret document that the government sees—can we take the chance that it is really Lennox King, a former banker from London, who is doing those tasks and making decisions on behalf of every Denbourgian?"

Casey knew on one level the concern was appropriate. "Why does it have to be me?"

"Because you are the best, Lucian, and I trust you to do this right."

Trust. Poppy had said she trusted her.

"Like I said, I'll do it my way." This was the only way she could bring herself to do her job and care for Poppy.

"Anything. And if you find nothing, then I'll work it out," Annika said.

"Have the security services been checking my employment status?"

"Yes, they did. They haven't questioned you, have they?" Annika asked.

"Yes, the Palace mafia has given me a big old warning, but nothing too worrying."

"Good, is there anything else you need?"

"Uh, no."

Casey squeezed her hot mug in her hands. The smell of fruit tea was making her think of sitting on Poppy's sofa, drinking her tea, and listening to her talking so passionately about her future plans, helping people, and generally being such a sweet person. She couldn't do this to her.

"Fair enough. Update me soon." Annika hung up.

Casey lifted her mug and walked through to her office. She stared at the pictures of Poppy and decided in that moment that if she was doing this, she was going to be as real with Poppy as she possibly could be.

She'd had enough of this life. When she had looked into the mirror at that motel room, she'd asked herself who she was. What if this was her? She had reconciled herself with the idea that it was the places she had to work, the people she had to work with, that dragged her down into the darkness, but what if this was truly who she was meant to be?

Casey pulled one of the pictures off the pinboard and looked into Poppy's smiling face. "I'm sorry I have to do this, but I'll do it the right way."

CHAPTER FOURTEEN

R oza was being driven home from an engagement at a new historical exhibition at Battendorf Library. From her seat in the back of the car, she was watching TV footage of Lex arriving in America. She was being met by the Denbourg ambassador and American officials.

Lex seamlessly moved from private person into her public Crown Consort mode. It was something she'd always admired in Lex. Roza showed more emotion. She couldn't help it—it was the way she was built. But was it a good thing in a Queen?

When she looked to her cousin George, Roza felt inadequate. Princess Olga of Vospya, with whom she shared ancestry and a bond, wasn't even queen, but with her uncle she had helped rebuild Vospya from a country torn apart by war, to a European country set to take its place on the world stage again.

Roza didn't believe she could do that. But Lex could do it.

Being consort to a regnant king or queen wasn't an easy task. From day one, Lex had taken to it like a duck to water and ran the Consort's office and charity concerns like a confident and efficient CEO.

Roza's car entered the gates of Ximeno Palace, and her mind wandered to this morning when she woke up and found a note lying on her bedside table. It was usually a romantic gesture, and Lex had left similar notes throughout their married life.

But this morning it was for quite different reasons, not to convey romantic words, but to build bridges.

My Queen, it breaks my heart to leave you like this. I have always believed we were a team, and I made a mistake. I admit to that. I'll no doubt make many more in our life together.

I won't try and justify what I did. I just hope these two weeks apart will make you realize that I was just trying to protect you, but I have made things worse. All I can say is I love you, and I'm going to miss you every minute I'm away. You are always in my heart.

Lex xx

Roza had cried after reading it, but she had to know if she was strong enough to do this on her own. Had she been propped up by Lex all these years?

The car stopped, and the door opened for her. She got out and went up the stone stairs to the entrance hall. One of the footman met her and took her coat.

"Has my sister-in-law arrived yet?"

"Yes, Your Majesty. Ms. King is in the family drawing room with Prince August and Princess Maria, ma'am."

"Thank you."

Roza had asked Poppy to stay with her and the children for the weekend since Lex was going to be away. She wondered if Lex had told Poppy of their problems.

Olly walked alongside the Queen as she walked as quickly as she could towards the family room in her private quarters.

"The dates for your state visit to Germany have been proposed, and you'll see them in your evening government papers, and—"

"Olly, can we do this later? I just want to see my babies."

"Of course, ma'am. Goodnight."

Roza remembered that there was one thing she had to ask, although she didn't want to. She turned around as Olly was walking away.

"Olly?"

"Yes, ma'am?"

"Could I have a word, just quickly?"

"Of course, ma'am."

Roza looked up and down the palace hallway. There were cleaners starting their evening shift, so she needed some privacy. To her left was a walk-in storage cupboard. That would have to do. She opened up the door and said, "In here a moment."

Olly looked a bit bemused by this unusual request but joined her. There were shelves along every wall with cleaning products and household items.

"I know this might seem a bit strange, but there are ears everywhere, and I need the utmost discretion."

"Of course, ma'am."

Roza rubbed her forehead. "I never imagined I'd ever be saying this. I need you to find me a doctor."

Again Olly looked confused. "The royal doctor can be here in minutes—"

"No, not that kind of doctor. I have some issues that I need help with, but where does a Queen go for therapy?"

"Say no more, ma'am. I know exactly what you mean, and I have the perfect person in mind," Olly said confidently.

"This needs to done very quietly, I don't even want my family to know at this point, and if you could schedule appointments while the crown consort is away…"

"Leave it with me, ma'am. I won't let you down."

"Thank you. I better go and see if my children are behaving."

She walked into the sitting room, and jumping on the couch were Poppy, Gus, and Mari. "You do realize that's a seventeenth century piece of furniture."

Poppy's face fell. "Oh, eh, sorry."

She helped Maria down, and she ran to her mother. "Hi, sweetie."

"Where's Mum?" Maria asked.

"She left on the aeroplane, remember? She's going to phone you later."

Poppy stood with her arm around Gus. You could see the King family resemblance in Poppy's and Gus's smiles. Just like Lex.

Roza's heart hurt. Lex was everything to her, to their family. She had to sort her thoughts and fears out. She'd taken a first step.

Roza lay with her feet across Poppy's lap, the TV playing in the background. Poppy was only half watching as Roza looked at her government papers.

"Roza, I wanted to ask you something."

"Yes?"

"Am I distracting you?"

Roza put her papers down on her knee. "A welcome distraction. Believe me."

"Remember I told you I'm working on a group project with my friends? It's a coffee shop business," Poppy said.

"Uh-huh. Sounds like fun."

"Joe and Brit, that's whose business we're working on, well, they have a building down on the square."

Roza looked impressed. "Nice piece of real estate."

"The building belonged to their grandmother. Anyway, since it's Restoration Square, we thought we could make the theme the revolution, and…"

"The Little Terror," Roza whispered. "It's bad luck in my family if you talk about it out loud."

"I never even knew that your family had ever been deposed," Poppy said.

"Oh yes, though to be super honest, many historians have claimed that Denbourg came out of it a better, stronger, happier country."

"How could that be?"

"My ancestor, King Harold V, wasn't the nicest of men. Denbourg was an absolute monarchy. No democracy, no representation of any kind. He was a cruel man, both to the people and to his family."

"And the upside to the revolution was democracy?"

"Exactly. An agreement was made to limit the powers of the monarch, and we've been living within those rules since. Quite happily."

"Wow, amazing," Poppy said.

"Queen Catherine has always been a hero of mine. In fact, there's a series of young adult novels about Queen Catherine. I loved them when I was a teenager."

"I can't believe I didn't know anything about her."

"So, tell me what it is you need," Roza asked.

"Any papers, first-hand accounts from back then, pictures, things like that."

"There's lots of material in our library and over at the Battendorf museum. Why don't I have my archivist get some things together for you and your friends?"

"That would be wonderful. It'll just be two of us. My friend Casey and me, we're in charge of theme and marketing," Poppy said.

A smile crept upon Roza's face. "Your cheeks are pink."

"They aren't." Poppy covered her cheeks with her hands.

Roza grinned and moved closer. "They are. Come on, you can't lie to your big sister the Queen."

"Oh, thanks for the direct order."

"Well?" Roza play-hit Poppy.

"There's nothing in it. Casey's…she's not even my type."

"What is your type? I think I've seen you with two girlfriends the entire time I've known your sister, and they were dull."

Poppy frowned. "They were not dull—they were sensible and reliable."

Roza rolled her eyes. "Well, that's two words to get your knickers wagging."

"There's more to a relationship than sex."

"Of course there is. But there's always that needy, desperate hunger for the one you love. That's what I felt, *feel* for Lex."

"No, I'm not listening." Poppy slammed her eyes shut and stuck her fingers in her ears.

After a few seconds, Poppy opened one eye and saw Roza had tears rolling down her face.

"Roza? What's wrong?" Poppy took her hand.

Roza wiped away her tears. "I'm sorry. I shouldn't be—"

"Hey, I'm your little sister-in-law. You can tell me anything."

"Did Lex tell you that we had a disagreement before she left?"

This was kind of awkward for Poppy. Whatever had happened was obviously more upsetting and serious than Lex had let on. "I asked if everything was okay because of that night at the theatre. You both looked stressed. Was it because of Story St John being there, and the film?"

Roza smiled and wiped away her tears and put a forced smile on her face. "Bad memories. Just something I need to work through. Don't worry."

"If my sister needs putting in her place, come to me. I can sort her out for you."

"So, anyway…" Roza said, changing the subject, "Casey. The not dull one."

"She's like the typical bad boy. Motorcycle, leather jacket, gorgeously butch, arrogant, full of herself, brash—"

"Sounds like your sister would love her." Roza chuckled.

"Yeah, I know. I judged her, I suppose—well, she told me I did."

"And did you?" Roza asked.

Poppy nodded. "But with good reason. The first day I met her, she was a complete dick. Honestly, just infuriating."

"I've often found that the people who can rile you up the best are the ones who attract you on some deeper level."

"Lex infuriates you, I know that," Poppy joked.

"Very true. So, tell me more about your bad boy."

Poppy frowned. "She's not mine by any stretch of the imagination, but as I've spent time with her, I've become sure that bravado is covering up something deeper. Anyway, she does this wink thing."

"What? A *wink* thing, Pops?" Roza laughed.

Poppy clasped her hands to her cheeks. "Why did I say that out loud?"

"You did, so you have to tell me."

Poppy groaned. "Do I have to?"

"Yes, the Queen commands it," Roza said formally.

"Fine. Casey has this wink that totally disarms me. My chest tightens, and everything else reacts. It's like, in my head, she winks and my clothes fall off."

Roza threw her head back and laughed out loud for the first time in ages.

"Oh God, don't tell my sister."

"I'm sorry for laughing, Pops. You've never spoken about someone like that before."

"Last night we all met up at Joe and Brit's flat, and she offered me a lift home on her bike, and we sort of kissed."

"Wow. You don't usually jump into things. Has Ravn had her investigated? You know, if something happened to—"

Poppy held up her hands. "I'm not jumping. We agreed to not let things be weird. It's not happening again."

Roza narrowed her eyes. "I'll tell you what. I'll ask the royal librarian to put together something for you both to look at. You can bring her to the palace, this Sunday."

Uh-oh, Poppy thought. She didn't want everyone's eyes on Casey. Judging her, thinking she was some kind of terrorist or philanderer.

"We can quite easily go to the library."

"No, Pops, bring her here. There are some items in my private collection. Unless you know that she wouldn't want to come here for some reason?"

Why did she have to even bring this up? "No, I just meant that I'd need to check if she was free that day. I'll ask," Poppy said.

"Computer, take a note. Ask royal archivist to put together a selection of materials for Poppy. Subject of Denbourg Little Terror, King Harold V, Queen Catherine with specifics on…?"

Roza prompted Poppy to speak. "The role of coffee houses around Imperial Square in the revolution."

"Good. By the way, what did the kiss feel like?"

"Honestly? Like I was melting."

Chapter Fifteen

Casey had hardly stopped for breath since her phone call with Annika. The pinboard in her study had been completely reworked, just like her investigation was ripped up and started again.

She pushed an old fashioned thumbtack into a picture on the board. At the top were King Christian and Prince Augustus. To the side and slightly above was Thea Brandt. Below, Poppy was no longer in the centre of the board, it was Queen Rozala and Consort Lennox. They were now the centre of her investigation.

Casey felt excited by the case, whereas before all she thought of was guilt. She walked over to Poppy's picture, just below Lennox's. For the first time in her career, someone on her job had touched something inside her.

She stood back and gazed upon the whole board. Casey remembered the first journalist she'd worked with as a youngster. He was an instinctive man and always told her to look deep down inside and find your gut feeling, because more often than not, you could trust your gut.

Casey crossed her arms and rubbed her chin. One picture stood out to her like a beacon. Roza's cousin, Prince Bernard. "Computer, take notes."

"Ready."

"Lennox, recovering drink and drugs abuser, runs one of Queen Beatrice's charities. Party girl Roza meets her, they fall in love, blah, blah, blah."

Casey was on a roll, the special feeling when she was following a lead, a hunch, and she had to track it down. She started to pace while she talked.

"Roza's ex kills her father and brother, thrusting the ill-prepared

Roza onto the throne. Somewhat against the odds, and with Lennox to support her, Roza shines as Queen, and nine years in all not a word about problems in their marriage, until the end of last year. The Queen has her tragedies along the way, mental health issues that brought some heartache, but she kept going and had an heir, and adopted a little girl."

She walked back to the board. "If Lennox King was abusive, why did no stories leak out before the end of last year? Before Roza's son was born, Prince Bernard was next in line."

It looked to Casey, if her hunch was right, that there were two heroes in this story. She gazed at Roza's and Lennox's pictures. But who was the villain? Her eyes flitted to the picture of Prince Bernard.

She needed to find out more about him. For some reason her eyes were then drawn to the very top of the board, above King Christian and Prince Augustus. The very top picture was the late Thea Brandt. She was known by her friends and enemies alike as the puppet master, and even though she was dead, everything in this story started with her, but did it end with her too?

Thea.

Casey shuddered as her mind replayed the shouts and screams she had heard in the prison. The one that haunted her was a woman being punished with boiling water and sugar. Casey didn't think she would ever get rid of the noises she'd heard that night.

Why do I get the feeling you are involved somewhere, Puppet Master?

Thea Brandt stared down from the window of the apartment. It was fifty-two floors up in a building apparently under construction. Scaffolding bordered the outside of the building, and mechanical diggers, heavy equipment, and construction materials of all sorts lay idle below and on each floor.

Only the upper two floors were completed and fully equipped with everything Thea would need to run her operations for the shortish time she would need them.

She looked across the city skyline and saw the top of Ximeno Palace.

"Hidden in plain sight."

Thea wandered over to her bar and poured herself a glass of

brandy. With her control over the prison she could get luxuries like brandy even there, but it wasn't quite as nice as enjoying it here, in the comfort of her own building.

She had been planning this place for years inside jail. A place to come and be virtually undetectable. As well as all the tech, designed by Rhys and built in to the structure to keep her undetectable, Thea had a more traditional security system: the perception of a building in progress. While her lawyers kept the building's plans under constant dispute, she could inhabit the top two floors undetected and undisturbed, for very few city officials, police, or secret service agents would want to climb into the rudimentary lift shaft.

Fortunately for Thea, a hidden section of the basement housed the executive elevator system, making her access an altogether more civilized journey to the top. She took her drink to a extremely comfortable office chair. On the floor below was her technical department where Rhys led his team to reach her objectives, and adjacent to this living area was a large apartment with bedroom, bathroom, and kitchen facilities.

With brandy in hand, surveying her objectives and business empire on the large holo screen, Thea thought, *I wonder what Mother would think if she could see me now?*

In front of her, on the right side of her screen, were her targets, her to-do list, as it were. The images were of the royal family, from the Queen and Lennox King, to the royal children, and to Poppy King and her parents.

Poppy King and her parents would be taken out before Lennox and Roza, so they'd have time to feel the pain of grief.

Then there was Lucian, or Luca, as she knew her in prison. All they had was that partial image when Lucian turned partway round to the camera. Thea would find her and make her ending painful and drawn out. She was at the bottom of the list, and perhaps not as important as the rest, but would still be satisfying to find and kill, as well as being one who had information that could help Thea.

On the left side of the screen were her contacts and links to her business empire all over the world.

"Computer, put me through to Rhys," Thea said.

"Hello?"

"Any news on Lucian?"

"Nothing yet. My systems are checking through all the relevant files. We just need a break. I'll find her."

"I know you will."

Just as she ended that call the computer said, *"Incoming call from Prince Bernard."*

"Ah, my little puppet. Computer, disguise face and voice."

"Activated."

From the start of their tentative alliance, Thea had never disclosed her true identity or place in the Brandt organization, purely to protect her anonymity. Although Prince Bernard needed and wanted her help for his own gain, he was not someone she could trust with the fact she was still alive. He was too power-hungry and easy to manipulate.

"Prince Bernard, how can I help you today?"

"Has there been any movement on our plans?"

"There is always movement, Your Highness," Thea replied.

He almost growled in frustration. "I've waited two years for your help. My backers want results."

What a fool, Thea thought. He had no patience. And patience was where Thea excelled. It had taken her nine years of careful planning to get to this point. Others might have rushed in to it, but not Thea. She had seen every moment of her plans come together in her mind before any firm plans were made.

Thea didn't agree with Prince Bernard's extremely far-right views—in fact, if he knew he was speaking to a woman, he probably wouldn't like it too much. But he was a means to an end, a puppet to be used and manipulated.

"If you want my organization's help, then you will have patience. If you think you can get anywhere on your own, then please just tell me, and we'll forget this whole deal."

"Now let's not be hasty," Bernard said. "I can wait on your timeline."

Thea noticed on-screen that her brother Morten was outside the door, waiting to see her.

"I'll be back in touch soon, Prince Bernard."

"But—"

"Computer, end call and unlock office door."

Prince Bernard's image disappeared from the screen, and Morten walked in. She turned around in her swivel chair.

"Morten?"

He smiled.

"We've got him? The prison governor?"

Morten nodded.

Thea felt a surge of adrenaline rush through her. She jumped up and patted her brother on the back.

"Well done, now we will get somewhere."

CHAPTER SIXTEEN

Poppy walked through the college gates with nerves bubbling in her stomach. This would be the first time seeing Casey since their kiss. The kiss that they both agreed was a one-off, and Poppy couldn't stop thinking about.

Her stomach lurched when she saw Joe, Brit, and Casey standing at the main entrance. It was a warmish day, and Casey had dispensed with her usual leather jacket. She was wearing just her black T-shirt with a white print of a motorcycle shop, jeans, and a leather wrist strap.

She's not sexy, not sexy, not—

Casey lifted her head and smiled.

Shit.

Brit must have seen her face and where she was looking because she said, "We're over here, Poppy."

"Uh hi, good morning, everyone."

"Morning, Pops," Joe said.

"Hi," Casey said with a twinkle in her eye.

God. Why did she have this overwhelming urge to just jump on Casey? This wasn't like her. She'd had sex before and been attracted to people before, but this was different. She felt pulled to Casey.

Brit walked ahead and said, "Come on, Joe."

Picking up on his sister's signals, he offered his arm to her and walked ahead, leaving Casey and Poppy.

Why did this feel like high school all over again? She was a grown woman.

"You okay?" Casey asked.

"Yes…um, we said this wouldn't be awkward and…"

"It'll be okay. It was just two people lost in a moment."

"Lost in a moment?" Poppy considered that. It made sense, and she wanted to cling to it rather than deal with what she was feeling. "Yes, and that moment is gone?"

"I guess."

"So we can just go back to being frenemies?" Poppy said with a smile.

Casey laughed. "Yeah, frenemies."

They walked into class, and Poppy sat in her usual seat beside Joe and Brit. Casey was still in the seat she'd had from the beginning. Poppy wasn't taking in a thing from today's class.

She could feel Casey's energy flowing from her, without even looking. Casey's eyes were burning in the side of her head. Poppy tried so hard not to turn around, but she weakened a few times and found Casey smouldering right back at her.

Their kiss was all she could think about. Casey was just filling her thoughts. Break time couldn't come quick enough because she needed to clear her head.

❖

Brit leaned against the sinks in the bathroom with her arms folded. "So, what happened after the bike ride home?"

"What do you mean?" Poppy knew exactly what she meant but wasn't going to say it.

"Did she come in for coffee…"

"No, she prefers fruit tea." Poppy closed her eyes, realizing she'd said too much.

"Ah, so she did come in."

Poppy went to dry her hands. "No, she didn't. I simply happen to know that she likes fruit tea."

"Something happened. There was a vibe this morning. The *Do you remember what we did?* kinda vibe. Not to mention the sexual tension that was going on at our flat that evening."

"There wasn't. We argued most of it." Poppy crossed her arms defensively.

"And the way you've both been looking at each other in class all morning."

"What way?"

Brit leaned in and whispered, "Like you want to lick each other all over."

"Look, she took me on a longer ride on the bike because I was enjoying it so much. We drove down to the harbour and talked."

Brit raised an eyebrow. "Just talked?"

A flushing sound came from one of the toilet cubicles, and they realized they weren't alone.

Please don't be anyone from our class. Please, Poppy begged internally.

She and Brit looked at each other tensely. The door to the cubicle opened, and out stepped Casey.

"Raspberry tea is my new favourite, actually," Casey said.

Poppy wished the ground would open and swallow her up.

Brit said, "I better go—see you later."

"Brit—"

Casey went straight to washing her hands, and now abandoned by Brit, Poppy was left to steep in this awkwardness.

"Brit was just…"

Casey dried her hands and said, "I know. It's okay."

Poppy could feel her cheeks were red hot. She placed her palms over her face. "We said this wouldn't be awkward."

She felt Casey grasp her wrists and pull her hands away. "Remember what we agreed this morning?"

Poppy shivered at the touch of Casey's hands on her wrists.

"It was a moment in time," Casey said.

Poppy ran her hands down Casey's arms. "A moment in time."

She looked up into Casey's smoky eyes, and all Poppy could think about was kissing her lips again. Poppy felt Casey's hands come to rest on her hips.

"I want another moment," Poppy said.

Casey looked around, then took Poppy's hand and drew her into one of cubicles. As soon as the door was closed, their lips crashed together.

Casey had been determined this wouldn't happen again, but Poppy's kiss was emblazoned on her mind ever since that moment at the lookout point. From the first moment she saw Poppy this morning, all she could think about was touching her again.

When their lips touched again it was like fire. Casey needed her, wanted her, even though she knew logically this was a bad idea. Their kisses became frantic. Tongues were tasting, needing, and Casey wanted more.

She grasped Poppy's hips and slipped under the hem of her blouse.

She ran her hands from Poppy's hips up over her ribs just below her bra strap. Poppy moaned in her kiss, then pushed her fingers into Casey's hair.

Poppy pulled out Casey's ponytail and tangled her fingers into Casey's hair. She grasped and tugged while Casey's hand pushed up the bottom of Poppy's miniskirt and squeezed her thigh.

God. Casey wanted Poppy so much. Even though this was wrong in many different ways. She was investigating Poppy's family, but she was burning for her.

Eventually they heard a few people entering the bathroom laughing, and they both pulled back.

Casey rested her forehead against Poppy's, and Poppy said, "Is this another moment, or is it more?"

Casey wanted to say no, she wanted more. More of this fire. She couldn't remember a woman making her feel as hot and hungry as Poppy did. But who they were and what Casey was doing made it difficult.

"Yeah, it's just a moment. No need to take it too seriously." She lied.

Poppy pulled back from her abruptly. "A moment of lust and you're done? Well okay, I must go. I have better things to do than waste *moments* with you."

"Poppy, listen—"

Poppy unlocked the door and got out of the cubicle quickly. It was clear that something had transpired between them, and clearly she had fucked up.

❖

Queen Rozala was sitting in the nursery, having some time with Maria in between appointments. Nanny was taking the chance to tidy up while Roza was keeping an eye on Maria, who sat on Roza's lap, holding her favourite toy—a stuffed lamb her grandma gave her when she joined the family. Roza was so happy Gus and Maria had wonderful grandparents. In the summer they went as a family back to Lex's childhood home, and the kids just loved it, and Jason and Faith came to visit them many times a year, since they were retired.

Roza hoped that her own mother and father were looking down and proud of their grandchildren.

"Mama, want Mum," Maria said sadly.

"I know, sweetheart, I miss her too, but we'll talk to her later." She did miss Lex so much. Her life and her bed were too empty without her. Roza pushed the dark curls from Maria's eyes to behind her ears. "Are you going to visit the kitchens today and get a snack?"

"Yes," Nanny replied.

The chef and the kitchen staff adored the children, and Maria often went down there with Nanny. Maria loved to visit the kitchen and experience all the sights, the shouts, the crashing pots and pans.

There was a knock at the door. Olly came in and said, "Ravn is here to see you in your office, ma'am, and then you have a private audience."

Roza sighed and nodded. "Thank you. Mari, I have to go now."

"Why?" Maria said.

"Because I have to do my Queen thing." She lifted Maria and stood up. Roza gave her a big kiss and hug, then handed her over to her nanny. "I'll see you later, beautiful girl."

Once Roza left the nursery, she walked to her private office where Ravn was standing at ease out front.

"Ravn, thanks for coming."

Ravn bowed her head. "Your Majesty."

"Come in." Roza sat behind her desk. "Sit down, Ravn."

Ravn did sit, but she managed always to look as if she was sitting at attention. "Thank you, ma'am."

"Ravn, I believe you had Jess protecting Poppy."

"Jess and Mattius, yes, ma'am. Until I was instructed to take them off protecting her," Ravn said.

"Yes, she managed to convince both me and Lex that she didn't need protection now. It wasn't something I or Lex wanted, but Thea is gone, and Poppy is such an independent spirit." Roza smiled. "A bit like I once was, if you remember."

Ravn chuckled. "Yes, ma'am. We did agree that she checks in with Jess before travelling to and from college, and if she goes out at night. Just to make sure she's safe, and of course, we always have a tracker on her."

"Has Jess said anything about a Casey James?"

"Yes, ma'am," Ravn said firmly.

"You said that quickly. Poppy seems to be quite keen on her. Have you any information on her?"

"Yes and no."

"What does that mean?" Roza asked.

"Her background check came back normal and ordered. Too normal and ordered if you ask me."

"Why? What's her background?"

"She works for a subsidiary of Ivanov Media Corporation, called Athena. A concert promoter, I believe. She has been given six months to study business on the same course as Ms. King."

"That sounds all right. What do you think?" Roza asked.

"There's something too ordered about her backstory. It's all too simple, too put together."

Roza started to worry now. "Do you think we should be worried? If I thought she was in danger, I—"

Ravn held her hands up. "No, not necessarily. Just something's bothering me about her. Jess and I went to talk to her the night Casey James gave Ms. King a ride home."

"Why?"

"They took a detour, and we wanted to just have a word and let Casey know Ms. King has protection."

Roza smiled. "You didn't scare her, did you?"

"I hope so, but if I did, she's the kind that would never show it. I only did what the Crown Consort would do if she was here."

Lucky for Casey, Lex wasn't here. She would be making life quite difficult for Poppy and her new friend.

"Poppy and her friend Casey are doing some research for their group project. It's on the revolution," Roza said.

"The Little Terror?" Ravn smiled.

"Exactly. I asked Poppy to come next Sunday with Casey, and my librarian would leave out some documents and books that will give them the information they need and give me and you a chance to have a look at Casey James and see if she's genuine or not."

Ravn looked worried. "It's a great risk to invite a virtual unknown in the palace, and even more so if you intend to meet her."

"I give you full authority to take any security steps you need to."

"Are you sure about this, ma'am?" Ravn said.

For a second Roza started to doubt herself. She looked up at the imposing picture of her father on the wall of her office. He never knew Roza the Queen, only Princess Roza, the disappointment. Normally she would bounce her ideas off Lex, and they would come to a decision together. Was that where she had been going wrong? Was she doubting herself and always looking for the approval of a stronger character?

She looked up again at the picture of her father. *Am I seeking your approval?*

Roza cleared her throat and sat up straighter in her chair. She looked at Ravn and said confidently, "I'm sure, Ravn. Those are my wishes."

"Yes, ma'am. I'll make sure everything runs smoothly."

❖

Thea let her guest, Prison Governor Kadal, stew on his predicament overnight. After breakfast she left her apartments and walked to the rudimentary lift shaft, which was meant to be for workmen on the so-called mammoth building project.

Morten and some of her people were standing near the lift. Kadal was covered in bruises and cuts and was sitting tied up on a chair near the edge of the shaft. The lift was a few floors above, so there was only a drop into the shaft below. His chair was so near the edge that if there wasn't a steel rope around his chest, he would plummet to his death When she walked out in front of him, he appeared genuinely terrified.

"You're dead," Kadal said.

Thea held out her arms and said, "Reports of my death have been exaggerated."

"Please, Thea. Pull me back from here. I'm afraid of heights."

"You are? My apologies then. One piece of Information and you can go. Who bribed you? You were asked to let Lucian into your prison to get at me. Who was it?"

"I swore an oath that I wouldn't tell. I owed a favour, and I can't break that confidence."

Thea nodded and calmly walked over to him. "I can understand that."

She grabbed his shirtfront and dangled him over the edge.

"No, no," he squealed.

"We call this The Drop, and anyone who crosses me ends up a bloody mess on the ground," Thea said.

"Please, please, don't," Kadal said.

Thea held on to a handrail at the side to steady herself. "It's not just the fall, all fifty floors. It's the fall into utter darkness, and you will not know from one moment to the next when you are going to hit the concrete, and then your head smashes like an egg."

"If I tell you, I'll be breaking an oath and losing trust," Kadal said.

Thea pushed him back even more. "And if you don't tell me, your brains will be dashed on the floor. Your choice."

She saw Kadal looked down into the inky abyss. He was terrified, and she knew she had him.

"Okay, okay, it was my contact at Ivanov."

"Who was your contact?"

"I never knew. I wasn't allowed to see their face."

"You sure?"

"Yes."

"Then you have just outlived your usefulness." She raised her hand and then dropped it.

The steel rope was cut while their prisoner screamed, "No, no, please, no."

When the rope was cut, the momentum pushed Kadal over the edge. He screamed in terror as he fell into the darkness. It wasn't long before the horrible, sickening thump at the bottom.

Thea turned to her brother. "Get the mess cleaned, and find me his contact at Ivanov."

CHAPTER SEVENTEEN

Casey had messed up. As soon as she implied that kissing Poppy was a bit of fun, Poppy's shutters came right down. Casey hadn't expected that, and she'd been avoiding her all week.

Poppy was so careful in her love life it seemed to Casey, but she had been really hurt by her brush-off. Casey didn't want to hurt her. She was feeling guilty enough for not sharing her true self with her, although she had changed the angle of her story.

Casey had to get back to being friends with Poppy, at least. She had her invitation to the royal library. That was the next step in her search for the truth.

She had marketing class this morning, and as soon as it was finished, Casey would try to make it up with Poppy. They didn't have class this afternoon, and she hoped they could talk things out and make up.

Professor Anderson said, "Okay, that's everything today. Remember, your first exam is in two weeks' time. Get studying."

Casey packed up her stuff quickly to try to catch Poppy, but she was waylaid by another student asking for advice about buying a bike.

"Can we do this another time? I'd love to help, but I'm in a hurry today."

"No problem. Catch you soon."

By the time Casey had turned around, Poppy was gone. Only Brit and Joe were still there. Casey hurried over. "Brit, where did Poppy go?"

"She had an appointment this afternoon. You upset her, by the way," Brit chastised her.

"Yeah, not cool, Case," Joe added.

"I know I messed up, but I need to speak to her. I'll see you later."

Casey ran out to the front of the building and saw Poppy entering a taxi. She ran and, to Poppy's surprise, jumped in the back of the taxi.

"What are you doing?" Poppy asked.

"I have to speak to you."

"I'm going to look at premises for my business. I'm meeting a property agent," Poppy said.

"I'll come too," Casey said.

"No, you won't. This is not group work at college. This is my dream."

"Then what could be better than a second opinion. Please, Pops."

"Fine." Poppy sounded exasperated. "And don't call me *Pops*. Only my family and close friends call me Pops."

Casey dramatically grabbed her chest. "That was like a dagger to my heart."

As quick as a flash Poppy replied, "Do you have a heart?"

"Somewhere in there, I think, honey."

She could tell Poppy was trying her hardest to contain a smile. At least this was a start. From not talking at all, to throwing banter and jibes back and forth was more like them.

"Where are we headed first?"

"East side of Battendorf."

They were at the third property. All three had been quite underwhelming, Poppy thought. Casey thought they were terrible and didn't feel shy about telling her. Why she had allowed her to tag along, she had no idea.

The agent who was showing them around, Kate, said, "What do you think?"

"It's better than the first two, certainly."

"Have you got anything else you could show us?" Casey said.

Poppy gave her a look. Why was she interfering?

"Not in this price range, no. We do have quite a few in higher rent areas, all the way from a space in Restoration Square to ones with even lower rents areas than this."

"Perfect," Casey said. "Could we see that one, please?"

Kate's face brightened up immediately, thinking of the commission, no doubt. "I could call and see if I can get the keys."

Poppy quickly jumped in. "No, I don't wish to see that property, but thank you."

"Kate, could you give us a minute?" Casey asked.

"I'll be outside when you're finished."

Poppy walked off to the back of the shop area. She was frustrated and angry.

"Poppy."

"What is your problem? You've criticized everything I've looked at. Why are you even here, anyway?"

"I'm here because I like you, and I want to help, as well as the fact that you haven't been talking to me all week."

"Why would that bother you? After all, we've only had *moments*, as you put it."

Casey let her head fall back in frustration. "Oh my God, that's what the silent treatment is about?"

"Despite what you think, everything isn't about you."

"It is in this case."

"Kissing someone might be an everyday thing to you, but not to me." Poppy tried to walk off, but Casey grasped her arm lightly. "Let me go," Poppy said.

"Don't run away, please. Talk to me? I called them *moments* just to save you us—thinking about what it meant. You were worried about things being awkward. I thought that gave you an out without worry. And kissing *isn't* an everyday thing to me. You're making assumptions again."

"I don't understand why this is happening. This never—"

"Listen, why don't we go for a drink and talk about these spaces, and whatever else we need to."

"Where?"

"What about my brother-in-law's place, Gold's?"

Poppy hardly knew a thing about Casey's life. Maybe this would be a chance to find out more about Casey and cool this aching need, this force, pulling her to Casey James.

"Okay. Let's do that."

Casey looked surprised. "Really? Great. Let's go talk to Kate and go."

❖

As I sit here at the window, looking out over the square, where I signed the new constitution, I wonder whether I would have been able to go through the hell of these last months without my dear husband.

Roza shut Queen Catherine's diary and walked over to the window. The exact same spot where Catherine stood. Restoration Square was bustling with people, all enjoying the sights and sounds of a special historical space.

How markedly different the square must be to what Catherine saw and experienced. So far in her diaries, Catherine had done nothing but praise her husband. But was it the times they lived in? Did she passively accept her husband's ideas and opinions?

From what she knew already about her ancestor, she was thought of as an extremely strong woman. But behind closed doors reality could be very different.

Roza saw a car come through the gates. It must be her. Olly had contacted a doctor who worked within the secret service, working with agents and special forces teams, and so bound by secrecy. If any mental health professional could be trusted, then one from within the service surely could, couldn't they?

She was attacked by doubts. Why had she agreed to this? A Queen needing a counsellor?

Roza hadn't opened up to anyone outside her family before, but if she did, she could be sure she'd get the truth. Lex had this unwavering loyalty thing, where even if something was blindingly obvious, like if a dress was too tight, or Roza declared she wasn't the best at some particular activity, Lex would always argue against her.

As sweet as that was, it meant she didn't always get the truth. Hence, why an outsider might be helpful.

Lex. Oh, Roza missed her so much. Not talking to her was killing her, but she had to sort her head out first.

There was a knock at the door. Her equerry Colonel Jude Marsden came in and bowed. "Your appointment is here, Your Majesty. Dr. Kenzie Rivers."

"Show her in."

"Yes, ma'am. Dr. Rivers," Jude said.

Agent Rivers walked in and bowed. She looked every inch the security agent she was, medical professional or not. She was dressed in a power suit and had long wavy brown hair.

"Welcome, Agent Rivers. Please take a seat."

"Thank you, Your Majesty. Call me Kenzie."

There was an awkward silence. Roza didn't know what to say to start off the conversation. She was good at small talk when meeting the public, dignitaries from all over the world. The question was, how, as Queen do you ask for help? For mental health advice?

Kenzie sat forward in her seat. "Forgive me, ma'am. I know there is protocol and such, but it seems that you might be finding difficulty."

"Yes, please speak freely, Kenzie."

"Ma'am, I want you to trust me, and trust in my methods. I believe it was explained to you that I work with governmental agencies and the Denbourg secret service."

Roza rubbed her hands together nervously. "Yes. It was. That's why I agreed to see you."

"As one of Your Majesty's agents, I swear an oath to Your Majesty and sign the official secrets act. If I did break your confidence, I would be behind bars."

Roza forced a smile through her anxiety. "Let's hope that doesn't happen."

"I can assure you it won't. When I work with agents or special forces, working through PTSD, or mental suitability to certain roles, I have to be trusted. I talk through special operations that the Denbourg population will not know ever took place. Does that put your mind at ease, ma'am?"

Roza cleared her throat. "It does, thank you, but I'm more nervous about other things."

"May I ask what, ma'am?"

Roza's mouth went bone dry. She lifted a glass of water and took a sip. "It's not the trust so much, it's...how does a Queen ask for help?"

Kenzie sat back and crossed her legs. "We just talk, nothing more complicated than that. I'm not a conventional mental health practitioner. I like to do things naturally." She held up her hands. "You'll see I don't take notes, I have no recording device. Your security swept me as I came in. It's just you and me, having a conversation."

Roza let out a breath. "I've never talked about personal issues, or the ones I need to talk about to you, apart from with my Consort."

Kenzie nodded. "I understand from the news that she is on an overseas trip."

"That's right. To publicize addiction charities. It's extremely important to her."

"I can see such pride on your face as you talk about her accomplishments," Kenzie said.

"I am. So proud. Lex never misses a week from her addiction group, apart from being away on royal business. All she has accomplished in the nine years we've been on the throne is remarkable."

Kenzie nodded. "It must have been difficult for the Crown Consort. You are the first gay couple on the throne of Denbourg. There were no templates from the past to follow, and I'm sure a strong figure such as the Crown Consort would have had difficulties carving out her own way of doing things."

Roza looked down at her clasped hands. "She did it with such ease. Lex tackles her job as Consort like a CEO of a company, or of a charity organization, as she was when I met her. Lex took to it like a duck to water."

"I feel there may be a *but* somewhere in your praise, ma'am."

Roza clammed up. Could she say this out loud to someone she had just met?

"If this is too hard to talk about at the moment, we can talk about something else," Kenzie said.

Roza hesitated. "I—I think she should have been Queen. I've come to wonder recently if I have just been there as the figurehead, and Lex has been propping me up all these years."

Tears started to fall as she said those words. It was so emotional saying it out loud.

Kenzie looked unreadable after Roza's declaration. Had she been too open in this first meeting?

Roza watched Kenzie's gaze fall onto the side table beside her. Kenzie stood and walked over to it.

"You have Queen Catherine's diaries. May I?" Kenzie asked.

"Yes, on you go."

Kenzie lifted the old book. "This brings back memories. I wrote an essay in high school on Queen Catherine, Denbourg's first regnant Queen. I titled it 'The Royals that saved the monarchy.' She was a fine Queen, and her Consort, Artur, was a good man."

"Yes, I read it when I was younger. My tutor made me, I think, but I haven't read it as an adult."

Kenzie tapped the book. "If you'd like my advice, ma'am, I would read this book carefully. You'll find parallels with your own life, and some excellent lessons to learn."

"I will, thank you," Roza said.

"Why don't we leave it there for our session, and perhaps we can discuss this book when I come next time."

Roza stood and offered her hand. "That sounds like a good idea. I must go and attend to my children soon, anyway."

Kenzie bowed her head. "Thank you for your time, ma'am. If you need to, call me anytime. Please feel free."

Roza touched a sensor, and Colonel Marsden came in. "My equerry will show you out, Kenzie. Thank you for your time."

"A pleasure, ma'am."

Roza let go a sigh of relief. That conversation had gone much better than she'd expected. Kenzie was different, and Roza liked it. She picked up Queen Catherine's diary.

Then Roza looked over to a full-length portrait of Queen Catherine that sat above the other fireplace.

"Queen Catherine, looks like we're going to be spending more time together. Any advice would be greatly appreciated."

CHAPTER EIGHTEEN

This was a first for Casey, taking someone from her current investigation into a family space. A *true* family space. She had sent a message ahead to Goldie that she was bringing someone and to have discretion.

Goldie was well-versed in discretion. He was married to her brother, a special ops officer, and their life was about keeping secrets. She trusted Goldie, and if it was anyone other than Poppy, they wouldn't be anywhere near here. But she was Poppy, and that fact made her different in Casey's eyes.

Casey held the door of Gold's open for Poppy. When she walked in, she said, "This is a nice place. Is that a stage at the back?"

"Yeah, there's performances, usually at the weekend. The monthly one is usually the best. There's lots of acts on then." She took Poppy over to a booth near the stage. "What can I get you to drink?" Casey asked.

"White wine, please."

"Coming right up." Casey walked over to the bar.

"Casey?" Jon said. "You've actually brought a beautiful woman in here. What's come over you?"

"I'm taking a course at business school. We're working on a group project together."

"What happened to driving all over Europe on your bike?" Jon asked.

"Changed my mind. I thought I'd add another string to my bow."

Jon smiled. "I'm sure. Your friend is very beautiful."

"Yes, she is."

Casey ordered the drinks and turned around to see Goldie at the booth, talking to Poppy.

Shit.

As soon as Jon brought the drinks, Casey was over to the booth like a shot. God knew what embarrassing things he was telling her.

Both Goldie and Poppy were laughing out loud when she arrived, and that made her feel extremely uncomfortable.

"Casey," Goldie said, "there you are. Where have you been hiding this beautiful woman?"

"Nowhere. We're in the same class at college."

Goldie rolled his eyes. "She told me that much herself. Honestly."

Casey gave Poppy her drink and sat down herself.

"I was just telling your brother-in-law that you came to look at some premises with me," Poppy said.

"Was she much help?" Goldie asked.

"Yes, she brought up some really good points, and we thought we'd come here to talk about them some more."

"Hmm. I think your friend gives you too much credit," Goldie said, laughing. Then he added, "We're having a special night here at the end of the month. Get Casey to bring you. She never gets out often enough. Speak to you later, my little treasure."

He didn't. Casey closed her eyes to try to hide her embarrassment. She could feel the heat on her cheeks.

When Casey opened them again, she saw Poppy grinning at her. Casey held up her hand. "Don't start."

"Okay, I won't, my little treasure." Poppy burst out laughing.

"Yes, yes, have your moment. Laugh." Casey took a swig of her lager.

"Wait till I tell Joe and Brit."

"I knew bringing you here was a mistake."

"Don't pout," Poppy said.

"Okay, I won't, honey." It was Casey's time to smile.

Poppy stuck her tongue out at her.

"Oh yes, very mature," Casey said.

Casey saw Poppy watching Goldie over at the bar, where he was helping out.

"Goldie is nice."

"Yes, he is. I say he's my brother-in-law, but he's more of a father to me. After my brother Albie died, we were all we had. So we made sure that we were both okay. Well, I say both—it was mostly Goldie helping me. Goldie is so strong. He kept me going."

"Do you mind me asking how your brother died?" Poppy asked.

This was a test. How open was she prepared to be with Poppy. Even though Casey wasn't being honest in many things, she wanted to be as honest as she could.

"He was in the army and died on an operation."

Poppy reached across the table and took her hand. "I'm so sorry, Casey."

Casey loved the feel of Poppy's hand. She was so caring and warm. Poppy had demonstrated that through her tireless work with UNICEF and now with her response to Casey's grief.

"Thank you," Casey said.

Casey jumped when Goldie came back over, carrying a tray. "Here you are. Two Sunset Surprises."

"You didn't have to bring us drinks," Casey said.

"Oh, be quiet, you. You're not too often able to have a drink. Enjoy. Oh, Poppy—it's our monthly show on Saturday night, Goldie's Showcase. If you'd like to come, you would be most welcome."

"Thanks—oh, Joe and Brit would love it here. They're our other two college friends."

"Casey has more than one friend?" Goldie mocked her.

"Yes, just a couple."

"Okay, I won't embarrass you any more, Case. I'll be off to help Jon," Goldie said.

"Goldie is quite the character," Poppy said.

"You aren't kidding. Apart from trying to embarrass me, he is the kindest, most generous man you could ever hope to meet. I'm so lucky Albie met him."

Poppy dragged her fingertip around the rim of her wine glass. "Tell me I'm being nosy if you like, but would you tell me what your brother was like? You told me a little, but I want to know more…"

Again Poppy was getting into uncomfortable areas. She had only ever talked about her brother to Goldie, but her first instinct was to tell the truth. She was taking a risk, but she wanted to take it for Poppy.

"My mum and dad were divorced when I was three. Mum relocated to Denbourg, and Albie chose to go with her. Dad was a bit of a tyrant, and he was hurt that Albie chose to leave, so he made sure I was staying with him. He was wealthy, and his lawyers managed to argue the case for him. I don't remember much except missing Mum and Albie so much."

"That's heartbreaking," Poppy said. "Did you get to see them?"

"I got summers with them. I counted down the days till I could go. Then, as I got older, and Dad's new wife didn't want me around so much, I spent longer and longer here. Until my father agreed to let me go live in Denbourg."

"You must have loved that."

"I did—"

"Is there a but?"

Casey gulped hard. She was so used to giving false information as she worked undercover that she wasn't at all used to saying these things out loud.

"Mum died suddenly, a month after I arrived."

Poppy gasped and took Casey's other hand. "That's awful. I'm so sorry, Casey."

The touch of Poppy's hands made her feel grounded in this moment, here and now. Normally her thoughts of that period in her life tumbled her down into a dark rabbit hole of sadness and despair. But now Poppy's hands were pulling her back.

Poppy entangled her fingers with Casey's, and she rubbed her thumb soothingly along Casey's. This was the emotion she had seen a few times behind the eyes of the normally overconfident Casey. Casey had been truly hurt.

"What happened after that?"

"Albie and Goldie took me in. Looked after me like I was their own teenage child. Albie was on duty often, so Goldie took care of me most of the time."

"You were really lucky to have them."

"I was."

She and Casey both noticed at the same moment that they were holding hands and pulled back, covering their awkwardness by taking a drink.

"Anyway…" Casey clapped her hands together. Obviously, their heartfelt conversation had gone as far as Casey was willing to go. "So, about your shop. Why not have a look at Restoration Square?"

"Not this again." Poppy sighed. "It's way out of my price range. I already have had Lex and Mum and Dad invest in the start-up of my company. I don't want to go back to them and ask for more."

"That's a shame. Because it would have been perfect for what you were going for."

Poppy swirled her remaining wine around her glass. "Oh, and what is it you think I'm going for?"

"You said that you want your brand, Simply Human, to draw

attention to the cause of low-paid workers. That you'll have simple basic designs and pay the workers a proper amount for their work. Basic designs at a premium price, so the wearing of your clothing becomes fashionable."

"Wow, you do listen," Poppy said with surprise.

"Of course I do, honey," Casey said with a wink.

No, not the wink again. It lit something inside her, and suddenly all she could think about was the time they kissed—or had a moment, as Casey put it. It was passion like she'd never felt before, and it was so addictive.

While Casey continued talking, Poppy's attention was drawn to a curl of blonde hair that had escaped from the topknot above her undercut hair. She remembered how that silky hair felt in her fingers and when she drew Casey closer to her lips…

"What do you think?"

Poppy was pulled sharply from her beautiful little dream, hearing Casey's voice.

"What? Sorry, what did you say?"

Casey let her head fall to the side in exasperation. "I just said some really important things here."

"Sorry, I do get distracted sometimes. Tell me?"

Casey sighed. "When we talked about the kind of people Joe and Brit wanted to pull in at their place, it's the high-end market and tourists. Let's face it, their coffee isn't cheap, even though it's for good reasons—paying the growers, those on the supply line, a fair price. You're in the same boat. You want the people who will pay a high price for brands, and especially brands that appear to have a social conscience."

"I think someone is going to do well in marketing." Poppy finished her wine and moved on to the cocktail Goldie had brought them.

"Seriously, what do you think?" Casey asked.

I think you're gorgeous. "Seriously?"

Casey nodded.

"On a lot of levels you're right."

"But?"

"But that was the reason I left my internship with a fashion magazine, after university. I hated the conspicuous consumption, the brand-is-everything mentality, while they're paying sweatshop workers in India and the Far East buttons to make this luxury wear. I don't want to be a part of that merry-go-round."

Casey grasped her cocktail. "I'm moving to the hard stuff if you're going to start using phrases like *conspicuous consumption*."

Poppy laughed and took a drink.

"You have a sweet laugh, you know," Casey said.

Poppy stopped mid-swallow. She expected to see a joking grin on Casey's face, but instead she saw a bashful smile.

"Thank you. No one's ever said that to me before," Poppy said.

"Well, they should've. You are beautiful too."

Poppy's heart started to beat harder. *Don't get drawn into this again.* She had twice and both times ended with a brush-off. She tried to play it cool.

"Really?" Poppy said that word dripping with sarcasm. "What, is this another *moment*?"

"No, not a moment. It is true, so I have to tell you because I feel like you haven't been told that enough."

This wasn't what she was expecting at all. An utterly sincere Casey was even more sexy and sweet than she already was. Poppy needed to take a step back.

"If you'll excuse me, I'll just visit the bathroom."

"Yeah sure, I'll get another round of drinks. Cocktail or wine?"

"Surprise me."

Roza was sitting in Gus's bedroom with Maria on her knee while they had their evening chat with Lex. With each passing day it was harder and harder not to just fall into old patterns. It was tempting, would be so easy, to say *Let's forget what we said and did, I miss you too much.*

But she couldn't. Roza knew that to make her marriage work, and for her reign to work, she needed to find out what the truth was. Was she capable of doing this job alone, or had she been propped up all along by Lex? And she needed to bring some dark trauma into the light.

"Gus, are you looking after your sister?" Lex asked.

"Yes, Mum, I am. We really miss you, though."

"I'm missing you so much. Mari, I met a friend in America."

"Who, Mum?"

"I went to visit the TV studio where Mr. Tiddles the elephant is made."

Roza smiled. *Mr. Tiddles* was Mari's favourite show.

Mari jumped up and down on Roza's lap. "Ooh, Mr. Tiddles!"

"He was sorry you weren't there with me but gave me a soft toy that looked just like him and said I was to bring him back for you." Lex reached over and brought Mr. Tiddles the elephant into camera range.

"Look, Mari," Gus said.

Mari reached out her arms saying, "Want him now."

"No, no," Roza said, "Mr. Tiddles is going to stay with Mum to remind her of you. Okay?"

When Roza and Lex were away without the children, they always liked to bring back a little present from where they were visiting. Nothing extravagant—they tried not to spoil their kids—but just a little memento of their trip.

"Don't worry, Gus. I got your American football jersey and baseball cap."

"Thanks, Mum." Gus had a big smile on his face now.

Now came the difficult bit. Roza kissed both kids and said, "Okay, you two, go to your rooms, and I'll be with you in a minute. I want to talk to Mum."

Gus got up from the chair and took Mari's hand.

"Horsey, Gus?"

"Okay." He knelt down and allowed his sister to clamber on. They galloped out of the room.

"I hoped we'd get a chance to talk," Lex said. "I'm missing you so much."

Roza didn't want to go down that emotional road again. She just wanted to say what she needed to and not get too emotional.

"I wanted to let you know that I started to see a therapist today."

Lex looked shocked. "Really?"

Lex had been suggesting Roza get some help for her mental health ever since her father and her bother were killed, but Roza had always resisted. Roza knew people thought she was being stubborn, but it wasn't that. It was fear, fear of being judged as weak, as a failure.

She was not unaware that everyone thought she would fail, that she would crumble as Queen. That's why she resisted, but things had gone too far. Her mental health was affecting her marriage, her family, and ultimately her fitness to be Queen.

"Yes, I think the time has come where I have to talk."

Lex put her hand on her chest. "You can always talk to me, you know that."

"I do, but it needs to be a dispassionate person not connected to me, and a professional," Roza said.

"So who did you get?"

"I asked Olly to seek advice, but she knew the right person. Her name is Dr. Kenzie Rivers. She works with the secret service debriefing, helping with any mental health issues. So as an agent, she can be trusted."

Roza could see Lex's jaw tightening, being very careful what she said. "Whatever you have to do to get peace of mind, then that's fine with me. Just remember that I love you, and I'm sorry for what I did. I'll call the children tomorrow. Goodnight."

She wasn't expecting Lex's abrupt goodbye, but she was clearly worried and feeling cut off by the distance between them. And perhaps worried that Roza might be second-guessing their marriage.

That was never going to happen. Roza loved Lex with all her heart, and she was never giving up on that.

❖

"Are you sure you know what you're doing?" Goldie asked Casey.

When Poppy had slipped to the bathroom, Goldie came and took her place at the table.

"I don't know what you mean," Casey replied.

"You do." Goldie leaned forward and lowered his voice. "You have never brought someone connected with your investigation here before, and that means something."

"I also never use my real name, but I wanted to be myself, and be as true to Poppy as I could. I didn't want her to be in any doubt of what you mean to me. That you're like my parent, and so was Albie."

Goldie's face softened. "You are truly my little treasure, Casey James. But think about that young woman. I can see the way she looks at you."

"What way is that?" Casey knew the answer to that question but wasn't going to volunteer the answer.

"In a way that she thinks of you as more than just friends."

Casey said defensively, "She hasn't been talking to me all week."

"Why?" Casey said nothing and Goldie said, "I won't ask you again, Casey James."

"Okay, we kissed and she thinks I gave her the brush-off."

Goldie shook his head. "Are you out of your mind? She's a lovely girl. I know you've probably faked attraction to get stories before, but she's an innocent."

Casey filled with anger, and her voice carried as she spoke sharply. "Do you really think I'd do that to Poppy?"

"I hoped you wouldn't, Case."

"I can't stop thinking about her. She's making me enjoy business college, and I've met new friends. I've nearly given up this story twice, but Annika has guilt-tripped me back into it."

"Tell Annika to fuck off, Case. You should have just left on your motorcycle that day. It's just a royal story. Anyone who believes Lennox King is some bad guy manipulating the Queen is an idiot," Goldie said.

Casey rubbed her face with her hands. "Annika says she is getting pressure put upon her, so instead of trying to investigate and expose the royals through Poppy, I'm going to prove all the salacious gossip wrong, and that it's artificially planted in the media. Just trust me."

Casey heard her phone beep—a text from Poppy. *Can you come down. Getting a bit overwhelmed here.*

She jumped straight up. "I need to go help Poppy."

Casey rushed downstairs and into the bathroom. She could just see Poppy's head in a circle of women and men taking pictures. Some were livestreaming, talking to their audiences.

One man said, "It's the Crown Consort's little sister in Gold's. Who has always suspected she was gay?"

Casey pushed past him. "Get your camera out of her face."

She grasped Poppy's hand and pulled her out of the crowd, and the man said, "Oh, she's got a girlfriend too."

"Wanker."

At the top of the stairs Goldie was waiting for them. "Everything okay?"

"It's fine, Goldie. Just some excitable people," Poppy said.

"I'm going to take Poppy home now, Goldie. I'll call you and hopefully see you at the weekend."

"Stay safe, both of you."

When they got outside, Goldie told the bouncers to get them a taxi.

"Are you okay? I'm so sorry for that."

Poppy was a bit shaken. "It's the cameras in my face I don't like, but thanks for coming to my rescue."

Casey opened up her jacket and pulled Poppy into a hug to keep her warm. Poppy went gratefully into Casey's arms. Poppy allowed her hands to sweep around her back and grasp Casey's T-shirt. She felt so warm, so safe, that Poppy hoped the taxi wouldn't arrive straight away.

But after a few minutes it did, and it took them to Poppy's flat. They held hands the entire way, and Poppy didn't want to give that up so soon.

"Do you want to come up for a raspberry tea?"

Casey smiled and squeezed her hand. "I'd love to."

Poppy led them upstairs, and she started to feel tension. Something was happening between them, like a threshold had been reached, and there was no way back.

Once they were upstairs Casey hung up her coat while Poppy went to stick the kettle on.

Poppy raised her voice to be heard on the other side of her flat, turned around, and said, "Are you sure tea is okay?"

She jumped when she realized Casey had followed her into the kitchen. "It's perfect."

Poppy was more than tense now—she was nervous. Probably because all she wanted Casey to do was pull her into a kiss. She busied herself getting the cups and teabags out while the kettle boiled.

Casey was leaning against the kitchen counter with her arms folded. Poppy's gaze lingered over her body. Casey didn't have to say or do anything, but she had a strong magnetism that pulled Poppy to her. She realized how much she was affected when the teaspoon started to clink against the cup of tea as her hand shook.

"Are you okay?" Casey asked.

Poppy cleared her throat. "Yes, um…you can see why the whole royal thing isn't fun. I'm always worried I'll do something stupid and embarrass my sister and the Queen."

"How could you embarrass her? You're the nicest, sweetest person anyone could ever meet."

"You saw—I was on camera. If I'd have reacted to those people, then it could have been an incident." Poppy set Casey's tea down beside her on the counter. "You think I'm nice and sweet."

"You said that as if it was a bad thing," Casey said.

"No, not a bad thing. But sometimes sweet girls…just forget I said anything." Poppy didn't quite know how to handle the feelings she was having or how to show them.

Poppy stirred her tea and Casey said, "Poppy, look at me."

She turned and Casey said, "Come here."

Poppy's heart started to pound. Casey had this energy, this aura that made Poppy weak at the knees. She was pulled by that strong energy, and Casey placed her hands on Poppy's waist.

"I'm sorry if I upset you."

"I'm sorry I stopped talking to you."

Casey touched her forehead against Poppy's. "I deserved it. I'm not good with emotions and understanding what I feel."

Poppy grasped Casey's T-shirt and held on to her belt. "What do you feel?"

"All I know is that I can't stop thinking about you, and not just for a moment, for every minute of every day, and more than that I don't know because I haven't felt it before."

Poppy looked at Casey, whose fingers were stroking her bare skin at her waist.

"Case? I want more than a moment."

Casey nodded and lowered her lips to Poppy's and whispered, "Me too."

As soon as Casey's lips met hers, she experienced that melting feeling again, and it was all she could do to hold on tightly around Casey's neck. Poppy was shaking inside, but she managed to be brave enough to take Casey's hand and lead her to the bedroom.

When they got through the door, their lips came together, and Casey whispered through the kisses, "Are you sure you want this?"

Poppy stroked her fingers through Casey's hair. "Yes, I want this, I want you, I want us."

They quickly dispensed with their clothes, and Casey lifted Poppy onto the bed, then joined her. Casey sat up and gazed down at Poppy. She stroked her fingers around Poppy's medium sized breasts.

"You are beautiful."

Casey could hear how much Poppy wanted this. She reached down to Poppy's sex and felt her wetness. "You really want me to make you come, don't you?"

Poppy arched her back when she pushed inside her. "Oh God."

Casey started to thrust inside her, slowly at first, allowing her to get used to the full feeling. Poppy reached down and covered Casey's hand.

"I want to feel what you feel," Poppy said.

It was such a turn-on to watch Poppy mirror her movements. Poppy's groans got louder.

"Please, Casey, I'm going to come." Poppy's hips and thighs bucked wildly and then clamped her hand still.

"God, that was amazing." Poppy tried to calm her breathing.

As soon as her breath would allow, Poppy turned Casey onto her back. She hovered at her lips. "I'm going to suck you till you come, baby."

Poppy kissed her way down Casey's body, until she got down to her sex. She ran her tongue along Casey's sex and circled around her clit.

"You keep doing that, and I'm going to come too early."

Poppy looked up at Casey's expression. Casey was loving every moment. She was enjoying having this kind of control over her lover.

She sucked and teased Casey until she cried out, "Oh Jesus."

Casey put her arm across her forehead. "That was amazing. You're too good at that, naughty girl."

Poppy kissed her lips and said, "I care about you so much."

Casey took her head in her hands and kissed her nose, cheeks, and lips. "I care too, honey."

❖

Roza was glad she had a super-king-sized bed when she had Maria on one side and Gus on the other.

Usually Lex was there too, and that made her miss her. She couldn't remember how many nights she and Lex had shared their bed with first Gus, and now Mari. A long time ago when she was Europe's party princess, she could never have imagined being a mum and going early to bed to read.

Life was funny that way. Roza didn't know she wanted a family until she found the partner who made her want to share all these things. Roza stroked her sleeping children's hair and gazed up at her wedding photo hanging on the wall. It was her favourite. They were cutting the wedding cake. Lex had organized it, and it was perfect.

"I miss you."

Roza picked up her book from the bedside table. Queen Catherine's diary.

I was taken from jail back to the palace to change and get ready for the ceremony. When the revolution started, I didn't think it would end like this, and I certainly didn't know I would become Queen this early in life.

I did love my father, the King, but he was a hard man, whose views about monarchy were horribly outdated. I will try to be everything my people ask me to be. I will pledge my service to them today, humbly and truthfully.

I could not take on this huge responsibility if it wasn't for my husband, Artur. Since it was proposed that the monarchy of Denbourg be reinstated, I had many days where I thought the job beyond me.

But Prince Artur has made me believe. I couldn't ask for a better husband or consort. Artur reminds me that where I feel I need help and support, he will be there. I know he will always be at my side. I am the first regnant Queen of Denbourg, but I'm sure I won't be the last. I only pray the Queens that follow me have an Artur to support them.

Roza closed the book and looked up at their picture. Was she just lacking self-confidence?

Maria snuggled into her side. She had everything—she should be happy. Then the still pictures from the movie flashed across her mind, and then the images of her brother and father being shot started flashing, and she couldn't get them to stop.

But she did have a Prince Artur of her own.

"That was more than a moment." Poppy was lying with her head on Casey's chest.

Casey took her hand and kissed it. "I want more of this."

"I know you've probably been with a lot of women, but have you had many relationships?"

Casey shook her head. "No, never wanted them. I was your one-night stand kinda person. What about you? Are you a relationship girl?"

"Yes, I've always wanted someone to love me. Have a relationship like Lex and Roza have."

This was really the wrong time for undercover reporting, but she had to find out if her plan to do the right kind of story was going to work.

"From the outside it looks like they have a great relationship."

"They are perfect, honestly." Poppy pushed her nose closer into

Casey's neck. "Don't get me wrong. They can be at each other's throats sometimes, but it's just because they're passionate. There's a natural spark that makes them work."

"Have you ever felt that spark?" Casey asked.

Poppy drew her fingernail down Casey's chest and around her navel. "I've had maybe one or two relationships, but nothing like this."

"What do you mean?" Casey asked. Casey lay listening, guilt creeping up on her inch by inch. *I'm going to make it work. I'm not going to hurt her.*

"What I feel when you touch me. It's like nothing I've felt before. It's a fire." Casey stiffened, and Poppy clearly felt it. "Oh, is this the point when you go running for the exit?" Poppy scratched her fingers through Casey's hair.

Casey had never had a relationship before or wanted one. Now, she had met someone so special, so beautiful, and Casey had to keep lying to keep her. She couldn't come clean now because she wouldn't find out who was planting these stories, and she couldn't prove to Poppy that she was going to write an exposé, not on the royals as she was meant to, but on the individuals spreading the lies.

She turned over so Poppy was underneath her. "Do you see me running, honey?"

Poppy slapped her bicep and laughed. "I told you—I don't like being called *honey*."

Casey raised an eyebrow. "Is that why you can't stop smiling and laughing?"

Poppy did laugh out loud now and put her arms around Casey's neck. "No, that's just because I've got this fiery bad boy naked on top of me. You were the type I secretly loved at school but wouldn't admit to wanting."

Casey grinned and started kissing her neck. "Tell me more…"

"I was always the good girl, spending time in the library, but secretly I dreamed of bad folks on motorcycles. I remember telling my sister that young people now don't label their types by gender, they just fall for the human."

Casey kissed her nose. "Simply Human?"

"Exactly, but then I got my biggest crush ever. In fact I swear she was my first love."

That pricked up Casey's ears. "Oh?"

Poppy giggled. "And she was as far away from a bad type as you could be. Total opposite. In fact I think she had rule following and *yes, ma'am—no, ma'am* stamped on her bones like a stick of rock."

Now Casey was super intrigued. She caressed Poppy's thigh with the back of her hand. "You have to tell me who this superwoman is."

"Roza and Lex came to visit us for the first time and brought Roza's police protection. Major Ravn. I was sixteen." Poppy sighed.

"Ravn? Tall scary Ravn? That's who you were in love with?"

Poppy nodded. "You know her?"

Casey fell back onto the bed laughing. "Oh my God. There's going to be a line of people waiting to kill me."

"How do you know her?"

"The night I dropped you off, Ravn, Jess, and a car full of security turned up like the mafia to warn me to…find out what my intentions were."

"Really? That's so embarrassing. Sorry."

"Don't be sorry. I'm glad there are people looking after you so well," Casey said.

Poppy became quiet and played with the dog tags around Casey's neck, "What will we do now?"

Casey turned onto her side and pulled Poppy's thigh up and over her hip. "I don't know about you, but I was planning on kissing and sucking your clit till you come."

Poppy looked all abashed. She was so beautiful and had such an innocent view of life. Casey loved that in her.

"I mean for us. Tomorrow, what will we do?"

Casey understood what she meant. "For me it's not a moment. Straight off. I think you're the most beautiful girl I've ever met. Tomorrow I'd like to go to college with you, meet Joe and Brit, and see what happens."

"Like, date, you mean?"

"Yeah, is that okay?"

Poppy laughed. "I'll need to clear it with Ravn and Jess, but okay."

Casey pretended to shiver and said, "Now can I make you come, or do I have to clear *that* with Ravn and Jess?"

Poppy pulled her closer and whispered, "Let's keep that to ourselves, hmm?"

"Yeah." Casey gently pushed Poppy onto her back and started to kiss her way down her body.

❖

Poppy became aware of her phone ringing, and then she opened her eyes and saw she was spread halfway over Casey's body. It felt nice. If only the bloody phone would stop ringing.

"Computer, who's calling?"

"Your caller is Britta."

Then Casey's started ringing. And someone started banging at the door.

"Oh, shit! I better check who it is." Poppy checked her monitor and saw Jess and Mattius at the door.

"Uh-oh."

"What is it?" Casey asked.

"It's Jess and Mattius," Poppy replied while jumping up to get her dressing gown.

"Fuck. They're here to kill me." Casey tried to pull on her jeans as quickly as she could.

"Don't be silly. You go and answer the door," Poppy said.

"No way, they'll shoot me or something."

"Coward," Poppy said as she made herself as presentable as she could. The banging was getting louder. Poppy shouted, "I'm coming." Then she opened the door.

"Is everything all right?" Jess said in a panic.

"Apart from being utterly embarrassed, I'm fine."

"Can we come in?" Jess asked.

Just then, Casey walked in from the bedroom. "Is there something wrong?"

"Were you at a club last night?" Jess asked.

"Casey's family's bar, Gold's," Poppy said.

Jess nodded for Mattius to stand outside and then said, "Computer, show footage from Gold's bar last night."

Poppy and Casey watched the video of themselves in the bathroom of Gold's last night.

"Shit, we're trending," Casey said.

"This must be why Brit phoned."

Jess shook her head. "I'm sorry to have barged in, but we thought you might be in danger."

Poppy looked at Casey and said, "Well, I guess our little secret is out."

❖

Thea got a thrill from walking in the crowded city. She'd adopted a female form today, wearing simple jeans, a shirt, boots, and a casual jacket. Thea walked with assured confidence. Yes, she was really enjoying being out in the world again.

Everyone in this country hated her, wished her dead, thought they had her dead, and yet here she was, walking amongst all the rats, the cogs in the wheels hurrying to get to work.

What a feeling of satisfaction it was to come from nothing and never need to be a rat, getting scraps from the big and powerful companies. Nobody controlled Thea's destiny but her, and she was going to enjoy every last second of the new life she had.

One of the holo screens that lined the street playing news, financial markets, film, and TV news caught her eye. It was Lennox King's brat of a sister. What did she do to make the news?

Then another woman joined Poppy King in the video. Thea only got a flash of her image, but something about her gave Thea a niggle of recognition.

She arrived at the Ivanov multimedia company. Thea had her press pass code under her skin, ready to be scanned at reception, but as she approached the front of the building, she saw Annika Ivanov walking out and into her limo.

Thea had wanted to try to see Annika, but instead she could have her limo followed. Any information on her movements would be good. She called Rhys and asked him to track the limo.

Just as she was about to hang up, she saw the video again of Lennox King's sister and her mystery woman that was trending on social media. Then she had a flash of the video of Luca, or Lucian, or whoever they were, leaving the motel.

"Rhys? That video that's trending this morning, the one of the woman helping Poppy King? Could you run it against the motel video of Luca? I might be wrong, but then I rarely am."

CHAPTER NINETEEN

For Casey, the next week was filled with spending time with Poppy, and trying to crack the story of who was behind the rumours about the royal couple.

Casey sat in her office gazing at the evidence she had gathered so far. She flicked through the computer screens in front of her, periodically looking up at her pinboard with all the players on it.

Her initial thought of Prince Bernard had borne fruit. A source that she had worked with during her story about the far-right biker groups confirmed that contact had been made by Prince Bernard's representatives with the higher levels of far right groups. If civil unrest was needed to help Bernard's cause, then they were ready. Bernard was supported by global groups more powerful than him trying to manoeuvre him into power.

Casey stood up and studied the pictures. Above Prince Bernard, Casey had put up a picture of a dark cloud representing the kingpin, the one who was making everyone else dance to their tune.

She had to find out who that was, and quickly. If Casey wanted to fully explore her feelings for Poppy, then she had to get this story worked out, so that she could come clean to Poppy.

This week had been the happiest that Casey could remember experiencing, but Casey had to come clean. She'd had enough of lying, fudging, and covering up what she was doing. Poppy had already questioned why they hadn't enjoyed time together at Casey's flat, and she was running out of excuses. But if Poppy found her office and the information she had, it would all be over.

But with luck Casey might get her breakthrough soon. Annika had asked her contact, the one feeding her rumours about the Queen, to liaise with Casey. Before long a call was coming in.

"Computer, answer."

"I was told you have information for me."

The voice was clearly disguised. "I have access to the very heart of the Denbourg royal family, something I believe would be valuable to you."

There was silence for a few seconds. "That depends on the information."

"Of course." Casey decided not to beat around the bush. So she'd follow her instinct and try to prove she was speaking to Bernard. His reaction to her questions would verify who he was. "Let's lay our cards on the table, shall we? I know you are Prince Bernard."

There was an even longer silence this time. Casey was sure she had him.

"I don't know where you got that idea."

"I know you've a contact at Ivanov Media."

"I'm going to hang up now."

"Wait. If you hang up, then I know you're Bernard."

Casey heard a sigh, and she knew she had hit home. "What do you want?"

"I know you're frustrated about the lack of movement in your quest to—"

"Put someone more appropriate on the throne."

It made Casey feel sick to say it, "Yes, and I can produce that investigative journalism. What I need to know is who is backing you, not your money or far-right backers. There's someone else orchestrating this campaign."

"I don't know who she is."

"She?"

"Yes, my friends used the word *she* when they were contacted originally, but since I've been in contact with this person, their voice and face have been disguised."

"So you first started talking to the woman instead of her associates, when?"

"About a month and a half ago. Now what can you tell me?"

"When my investigation is finished, I'll pass on what I have."

"This has been a waste of time. Goodbye." Then he hung up.

"Not for me." Casey went over to her picture of a dark cloud and wrote on it: *She.*

It wasn't much, but it was something. Why would Prince Bernard have not talked to this kingpin before?

Casey had to think.

❖

Roza had a long day. After a visit to open a new navy training camp, she went on to meet with Dr. Kenzie, then dinner with the children. She had let the kids talk to Lex on their own and promised she'd speak to Lex later.

Roza went to her bedroom, kicked off her heels, and slipped onto the bed. She called up a holo screen from the side of the bed and called Lex, but she didn't answer, although Roza heard a ringing from the Consort's bedroom.

The connecting doors opened, and Lex walked in and smiled. "Sweetheart. How are you?"

Roza jumped up. "How can you be here?"

"I thought I'd surprise you and get an earlier flight," Lex said.

Roza jumped into her arms. "I've been missing you," Roza said.

"Really?" Lex said hopefully.

Roza felt bad. That must have been the first time she'd said it since their argument. She nodded and kissed Lex deeply.

"Roza, I'm sorry—"

"Don't, I'm sorry too. Just kiss me, everywhere. I need you so much."

She took Lex's hand and pulled her towards the bed.

❖

Lex and Roza lay in the dark of their room, holding hands, with the moonlight shining through the windows.

"You have no idea how much I've missed this," Lex said. "I'm sorry for what I did—I can only say I thought I was protecting you, but I know I went out of my bounds."

Roza turned and laid her head on Lex's chest. "You did, but I shouldn't have reacted that way. I've been doing a lot of thinking, and I've seen Dr. Kenzie a few times now."

Lex ran her hand up and down her wife's back. "How has that been going?"

"Good. I like her. We have conversations, and she gets me to think about things in a different way."

"I hope not about me?" Lex said.

"Don't be silly." Roza kissed her chest. "In fact, she has been encouraging me to talk to you."

"You can always talk to me, sweetheart."

"I know that, but that's hard when I didn't understand what was wrong myself. I see you were right all along now."

"About what?" Lex asked.

"Getting help from a therapist after my family was murdered."

Lex pulled her closer and kissed her forehead. "You needed to take your own time to do these things. I didn't get help until drugs nearly killed me."

"I get that, and like you I realize I'll probably need help with my issues as an ongoing thing, but talking to Kenzie, I've come to realize why I couldn't make myself take the help all these years."

"Why?"

"Because I felt if I did, I would be exactly what my father thought I was. Weak, a let-down, a disgrace to the throne."

"Don't say that. That's not true."

"It's how I felt. I mean, Father wouldn't have needed a psychiatrist, neither would Gussy."

Lex turned Roza onto her back and leaned above her. "With all you've had to face? You don't know that."

"I've been worrying that you have been keeping us afloat. That I wasn't strong enough to be a Queen in my own right. That's why I was so angry and took it out on you."

"Strong enough?" Lex shook her head. "Losing my family and then being thrust into a role I wasn't prepared for, keeping your country together at one of the worst times in its history, and doing your job as Queen? There's no way I would have been as strong as you."

"It's been a hard nine years, and when I saw those pictures from the film, it just came crashing down upon me."

Lex put her hand on her chest. "I swear to you that I'll never keep anything from you ever again."

"I did something today. I asked Olly to get me a preview copy of the film," Roza said.

"You did?"

Roza nodded. "I wanted to see it before I was ambushed by it. I watched it with Kenzie."

"Were you all right?" Lex caressed her cheek.

Roza smiled. "I was. I actually was. It was nothing like our lives. I didn't recognize any part of us in the script. I don't know why I was so worried."

Lex kissed her on the lips. "I'm so proud of you."

"No one out there, outside these walls, knows what our lives truly are, only what we share."

"Wait," Lex said, "did you not know I was placed on the throne by either the global banking elites, reptilian aliens, or both?"

Roza laughed out loud. "Of course you were. I love you, Lexie."

"I love you too. Any other news that I should know about?"

Roza pretended to think hard and then joked, "Oh yeah, your baby sister is dating a leather-clad motorcycle butch."

"What?"

CHAPTER TWENTY

Joe held open the door to the coffee shop as Casey carried a big box in. Poppy was super excited. It was her first delivery of her T-shirts, and she couldn't wait see them in the flesh.

"You've managed to let go of one another for a few hours," Joe said.

Casey smiled and winked at Joe.

Poppy could only smile. It was true—they could hardly put one another down. Everything appeared to be going to plan. She was dating her dream woman, she had fantastic friends that she trusted, their school life was going great, and she was helping her friends set up their business.

Casey put the box down on one of the tables.

"What's this?" Brit asked.

Poppy said, "My first box of T-shirts for my new clothing range."

Joe clapped his hands. "Let me see."

Casey ripped the tape off and let Poppy lift the first one out.

Poppy ripped open the sustainable packaging and pulled out a white T-shirt with the slogan *Simply Human...*

"Wow. I can't believe my designs have come to life," Poppy said.

Casey put her arm around her and kissed her brow. "I'm so proud of you."

"Take a look—I went for simple black with white writing, and white with black. There's tight fitting and a relaxed style."

"These are fantastic," Brit said.

"Choose whichever ones you want. Goldie is going to give some away as prizes at his big night on Saturday."

Joe held up the white one to his chest. "Hey, we could all wear them that night. We could be good influencers."

"Excellent idea," Brit said.

Joe looked at Casey, who was being unusually quiet. "Are you okay?"

"She's nervous. My sister got back early from her trip, so she's going to meet the Queen and my sister when we go up to see the library for our project."

"Uh-oh, you're in for the third degree, Case," Joe said.

"Thanks, Joe," Casey said. "That really gives me confidence."

❖

"Wow! What a beautiful space," Casey said. She walked around the library at the palace, head tipped back, looking at the ceiling. The ceiling paintings celebrated ancient Greek thinkers.

"It's stunning, isn't it?" Poppy put her arms around Casey.

"But not as gorgeous as you." Casey cupped Poppy's cheeks and pulled her in to a kiss.

Poppy pushed her hands under Casey's T-shirt and stroked the skin she found there. When she scratched her fingernails on Casey's back, Casey moaned and pushed her back against one of the bookshelves. Their kisses became deeper, and they found the edge of one of the library tables, and Casey lifted her up onto it.

While Casey kissed her neck, Poppy giggled. "This feels so wrong."

"But exciting?"

"Remember last night?" Poppy said.

Then, worryingly, another voice entered the conversation. "I don't think I want to know about what happened last night."

Casey jumped away from Poppy to find a smiling Queen Rozala and a second woman in the room with them.

"Shit, ma'am, Your Majesty—" Casey rambled.

"Sorry, Roza, I mean Your Majesty," Poppy said.

Roza laughed. "Don't worry about it. I remember Lex and I had a little tryst in Buckingham Palace's secret corridors."

"You did?" Poppy asked.

"I see you two have become better acquainted. Pops, will you introduce me to your friend."

Poppy stood forward. "Queen Rozala, this is Casey James. Casey, my sister-in-law the Queen, and Olly, her private secretary."

Roza held out her hand to Casey. "It's nice to meet you, Casey."

"It's an honour, ma'am," Casey said.

Roza wrinkled her nose. "She's very polite. If Crown Consort Lex had found you in that position, her reaction would have been less favourable. She'll be here in a few minutes."

"Yes, I know. Thank God," Poppy said.

"I presume I don't need to give the talk about how precious Poppy is to us."

"Roza, really?"

Casey smiled. "No, Your Majesty, Ravn already gave me my warnings."

"She is very fond of Poppy, and you can expect the Crown Consort to say something similar when she gets here."

Casey was not looking forward to that. She'd never had to impress a family member before. This was new territory.

"Let me show you what my librarian has put together for you. I have a prior appointment, so I won't be able to stay long, but you can both stay as long as you wish."

The Queen guided them over to the table. On the long table by the window were copies of pictures, pamphlets, letters, diary entries, and military records.

"This is fantastic, Roza. Thank you so much for doing this."

"Not at all. Anything I can do to help my little sister."

Casey watched Roza and Poppy hug each other with such family love. She just couldn't see the unhappy coercive control that some sections of the media were portraying.

"Ma'am?" Casey said, "Could I ask you one question?"

"I don't generally do interviews, but since you're Poppy's friend, on you go."

This was her moment to get the one-on-one with the Queen. At the start of this journey, her questions would have been quite different. Then Casey was trying to find out if there was scandal at the heart of Denbourg's monarchy. Now she wanted to prove her theory that this was a conspiracy.

"When you look at these items, the history of The Little Terror, and you look down on Restoration Square, how do you feel about the revolution?"

"Off the record?" Roza said.

"You have my word." And Casey meant that.

Roza walked over to the window that looked out to the square. Casey felt Poppy slip her hand into hers.

"People were killed mercilessly, on both sides, but revolutions rarely start with no good reason. My ancestor King Harold V was a tyrant by all accounts, as was the leader of the rebels, but what came out the other end were good things." Roza turned to face them. "The very first regnant Queen, Queen Catherine. A bill of rights. A constitutional monarchy, to make Denbourg a true democracy. Maybe things turn out the way they are meant to, in the end."

Queen Rozala didn't disappoint. Casey was sure she had the measure of the woman.

"Catherine seems like she was a great Queen," Poppy said. "I like to sit by her statue on the square—it has such a historical atmosphere."

"She was. Of course I heard stories passed down through the family and studied her at school, but I've never appreciated her properly until recently. I've been studying her diaries. Catherine has some sage advice about choosing the right consort, Pops."

Poppy screwed up her face like a moody teenager. "Lex might be annoying and overbearing at times, but it's just because she cares."

"She does."

Just at that the door to the library opened. Lex walked in, and Poppy jumped into her arms. "Lex! I've missed you," Poppy said.

"I've missed you too, Pops."

Poppy took Lex's hand. "Come and meet my…"

Poppy stumbled, not knowing how to describe her. She and Poppy would need to talk about that, but she was more worried about the Crown Consort coming towards her with a look of steel.

"Lex, this is Casey. Casey, this is my sister, Crown Consort Lennox."

Casey bowed. "Your Royal Highness."

Lex offered her hand and didn't take her eyes of steel away for Casey's for one moment. Casey felt the strong grip and realized that Lex was going to be tricky to get on her side when she came clean about her background.

"Hello, Casey. You go to college with Poppy?" Lex asked.

"That's right. I've taken six months off work to take the course."

"What line of work are you in?"

"Event promotions. Concerts, theatre, comedy. That kind of thing."

Lex smiled at last. "Good, good. Just remember, Casey, my wife has the command of the armed forces, special forces, and the secret service."

Although Lex was playing it as a joke, Casey saw the warning behind the statement.

"Stop it, Lex." Poppy playfully hit Lex.

And Roza said, "Don't worry, Lex. I've already done the warning thing."

Casey had enough to write her story now. She had satisfied herself that this couple was not as they had been portrayed in the media. The two women in Lex's life adored her and had such an easy way with her. This nonsense was coming from Prince Bernard and his backers. They might never identify the kingpin, but she could prove these rumours wrong.

"Now, if you'll excuse us, we have an appointment to keep," Roza said.

"See you, Pops," Lex said. "Casey, it was nice to meet you."

Casey bowed her head. "A pleasure, Your Majesty."

Once they left the library, Casey said, "She hates me."

"No, she doesn't. Lex would be overprotective no matter who you were."

"If you say so."

CHAPTER TWENTY-ONE

The week was flying by for Poppy, although she hadn't seen as much of Casey as she would have liked. Poppy was at Brit and Joe's for the afternoon, finalizing the choices of historical posters and drawings to decorate the coffee shop.

Britta was holding up a mock-up of the brand logo Poppy had drawn for them.

"I can't get over how perfect this logo is."

"I'm really glad you like it."

Joe jumped down on the couch. "It's truly perfect, darling."

Poppy had drawn up a few different designs for them to choose from, the winner being the one that made them decide on a new name for the shop-cum-bar. It was an image taken from one of the original call to arms posters from the revolution, showing people with weapons above their head, in silhouette, and the address—and the name of the shop—6 Restoration Square.

"I hoped you'd like this one best," Poppy said. "It ties in with the whole marketing strategy, the square, the palace, everything."

Joe pointed to the couch where the other posters based on paintings they found at the palace sat. "How lucky were we, Brit, to get the Queen's sister-in-law in our course?"

"Exactly. I just wish Casey was here to help make the choices," Brit said.

"Oh well, we can't have the pleasure of her company all of the time," Joe said. "Where did you say lover girl was today?"

Poppy laughed. "Don't let her hear you call her that, Joe. She's doing a side job for her boss."

"I thought she'd gotten six months off to do our course?" Brit asked.

"She did, but it's a special favour or something."

Joe raised his cocktail in the air and said, "I suppose she has to let you out of bed sometime."

Poppy grabbed a cushion and threw it at Joe. "Stop it. I'll tell her you said that tonight."

Brit squeezed her arm. "So, is this serious, then?"

The feeling Poppy hadn't dared to give a name to rose up in her body. "Yes, it is. I'm falling in love with her."

"Whoa," both Joe and Brit said at the same time.

Poppy giggled, and Joe shouted over to his sister, "I think I'm going to need a new hat for a wedding at last, Brit."

❖

Thea sat in her office in her building, slicing pieces of apple with a knife and popping them into her mouth as she watched their new guest.

Annika Ivanov was slowly starting to come around after being drugged and bundled into a van. She opened her eyes, and as soon as she focused she said, "You're dead."

"People keep saying that to me." Thea smiled.

"What do you want?"

Thea stood and walked around, slapping her knife against her thigh. "I did want to know who Luca Connell or Lucian was, but I found that by myself."

The two pictures she had of her nemesis appeared on a screen. "This is Casey James, also known as Lucian, currently undercover as Poppy King's girlfriend. Sister of our wonderful Crown Consort, Lennox King. So now you're going to be bait."

"I won't be bait. She won't come for me—she's just a writer for my company. She won't care," Annika said.

"Of course she will." Thea walked around. "You've been her mentor since she was eighteen."

"So you're the one behind Prince Bernard?" Annika asked.

"Yes, he'll be a useful puppet king, don't you think?"

"You won't get Queen Rozala and her son," Annika spat.

Thea laughed. "I got you, didn't I? Multi-millionaire and CEO of one of the biggest media empires in the world. Don't bet against me."

❖

Casey was getting ready for their night out to Gold's. She had suggested to Poppy that they get ready to go out at her flat, simply because Poppy kept asking why they didn't spend any time at Casey's. Her office just needed to be locked up tight.

Poppy was finishing drying her hair by the sound of it, then came back into the bedroom. "You look so sexy," Poppy said.

Casey was wearing black jeans, one of Poppy's black fitted Simply Human logo T-shirts, and her usual black leather wristbands.

"Nah, that's you, honey."

"I've got a surprise for you." Poppy grinned. Poppy slowly untied her silky dressing gown. Casey's jaw dropped when she saw the black lingerie Poppy was wearing.

"God, you're beautiful." Casey's sex started to throb and made her own surprise react with her body.

"This is your prize for later," Poppy said.

Casey stalked towards her with a hungry look in her eye. "Not for later."

Poppy giggled and held up her hand. "For later."

She walked between Poppy's legs and lifted Poppy's hand on her denim-clad thigh. "I've got a surprise for you too."

There was a spark of recognition in Poppy's eyes. They had talked about using an Intelliflesh dildo. Poppy hadn't used one before and was excited to try it. Casey thought she'd get one as a surprise.

"You got one?"

Casey nodded.

With one hand Poppy grasped Casey's belt buckle, and with the other scratched her nail over the hardening dildo.

It had been too long since Casey had used one of these. It felt amazing. Instead of showing her growing need, Casey grasped Poppy's hand on her belt.

Casey smiled and raised an eyebrow. "For later?"

Poppy shook her head and started to undo her belt. "For now."

"We'll be late." Casey pulled off her T-shirt and sports bra.

Poppy kicked off her tiny G-string and pulled Casey onto the bed. There was no one else she trusted to try this with. Casey touched her skin, and it was like fire all over her body.

"Kiss me," Poppy asked.

Casey put Poppy's leg over her shoulder and placed a kiss on her thigh.

Poppy couldn't help but grasp Casey's hair, while Casey licked around her navel and kissed her belly.

"Yes, hmm…more." Poppy took Casey's hand and made her squeeze her breast.

Casey moved up and sucked her nipple through the black mesh of the bra.

Poppy pulled Casey's head up to her and whispered, "I'm hot and wet. I want you inside."

Casey didn't have to be asked twice. She unbuttoned her fly and took her strap-on from her underwear.

She inched inside. "Are you okay?"

"Yes, keep going. I need you."

When Casey pushed fully inside, the feeling was incredible. "Fuck."

Poppy held on to Casey's neck as she started to thrust. "I feel so full. Is it good for you?"

"Jesus, yes."

They kissed hard, and Poppy wrapped her legs around Casey's hips. "Faster, baby."

Before long they were moving in sync. Poppy could feel her orgasm building, and inside she was gripping Casey's strap-on. "Please, Case, make me come."

"Yeah, deeper, honey." Casey's pace was getting faster all the time. "Going to come."

Poppy felt Casey take her to the edge, and there was no way back. "Now, now, Case." As she tumbled over the edge into searing, exquisite pleasure, Poppy dug her nails into Casey's back.

She thrust fast and shouted out, "Fuck, yeah, fuck."

They both shuddered as their breathing calmed.

"Are you okay, honey?"

Poppy held Casey close and said, "You are so good, bad boy."

"The good girls like the bad boys?"

"Yes," Poppy said, then kissed her lips tenderly.

"Pops?" Casey said. "I think I'm falling in love with you."

Poppy felt her heart flutter. "I'm falling in love with you too."

❖

Casey hadn't felt happiness like this before. For the first time she was looking forward to the future, not searching the gutter for corruption.

She smiled as she sat on the bed and listened to Poppy sing in the shower. Casey had showered first because she was quicker and generally didn't stay in long enough to sing, but she loved hearing Poppy.

Joe and Brit were going to be annoyed they were late, but it was worth it, and Goldie would understand. Casey pulled on her T-shirt, and as she popped her head through, she saw something that filled her with fear.

Thea Brandt was on the holo screen on the wall. "No, it can't be."

"Reports of my death have been greatly exaggerated. Did you miss me, Luca? Or is it Lucian, or Casey? You pick."

"Casey, I'm Casey James."

"The first truthful thing you've ever said to me or Poppy King."

That sent a chill through Casey's bones. She ran to the window and saw a car running at the front of her building.

She turned back to the screen. "What do you want?"

Thea walked across the room, and Casey saw a woman hanging by her arms, with her mouth taped up. Her head was hanging down, so Thea pulled it up, and Casey was shocked to see it was Annika.

"Annika?"

"Yes, your mentor. The woman that gave you everything."

"Wait, you're the kingpin behind this conspiracy against the crown?" Casey's heart was hammering.

"The king? Sounds right. So here's the plan. You get into the car below your apartment, or I kill Annika and have someone visit your precious Poppy."

"Okay, okay. Don't do anything. I'm going right down." Casey grabbed her shoes and pulled them on.

"You know it makes sense," Thea said.

The screen went blank, and Poppy was still in the shower singing. Casey's hands shook as she tried to think what to do. She looked over at her locked office.

❖

Poppy came out of the shower for the second time tonight. It was worth it, though. She felt on top of the world. What she had with Casey was what she had always read about. True, passionate need, want, and love.

"Case?"

She couldn't see her on the bed. "Casey James, if you are playing tricks on me, I'll kill you."

There was an earie silence to the flat, and Poppy started to worry, especially when she saw the door to Casey's office ajar. She knew it was kept locked—Casey'd told her.

Poppy pushed open the door slowly and looked around, not comprehending what she was seeing. There was a pinboard with pictures of her family. Above was a picture of Prince Bernard, and above him a hastily scrawled note saying, *It's Thea Brandt. Thea is the kingpin. Give Ravn the folder on my desk.*

Poppy could hardly breathe. She'd been lied to. All this time Casey was undercover, looking for a story. She clasped her hand to her mouth as the tears started to fall.

She turned her gaze to the desk, where she saw a large paper folder. On it was a note: *What I feel is true. I love you.*

"Computer, call Jess."

❖

An emergency meeting was set up in the Queen's family room. Ravn, Jess, and Olly met with Rozala. Ravn had just stepped out to call her superiors at HQ.

Poppy was standing by the window, all cried out by this stage. The documents in the folder had been passed around, and they were in sheer disbelief.

"Your Majesty, I'm sorry any of this was going on under my watch," Jess said.

"It wasn't your fault," Lex said. "She had a perfect backstory. It seems that Casey James was brought in to either prove or disprove the ridiculous rumours about me and Queen Rozala. The best way to get to us was through my sister, but when she realized it was a conspiracy to undermine us, Casey changed the direction of her story."

"Have you read this story by Casey? The one for the newspapers about us?" Roza said, "Its title is 'The Royals who Saved Denbourg.'"

Lex nodded. "Yes, I did. It's more like a love letter to the monarchy, rather than a sensational tabloid piece."

Roza handed her the story and walked over to Poppy at the window. "Pops?"

"She lied to me, Roza."

Roza took Poppy into her arms and hugged her. "I honestly don't think she was lying about her feelings. The piece she wrote about our family is beautiful."

Ravn came hurrying back in. "Let's go, Jess—we've got a lock on her."

"Ravn?" Poppy said. "Please save her."

Ravn nodded and set off to find her.

❖

Casey was brought into a large room where Annika was hanging by her arms. Thea was there, pacing slowly around her.

"So this is where you have been hiding?"

"Luca—sorry, Casey, you made it. Yes, it was quite ingenious. Hiding in plain sight."

"Let Annika down. It's me you want," Casey said.

"I do, but I want you to suffer. You made a fool of me. I let you into my inner circle, I felt like you were my protégé, and all the time you were working for Annika Ivanov."

Thea pulled up Annika's head and slit her throat.

"Fuck! Annika, I'm sorry." Casey tried to get to her, but the men with the guns were holding her back.

Thea walked right up to Casey and said, "I'm going to kill everyone you care about, and I'm going to destroy her family."

"Don't touch them!" Casey screamed.

"Boss, we've got company," one of her men said. "Vans full of armed police are getting out. We don't have the numbers."

"Fuck. Computer, call Morten. Get the chopper ready on the roof now."

She grabbed a gun off the table and placed it against Casey's head, as she instructed her guards, "You go down and slow them up."

When her guards left, Thea said, "Change of plan. I'm getting the chopper out of here, and you're going to take a dive off the roof."

❖

The gunfire was incessant from the floor below. "You might kill me, Thea, but you're not going to win. You can either walk out of here alive with the authorities, or dead."

"I'm not going for either of those two options."

When Casey saw Major Ravn and two of her people walk up

the final few stairs and point their guns at them, she was so relieved, because even if she was killed, Thea would be heading straight after her into oblivion.

"Put the gun down," Ravn said.

Casey felt Thea push the gun harder into her head.

"You think my world is going to end like this?"

Casey knew Thea was losing control, and both of them were probably going to die.

"Thea Brandt is not going to end that way," Thea ranted.

"Ravn? Tell Poppy that I love her, and I'm sorry I had to lie," Casey said.

"Love? You're pathetic, Casey."

Again Ravn shouted, "Drop the gun."

"Stay back. I need to get to the roof, or she dies," Thea shouted.

In the commotion and the noise, Thea didn't hear the service lift moving, but Casey did. It was probably some of Thea's people. The game was up. This was how it ended.

I love you, Poppy.

Just as she was expecting the bullets to start flying, and one to end her life, there was a crack, and Thea fell, like a dead weight to the ground. Casey spun around and saw Jess in the lift, holding her gun.

Casey fell to her knees and said, "I've never been happier to see you, Jess."

CHAPTER TWENTY-TWO

A re you going to mope about at my bar every day?" Goldie asked. Casey swirled the whiskey around in her glass. "Yes, what else is there to do?"

Goldie pointed to the glass and said, "Alcohol won't mend a broken heart."

"Maybe not, but it can make me numb."

Letting Poppy down, lying to her, the guilt and hurt were threatening to sink her.

"Give her time," Goldie said.

"There is no time. You think her family would let me see her now? Even if she wanted to?"

"You don't know that."

"I know. Her sister would probably have me shot if she could." Casey looked up at the news playing on the screen above the bar.

"Famous and elusive investigative reporter Lucian, unmasked as she helps expose Thea Brandt and her criminal empire. In addition to Thea Brandt's death, arrests have been made all over Europe—in Belgium, France, Germany, and Spain—and most notably, Prince Bernard, the Queen's second cousin, has been arrested."

"Can you hear that?" Goldie said. "All of those arrests have been made because of you."

"But the price was my heart."

"What are you going to do now?"

Casey shrugged. "I think I'll make that bike ride through Europe I was meant to be doing, before Annika got me involved in this story."

The bar door creaked open and Goldie said, "Case? Look."

Casey turned around and saw Poppy standing there. "Poppy?"

"I need to speak to you, Casey," Poppy said.

Goldie pointed to the back of the bar. "Use my office."

Casey nodded and led Poppy to the office. Casey was sure her heart was going to break some more when she led Poppy in there.

When the door shut, Poppy said, "I'm sorry it's taken me so long to come and see you."

"You didn't have to come and see me. You could just have sent me a message."

"Saying what?" Poppy asked.

"That you don't want to see me again," Casey said.

"I read your letter." Poppy stepped closer. "And your story, and all the evidence."

"At least Thea's gone. That's one good thing to come out of this mess."

Poppy reached out and took Casey's hand. "How about love? I needed some time to think through everything, but I know why you did this, and how you tried to disprove the gossip about Lex."

"What are you saying?" Casey asked. "I don't understand."

"I know you…we didn't intend to fall in love, but we did, and I cannot live without you."

Casey was struggling to take this in. "You love me? Even though I lied about things?"

"You saved lots of lives by exposing Thea, and I'm proud that you followed the story to the end."

"Seriously?" Casey's heartache was turning to hope.

Poppy leaned in and, just before she kissed her lips, whispered, "Seriously, I love you, Casey James."

Casey pulled Poppy close and kissed her, then lifted her up and twirled her around. "I can't believe it. I love you so much. Wait, what about your family?"

"The Queen and my sister have invited you to join us for Sunday dinner. If you hadn't done this story, my family might have been gone."

Casey held Poppy's head in her hands and said, "I will never keep anything from you again."

Poppy smiled. "Kiss me then, arrogant biker."

Casey was so happy she could be doing backflips. "Okay, honey."

❖

They had come back to Casey's place to talk, but as soon as they got into the flat, need and hunger took over, and Poppy pulled them to Casey's bedroom.

Casey didn't know if it was the truth finally being known or that Poppy truly believed in their love now, but Poppy was more confident than she had been since she met her. Poppy led her to the bedroom, kissed her deeply, and told Casey what she wanted, and Casey loved that.

That was what led to their current position. Poppy was on top of Casey, lifting and undulating her hips on Casey's Intelliflesh strap-on. Every lift, every movement that Poppy made was pure pleasure for Casey.

Casey gazed up as she watched Poppy lean her palms against the wall above the headboard as she lost herself in the moment.

"Oh God, Case."

Poppy wobbled, then Casey reached up and said, "Take my hand." They clasped hands, fingers entwined, and Poppy quickened their pace.

"You're so beautiful, Pops."

"I never—" Poppy struggled to keep her breath. "It's so good."

"I love you. Jesus, I don't know how much longer I can—" Casey was losing a bit of control. She put her free arm on Poppy's waist and encouraged a faster pace. Poppy too was losing it. She dropped her arms and let her hair brush Casey's face.

It only took a few more thrusts, and Poppy shouted out. Casey lost complete control and held Poppy's hips while she thrust herself inside Poppy a few more times.

The orgasm took Casey by surprise. Nothing had ever been as intense before. She couldn't even shout, just let out a long groan of pleasure.

Poppy collapsed into Casey's arms. "That was amazing."

A thought made its way to the surface of Casey's scrambled mind. "That was the first time I've made love with someone who knew exactly who I am."

Poppy laid her head on Casey's chest. "I'm glad you have."

They were silent for a few minutes, Casey stroking Poppy's hair. Then Casey said, "I never thought I would have this."

"But we do, and no one is going to take it away from us," Poppy insisted.

"Life's going to be different. I'll need to find a new job."

Poppy lifted her head and smiled. "I know an up-and-coming fashion company that's hiring."

Casey laughed. "Really? I'll have to"—she flipped Poppy onto her back, making Poppy giggle—"make contact with the boss."

Poppy pulled her head down to kiss her and whispered, "I think you already have."

❖

Lex knelt down in front of her son and straightened his tie. He was wearing blue trousers and a fashionable grey suit jacket.

"Do I have to wear this tie, Mum? Every time I wear one, people make fun of me at school."

"Let's go and ask Mama—she's the Queen around here." Lex smiled.

They opened the door to the Queen's bedroom and saw Nanny helping Roza to put on Maria's jacket.

"There's my two beautiful girls," Lex said.

Maria ran to Lex, and she lifted her up in her arms.

"New dress, Mum."

Lex kissed Maria's cheek. "It's pretty."

They were all coordinated in blues and greys today since those were Queen Catherine's favourite colours. Today was the anniversary of the restoration, and Roza felt Queen Catherine should be celebrated, especially as she had been such an inspiration to Roza.

So the people of Battendorf were coming to the square today to celebrate her.

Lex walked over and kissed Roza. "You look stunning as usual. Gus wants to ask something."

"What is it? You look handsome, by the way," Roza said.

"Do I have to wear a tie?" Gus asked. "The other kids at school laugh at me."

"Of course you don't." Roza pulled it off for him. "Whatever makes you comfortable."

"Thanks, Mama."

Roza hugged him. "Follow me, family. I've got something to show you."

Roza couldn't wait to show Lex.

"Roza?"

"Just follow and you'll see."

"Mum, is Aunt Pops going with us?"

"No, she's going to watch in the crowd with her friends," Lex said.

"Her girlfriend and their friends, Lex."

"Whatever," Lex groused.

Roza just laughed. Lex was having a little difficulty getting adjusted to her baby sister being in a committed relationship.

"Where are we going?"

They arrived at a large room that was usually empty. Roza opened the doors and said, "Welcome to our new office."

"*Our* new office? You've put our desks together back to back."

"Yes, just like Queen Catherine and Prince Artur. We're a team, and we are going to govern this country together."

Roza could see how touched Lex was. "Thank you, Your Majesty."

"A new start. Queen and Crown Consort are a team." Roza held out her hand.

Lex took it and kissed her knuckles. "Always a team."

Chapter Twenty-three

Two weeks later

"What do you think?" Poppy asked.

The letting agent was showing them around another potential space for Poppy's clothing line.

"I think it's perfect," Casey said. "There's so much light coming in from the windows."

"It used to be an art studio," Kate, the agent, said.

"What about the area?" Poppy said with a twinkle in her eye.

"It's not too bad." Casey grinned.

Kate didn't get their inside joke and said, "It's a very up-and-coming area. An artistic, bohemian area."

Poppy was so excited. Her dream was finally happening, and with someone she loved.

"We'll take it," Poppy said.

"Yes." Casey kissed her.

Kate looked equally as delighted for the sale. "I'll let the owners know you've met the asking price."

As she called her office, Casey and Poppy went outside.

"We did it," Poppy squealed. "I didn't want to seem too excited in front of Kate."

Casey took her hands and nodded her head across the road. "The area is quite good too."

Across the road was Gold's bar. "Perfect, next to Goldie, and it's all ours too."

Instead of renting, Poppy and Casey decided to buy a premises. Casey invested in the business to make them partners.

Poppy put her arms around Casey. "So, how do you think you'll cope working in the retail business, rather than as a secret undercover reporter?"

"I'm going to love it. I've been searching to find out who I am. Whether I was just as bad as those I investigated."

"You weren't—"

Casey put her finger on Poppy's lips. "Let me finish. I used to think that I wanted to save the world being the journalist I was. Then I lost faith, but you've given me back that faith. So how about we go and save the world, honey?" As Casey said it, she winked at Poppy.

"That wink gets me every time. I love you."

"I love you." Casey kissed Poppy's nose. "Let's go and get Goldie and head down to the square."

About the Author

Jenny Frame is from the small town of Motherwell in Scotland, where she lives with her partner, Lou, and their well-loved and very spoiled dog.

She has a diverse range of qualifications, including a BA in public management and a diploma in acting and performance. Nowadays, she likes to put her creative energies into writing rather than treading the boards.

When not writing or reading, Jenny loves cheering on her local football team, cooking, and spending time with her family.

Jenny can be contacted at www.jennyframe.com.

Books Available From Bold Strokes Books

The Artist by Sheri Lewis Wohl. Detective Casey Wilson and reclusive artist Tula Crane are drawn together in a web of passion, intrigue, and art that might just hold the key to stopping a killer. (978-1-63679-150-0)

Cherry on Top by Georgia Beers. A chance meeting leaves Cherry and Ellis longing for a different life, but when Ellis's search for truth crashes into Cherry's insta-filter world, do they have any hope at all of a happily ever after? (978-1-63679-158-6)

Love and Other Rare Birds by Angie Williams. Ornithologist Dr. Jamie Martin and park ranger Rowan Fleming are searching the Alaskan wilderness for a bird thought to be extinct, and they're about to discover opposites really do attract. (978-1-63679-108-1)

Parallel Paradise by Mayapee Chowdhury. When their love affair is put to the test by the homophobia of their family, community, and culture, Bindi and Rimli will need to fight for a chance at love. (978-1-63679-203-3)

Perfectly Matched by Toni Logan. A beautiful Cupid named Hannah, a runaway arrow, and just seventy-two hours to fix a mishap that could be the best mistake she has ever made. (978-1-63679-120-3)

Slow Burn by Missouri Vaun. A wounded wildland firefighter from California and a struggling artist find solace and love in a small southern town. (978-1-63679-098-5)

The Inconvenient Heiress by Jane Walsh. An unlikely heiress and a spinster evade the Marriage Mart only to discover true love together. (978-1-63679-173-9)

Closed-Door Policy by Erin Zak. Going back to college is never easy, but Caroline Stevens is prepared to work hard and change her life for the better. What she's not prepared for is Dr. Atlanta Morris, her gorgeous new professor. (978-1-63679-181-4)

Homeworld by Gun Brooke. Headed by Captain Holly Crowe, the spaceship Velocity's crew journeys toward their alien ancestors' homeworld, and what they find is completely unexpected—and they're not safe. (978-1-63679-177-7)

Outland by Kristin Keppler & Allisa Bahney. Danielle Clark and Katelyn Turner can't seem to stay away from one another even as the war for the wastelands tests their loyalty to each other and to their people. (978-1-63679-154-8)

Royal Exposé by Jenny Frame. When they're grouped together for a class assignment, Poppy's enthusiasm for life and love may just save Casey's soul, but will she ever forgive Casey for using her to expose royal secrets? (978-1-63679-165-4)

Secret Sanctuary by Nance Sparks. US Deputy Marshal Alex Trenton specializes in protecting those awaiting trial, but when danger threatens the woman she's falling for, Alex is in for the fight of her life. (978-1-63679-148-7)

Stranded Hearts by Kris Bryant, Amanda Radley & Emily Smith. In these novellas from award-winning authors, fate intervenes on behalf of love when characters are unexpectedly stuck together. With too much time and an irresistible attraction, anything could happen. (978-1-63679-182-1)

The Last Lavender Sister by Melissa Brayden. Aster Lavender sells her gourmet doughnuts and keeps a low profile; she never plans on the town's temporary veterinarian swooping in and making her feel like anything but a wallflower. (978-1-63679-130-2)

The Probability of Love by Dena Blake. As Blair and Rachel keep ending up in the same place despite the odds, can a one-night stand turn into forever? Or will the bet Blair never intended to make ruin their happily ever after? (978-1-63679-188-3)

Worth a Fortune by Sam Ledel. After placing a want ad for a personal secretary, a New York heiress is surprised when the woman who got away is the one interested in the position. (978-1-63679-175-3)

A Fox in Shadow by Jane Fletcher. Cassie's mission is to add new territory to the Kavillian empire—murder, betrayal, war, and the clash of cultures ensue. (978-1-63679-142-5)

Embracing the Moon by Jeannie Levig. Just as Gwen and Taylor are exploring the new love they've found, the present and past collide, threatening the future they long to share. (978-1-63555-462-5)

Forever Comes in Threes by D. Jackson Leigh. Efficiency expert Perry Chandler's ordered life is upended when she inherits three busy terriers, and the woman she's referred to for help turns out to be her bitter podcast rival, the very sexy Dr. Ming Lee. (978-1-63679-169-2)

Missed Conception by Joy Argento. Maggie Walsh wants a relationship with Cassidy, the daughter she's only just discovered she has due to an in vitro mix-up. Heat kindles between Maggie and Cassidy's mother in a way neither expects. (978-1-63679-146-3)

Private Equity by Elle Spencer. Cassidy Bennett spends an unexpected evening at a lesbian nightclub with her notoriously reserved and demanding boss, Julia. After seeing a different side of Julia, Cassidy can't seem to shake her desire to know more. (978-1-63679-180-7)

Racing the Dawn by Sandra Barrett. After narrowly escaping a house fire, vampire Jade Murphy is unexpectedly intrigued by gorgeous firefighter Beth Jenssen, and her undead existence might just be perking up a bit. (978-1-63679-271-2)

Reclaiming Love by Amanda Radley. Sarah's tiny white lie means somehow convincing Pippa to pretend to be her girlfriend. Only the more time they spend faking it, the more real it feels. (978-1-63679-144-9)

Sol Cycle by Kimberly Cooper Griffin. An encounter in a park brings Ang and Krista together, but when Ang's attempts to help Krista go spectacularly wrong, their passion for each other might not be enough. (978-1-63679-137-1)

Trial and Error by Carsen Taite. Attorney Franco Rossi and Judge Nina Aguilar's reunion is fraught with courtroom conflict, undeniable chemistry, and danger. (978-1-63555-863-0)

A Long Way to Fall by Elle Spencer. A ski lodge, two strong-willed women, and a family feud that brings them together, but will it also tear them apart? (978-1-63679-005-3)

Forever by Kris Bryant. When Savannah Edwards is invited to be the next bachelorette on the dating show *When Sparks Fly*, she'll show the world that finding true love on television can happen. (978-1-63679-029-9)

Ice on Wheels by Aurora Rey. All's fair in love and roller derby. That's Riley Fauchet's motto, until a new job lands her at the same company—and on the same team—as her rival Brooke Landry, the frosty jammer for the Big Easy Bruisers. (978-1-63679-179-1)

Perfect Rivalry by Radclyffe. Two women set out to win the same career-making goal, but it's love that may turn out to be the final prize. (978-1-63679-216-3)

Something to Talk About by Ronica Black. Can quiet ranch owner Corey Durand give up her peaceful life and allow her feisty new neighbor into her heart? Or will past loss, present suitors, and town gossip ruin a long-awaited chance at love? (978-1-63679-114-2)

With a Minor in Murder by Karis Walsh. In the world of academia, police officer Clare Sawyer and professor Libby Hart team up to solve a murder. (978-1-63679-186-9)

Writer's Block by Ali Vali. Wyatt and Hayley might be made for each other if only they can get through nosy neighbors, the historic society, at-odds future plans, and all the secrets hidden in Wyatt's walls. (978-1-63679-021-3)